TIMECOP
VIPER'S SPAWN

By Dan Parkinson
Published by Ballantine Books:

The Gates of Time
THE WHISPERS
FACES OF INFINITY*

Timecop
VIPER'S SPAWN
THE SCAVENGER*

forthcoming

TIMECOP

Viper's Spawn

Dan Parkinson

Based on the Universal Television Series
created for Television by Mark Verheiden

Based on the characters created by
Mike Richardson & Mark Verheiden

A Del Rey® Book
THE BALLANTINE PUBLISHING GROUP • NEW YORK

This book contains an excerpt from *The Whispers* by Dan Parkinson, published by Del Rey® Books. Copyright © 1998 by Siegel & Siegel Ltd.

A Del Rey® Book
Published by The Ballantine Publishing Group
Copyright © 1998 by Universal Studios Publishing Rights, a Division of Universal Studios Licensing, Inc. All Rights Reserved.

http://www.randomhouse.com

Library of Congress Catalog Card Number: 98-92817

ISBN 0-345-42195-7

Manufactured in the United States of America

First Edition: October 1998

10 9 8 7 6 5 4 3 2 1

The Spanish Main, Outer Bahamas
July 1534

Good evening winds and a running tide had worked in favor of the flotilla in the first week of its eastward passage. Though south of the preferred lanes, the five laden galleons and their escorting caravels had logged near twenty leagues each day under fair skies. But now, for the third consecutive day, the morning dawned gray and misted over a flat sea where becalmed ships sat like ghosts on fog-shrouded still waters.

They had drifted during the night, and the transport *Santa Ysabela* lay now three miles to starboard of the rest, her fleet mooring frayed and dangling from her port rail.

With first light, one of the limp-sailed caravels crept out from the flotilla, sluggish and balky under the power of awkward oars. In the mist the little vessel struggled for an hour to come within clear sight of the straying galleon. Only when the lieutenant in command saw the larger ship's mast tops and made out the colors of Imperial Spain at its maintop did he rest his oarsmen and take up his trumpet.

"Saludos a la Ysabela!" he called. "Ahoy, *Ysabela*! You are adrift! Are you secure?"

Moments passed. A bank of fog crept across the stillness, completely obscuring the distant masts, then in its languid passage he could see them again. It seemed the devil's own weather at work, but in the movement of the fog there was a promise of respite. Today the vagrant winds might return, and the little fleet could continue its voyage.

Like every officer of the flotilla, Domingo Sanchez was nervous about this voyage. The treasures aboard the galleons were fabulous—especially the ingots in the holds of *Santa Ysabela*—and not a man among them would rest easy until the dome of Gibraltar lay abaft the transports' slogging sterns and the carronade ships of Spanish sovereignty closed about them to see them safely into port.

Atahuallpa's ransom lay beneath the big galleon's grates, whispered rumors said—a roomful of Inca gold, melted down now into stacked ingots. The ransom of a pagan king—four million sovereign *dólares* in gold bullion bound as tribute to the Spanish king, Charles V.

It was only rumor, but the big galleon did ride deep, and a full company of Governor Pizarro's best lancers was posted on her deck.

Four million and more reasons—just on that one ship— for every man at every station in this convoy to keep his wits about him and sleep with his eyes open.

At the caravel's after rail, Sanchez swept his crew with fierce, dark eyes, demanding silence. Again a bank of dense fog had closed the view. But now he heard the answering hail, muffled and distant, from the galleon.

"All's well!" The thin voice carried through shrouding mist. "I'm making sail now, to catch the new breeze!" Even at this distance, distorted by the speaking trumpet and muffled by fog, the voice was curt, angry, and dismissive.

Again the intervening mists thinned slightly, and Sanchez raised his glass. Vaguely he could see header spars climbing the masts of the distant galleon, and as he watched, the foresail began to unfurl.

"It is enough." Sanchez nodded. "*El capitán* is quite capable of reckoning his course to rejoin the fleet." He put away his glass, his nostrils twitching as he sensed the beginnings of a sailer's wind. He had assured himself of the galleon's safety. Now it was his duty to return his own vessel to its station at the convoy's starboard flank. "Come about!" he ordered. "Beater, set twenty strokes' count! Rowers, man your sweeps!"

Like an awkward bird shorn of its wings the caravel lurched about and started back into the fog, heading for the remaining convoy. Listening to the grunts of his crew as backs bent to the labor of rowing, *Teniente* Domingo Sanchez cursed beneath his breath, then bowed his head and crossed himself, a devout young man atoning for a moment's weakness.

He should be grateful, he reminded himself. There were no pirates or enemies in these waters, only the vagaries of a tropical sea. He who cursed the weather risked his soul, for no man could rule the winds. Only God had such powers.

And yet, in the back of his mind, it troubled him that *Santa Ysabela*—of all the ships in this little fleet—should be the one to break her cable and drift in the night. The fortune she carried from the New World, he suspected, would buy a dozen of everything aboard all the rest of the transports.

The broken cable puzzled him, as well. He himself had inspected its trailing end, still lashed to the starboard cathead of *Puerto Sancto*. The simple mooring reef—a length of cable to keep ships together—had parted sometime in the dark hours. Sisal and hemp were always unreliable, under strain, and the breaking of a cable was a common occurrence. But this raveled end had an odd, blackened look to it.

Sanchez could not shake off the impression that the cable had, somehow, been burned apart.

* * *

Through the night, Ramon Quintaro Obregon de Vasquez-Luz, *capitán* and *comandante* of His Majesty's galleon *Santa Ysabela*, had heard the turning of the bell and the muffled steps of men about their duties. The parting of the cable line had been reported when it was discovered, but for a time there had been lantern glow to keep them abreast of the galleon *Puerto Sancto*. Then the mists had come upon the sea, mast-high and dense, and only with first light was the topman able to report with certainty that *Ysabela* had somehow drifted from her course.

Full light lay upon the shrouded sea when lookouts caught a glimpse of the caravel coming out in search, and by the time the speaking trumpet's hail was heard, a first touch of breeze had stirred the mist and Quintaro no longer felt the need of the little escort's assistance. *El capitán* was a proud man. There were no *Ingleses* devils here, no Moorish pirates, not even any ships of Portugal or *Alemania*. These waters were Spanish waters and the idea of being escorted back to convoy position by a little subaltern vessel—like a strayed sheep led back to the fold—was repugnant to him.

The breeze strengthened within the hour, as Quintaro had known it would, and *Santa Ysabela* spread her wide wings and took the flat sea on her breast, heavy-laden and plodding but now spreading a respectable wake astern.

"Come north three points," Captain Quintaro ordered, not looking around. At his elbow, the deck officer turned. "Come north—" he started, then went silent.

Quintaro glanced around, then spun and crouched, his hand going to the Toledo blade at his side. A stranger stood beside the tiller—a big man, fair-haired and dressed in clothing unlike any Quintaro had ever seen. He wore polished black boots over gray breeches flared wide above the knees. A buttoned gray coat with silver-and-black epaulets covered him to the neck, and the cap on his head was flare-crowned, rising in the front to display a metal emblem above a shiny, black short bill that shaded his eyes.

Behind him and spreading to command the afterdeck were three others in similar uniforms, and at their feet lay Quintaro's two helmsmen and a junior officer, all with their throats cut.

The first man raised a weapon of a kind Quintaro had never seen. It was a thing of black metal, with a wooden stock as on a crossbow, and at its breech was a wide, circular cannister like a shallow, metal drum. "Alteration of course, *Capitán*," the man said in clipped, precise Spanish with a strong accent. "We turn south now, not north. Lay down your weapons, and instruct every man of your crew to do likewise . . ." The strange, ugly instrument in his hands twitched slightly, pointing past Quintaro. Behind the captain, lancers of *el gobernador*'s crack company were scurrying astern along both rails. "Including the marines, if you please," the gray man snapped.

"Who are you, señor?" Quintaro demanded. "By what right do you give commands on my vessel?"

The man smiled, a slight, cold smile. "By right of arms," he said. "I am the new master of this ship. I ask you once more, will you lay down your sword and do as I command?"

"I will not!" Quintaro shouted. Throwing back his cape, he drew his saber. "You will not take my—"

The weapon facing him seemed hardly to twitch as it came to point, but the last thing Ramon Quintaro Obregon de Vasquez-Luz, captain and commander of His Majesty's galleon *Santa Ysabela*, ever saw in this life was the fire that blossomed from its dainty muzzle—fire that went on and on as thunder built upon the echoes of thunder. He felt the bullets explode within him, saw those around him falling even as he fell, and heard the screams of his crewmen, blending with the screams of falling Spanish expeditionary soldiers. He heard the whine of impossible swarms of bullets, driven by the staccato thunder of machine-gun fire, then the bloody deck rose to meet him and there was nothing more to see or hear, ever.

Oberkommandeur Helmut von Steuben released the trigger of his Thompson .45-caliber submachine gun and lowered it, hot and smoking as sudden silence fell over the ancient, creaking wood-hulled ship. It was not his favorite weapon, but its noise and its methodical killing power were awesome attention-getters. All around him, antique Spaniards lay in their own pooling blood while stain-darkened sails throbbed overhead, swelling against their sheet lines as a cool, wet wind grew astern, driving the fogs and the sluggish old ship ahead of it.

There were still dozens of bug-eyed Spanish sailors amidships, at the main-sheet tackle, and several aloft, clinging to the rigging. Swarming among them were uniformed SS troopers, armed with deadly repeating rifles. As the reek of nitro-powder smoke drifted among them, punctuating the shock and amazement of what they had just seen, von Steuben raised his voice. "You men!" he shouted in perfect, though accented, Spanish. "This ship is a prize of war, and you are my prisoners! Obey my commands, to the letter, and you may live to see another day. Otherwise, you will die as these before you have died!" To his own men he said, in German, "They are less than half a crew for a ship this size. Work them until they drop, but not past recovery. Use whips if necessary, but no boots or clubs. Men cannot make sail with broken bones."

"How long must they be kept alive, *Oberst*?" a trooper asked.

"Our destination is east of south, eight hundred kilometers," von Steuben said. "I intend to reach it within five days."

Four days later, the galleon *Santa Ysabela* anchored in a deep channel south of an unnamed island off a tropical coast that would one day be Venezuela. SS troopers stood guard as the surviving Spaniards emptied her holds, boat-load by boatload, and rowed the cargo ashore. In a hillside cleft above the tidal range, they made their prisoners dig a pit and bury the treasure. Then the wretches were herded together and gunned down by concentrated small-arms fire. Their bodies were thrown into the sea.

Once more aboard the ancient ship, the SS company—with von Steuben supervising—dutifully cut loose all anchors and used axes to destroy the rudder and the cable braces.

Good soldiers, von Steuben thought wryly as his sub-ordinates methodically destroyed the galleon's survival mechanisms. Not even real soldiers, only SS—and likely a Gestapo spy among them—but they obeyed his every command without hesitation.

They don't even know where we are or how we got here, von Steuben reminded himself. Yet they salute the Führer, praise the Fatherland, and do exactly as they are told. Good German soldiers!

When all else was done, he ordered them to destroy the ship's boats, stave in the water kegs, and wreck the bilge pumps. They hurried away, scurrying to perform these tasks. Then they formed on deck, awaiting further orders.

But there was no one to give orders. Helmut von Steuben, the commander, was nowhere to be found. Rudderless, her boats gone, half her sails loose-set, and all of her sheets sabotaged, *Santa Ysabela* drifted southward, away from any charted land, riding the hot winds of equatorial solstice.

Krakenfjord, Norway
February 1945

Helmut von Steuben paced the subterranean corridors of Lundsgrofenwerk, the smallest and most secret of all the Reich's research facilities outside of Germany. For hours, they had grilled him—the scientists, the administrators, and even a pair of Himmler's aides. He had given them, in exquisite detail, his report on experiment nineteen, exactly as he had planned.

They were full of questions, but he—the loyal soldier—had no further answers. No, he did not know where he had been. It was a place, but in total darkness and silence, and he had been there for only a few moments before his retrieval. No, he did not know what had become of the SS volunteers with him, or even of the Gestapo observer among them. In the place of darkness, he had seemed to be alone. Possibly the device had not worked for them.

They questioned him endlessly, but finally they had no choice but to believe what he said. And, believing, they would put an end to this line of experimentation and turn their attention elsewhere.

Inside, he was wild with relief, but nothing about him showed it. He had simply volunteered for an experiment that failed, and he was the lucky one—the only survivor. He had done his duty as a soldier of the Reich.

Privately, though, von Steuben knew far more than he let on. He had some idea of the enormous effort that had gone into this undertaking, and he knew exactly what it was that the scientists—that Himmler himself—had hoped to accomplish. Next to that head-scratcher Heindl himself, von Steuben probably knew more about the experiment here than anyone else in the Reich. He had seen the significance of this thing from the first moment, and had made it his business to know.

"Heinrich, you have had your grand test," he muttered as he closed the door on his private quarters. "Make what you will of my report, and puzzle if you will over what went wrong. You and all your scientists, you told me nothing of what you tried to do. How can I possibly know that you have been working on a time machine, when I was told nothing? I was no more than a guinea pig in this. I might have received the Iron Cross, though Heindl and the rest of your scientists will be fortunate if they survive their interrogation."

He stripped to the waist, scrubbed his face with cold water, then stretched out on his cot. They will never know why their machine didn't work, he thought. Heindl might suspect, but they will never know what I know—that it did work! Just as its progeny will work again. He gave no thought to the men he had killed. They would have died soon anyway, of disease or war.

He took a small, worn wallet from his boot pocket and opened it. Inside was a fading photograph of a young, dark-eyed woman, standing beside a Pierce Arrow automobile. In the background was a low, stucco-dressed building fronted by curved, shadowy arches. Beyond the building, an ornate church steeple stood against a rising terrain—forest, sweeping high meadows, and the smoky silhouette of tall mountains.

I will see you soon, Elena, von Steuben told himself. I will come to you, and you will give me a son—a son to grow up strong and capable. A son whose hands might grasp the world and crush it in his fist. It is all there for the taking, Elena. Everything! You will bear a son for me, Elena, and I will teach him.

Adolf Hitler's insane Reich was toppling, just as the precarious, bizarre fantasies of madmen always toppled. Once again Germany had tasted glory, and once again it would know defeat. It did not matter. The future—von Steuben's future and his unborn son's—lay oceans away.

He would require a ship, and he had one. Swiss registry, an innocuous cargo, and a carefully selected crew completely ignorant of their real mission. The commandeered steamship *Krofft* lay now in Lisbon harbor, awaiting its claimant. The papers for that vessel were in a safe place, along with the only complete, unaltered copy of Heindl's notes, equations, and plans.

They chose the wrong guinea pig this time, von Steuben told himself wryly. This time, it is the guinea pig that walks away with all the winnings.

||

Addis Ababa, Ethiopia
May 5, 1936

In the rainy season, it was said, the muddy incline of King Menelik Avenue, the steep road leading up to Old Ghibbi Palace, flowed with the sweat of Egyptians, the tears of Muslims, and the blood of Italians. All of these, since the time when this place was only Finfinnie, stronghold of the kingdom of Shewa, had come to conquer this land. And all had spilled their blood here before being driven away.

But it was different now. Shewa and the other kingdoms of ancient Nubia were now the nation of Ethiopia. Finfinnie had become Addis Ababa, capital and seat of Emperor Haile Selassie. And this year's rainy season was still a month away. The blood that trickled now on the hard-packed slope, and here and there around the city, was more Ethiopian than Italian. The incident at Welwel had become a cause for war, and Il Duce had revoked the old treaty. Marshal Badoglio had marched, and defeated the Ethiopians at Mai Cheo, near Lake Ashenge.

In the five weeks since, the Italian advance had been unstoppable. Addis Ababa's gates had fallen at first light, and now Mussolini's expeditionary troops swarmed through the city. Before the sun went to rest behind the Simen Mountains, Italian occupation of Ethiopia would be complete.

Already, the viceroy Rodolfo Graziani was proclaiming Ethiopia's annexation—with Eritrea and Italian Somaliland—to form the new province of Italian East Africa.

By midday, only Ras Imru Mekole's fighters at Old Ghibbi still held out against the invaders, and that was hardly more than token resistance. Emperor Selassie was no longer in residence. He and a small escort provided by Ras Abebe Aragawi were making their way out of the city. Two twin-engine airplanes waited at a eucalyptus-lined landing strip a few miles away. One would carry Ras Abebe Aragawi to Gonder, to rally his resistance forces. The other would take Haile Selassie and his little entourage to Djibouti and then to Jerusalem, where supporters waited to escort him to Geneva.

The road to the private airstrip wound upward through coffee fields and produce farms, and the open car of the emperor led the way, as was expected. No one followed the four fleeing vehicles as they climbed slowly toward the summit of the Hill of Six Flames. Ras Imru Mekole and the palace guard were doing all they could to keep the Italians busy at Old Ghibbi. But nearly two miles west of the winding road, a man with a tripod-mounted telescope watched intently as the emperor's open Daimler and its accompanying vehicles rounded a rock-walled bend into clear view.

The man was tall and bearded, his skin the color of rich coffee. He wore the jodhpurs and *shemma* of native custom, but the sixteen little gold rings in his ears—eight per ear—were pure U.S. Street Scene. Beside him, carefully positioned and presighted, a large, long-barreled rifle rested on bipod mounts. The three-foot-long sight forward of its

Benchmark target stock was as powerful as the spotting telescope mounted on its side.

When the cars were in clear view, the man flattened himself behind the rifle, snugged its butt into the curve of his shoulder, and squinted through the sight. At a magnification factor of thirty-six, the dark, somber face and bright robes of Haile Selassie were as clear as though the emperor of Ethiopia were just a few yards away.

The man on the hill eased himself into firing position and thumbed the safety lock open, his hands caressing the wood of the big gun. "Bye-bye, Haile ol' bro'," he breathed. "Here come th' new top dog."

He squeezed the set trigger, eased his finger onto the firing trigger . . . and was crushed to the hard ground, flattened by the full weight of a man landing atop him. The rifle flipped off its rest and clattered on the stone. Stunned and bewildered, the wind knocked out of him, the sniper scurried aside as the man sprawled atop him slid away and stood. He looked up, squinting into the muzzle of a gun.

The man now standing over him was tall and solid-looking, with brown hair and dark, piercing eyes that hid an ironic mirth behind steely authority. He wore a dark, gray uniform like a reinforced flight suit, with a small shoulder patch—a stylized hourglass design and the letters *TEC*. His air of authority, his obvious control of the situation—everything about him said police.

He squatted, languidly, and the sniper looked into the businesslike bore of a laser-sighted automatic pistol. Behind it, the squatting man shook his head. "Bad career choice, B. J.," he said. "You should never have left New Orleans."

Scuttling back, the sniper stared at the intruder. "I didn' do nothin'," he said. "You—you some kind'a cop? Man, I wasn' gonna shoot."

"Yes, you were," the policeman said matter-of-factly.

"You did shoot. You assassinated Haile Selassie, then tried to take his place by throwing in with Mussolini's goons. You changed history, B. J. You made a real mess. But now it won't happen."

"Who—who you be, man?"

"A cop, like you said," the man told him. "Force you probably never heard of. Time Enforcement Commission. Name's Logan. Now just ease back, please, away from that weapon."

As B. J. sidled backward, staring into the steady bore of the laser-sighted pistol, Time Enforcement Commission agent Jack Logan glanced at the big sniper rifle still resting on its bipods. "How did you get here?" he asked. "And where did you get this? A Baldwin Custom, for God's sake. Fifty caliber, studded bolt action, five-mile effective range, optional armor piercing . . . there never were more than about fifty of these babies. All handmade for the U.S. military, starting about 1996. This must have set you back a bundle, B. J."

In the distance, across the valley, the four automobiles had rounded another curve, out of sight. Logan turned his attention again to the sweating, bearded black man lying on his belly a few feet away. "Now, how did you get to 1936, B. J.? Who sent you?"

B. J.'s eyes widened. "Man, I don' tell you that! Nobody mess wit' the viper, man! Nobody! Viper go anywhere. Anytime! Mess you up bad! Mess up you whole family . . . viper strike, maybe you don' even know it. Maybe then you gone, maybe you jus' wish you was!" His wide eyes went moist with terror. "Man, jus' le' me go! I won't do—"

"It doesn't work that way, B. J." Logan shook his head. "In our time, you already did it. Hell of a ripple, too. There are no second chances."

Just for an instant, the air behind Logan shimmered.

There was a grunt, a scuff of boots on stone, and Logan felt the cold muzzle of a gun at the base of his skull. "You got that right, luv," a woman's voice said. "Now just put it down, easy!"

Carefully, still crouching, Logan lowered his gun and laid it aside. "Good boy." The woman chuckled. "Now let's see . . ." She moved around him, then stopped. "Well, w'at 'ave we 'ere? TEC, is it? Me, too. AusTEC. 'Ow 'bout some ID, matey? You show me yours, an' I'll show you mine."

With the sun in his eyes, Logan looked up at a blond halo under a flop hat. "Hello, Harriet," he said. "What's a nice girl like you doing in a place like this?"

She tipped her head, staring at him. "You know me?"

"I've read your file." Carefully, Logan retrieved his weapon and rose to his feet. Looking down at her now, he grinned. She was smaller than he would have thought, considering what the exchange files said. Not more than five feet two, and there was a baby-doll prettiness behind her determined, hard-as-nails crust. "You're Harriet Blevins, aren't you?" he said. "Nickname: The Angel. AusTEC's best operative, they say. The best of the best, and licensed for final judgment. You're twenty-seven years old, Brisbane-born, run the mile in four-twenty, and you are an expert in martial arts, linguistics, and criminal psychology. You have vaccination marks on your right—"

"That'll be enough of that, cobber! Exchange files don't say that!" She started to lower her gun, a stud-muzzled Webley AF-44, then spun and pointed it at the black man now on his knees a few feet away. "Is 'at a dart in y' tucker, B. J.?" she snapped. "Get rid of it! Now!"

The sniper glared at her, then slowly withdrew his hand from the folds of his flowing *shemma*. The thing that dropped from his fingers was a stubby missile that looked like six inches of broom handle, with metal feathers at one end and a glittering, needle-sharp spike at the other.

Carefully, Harriet approached and kicked the dart aside. Taking another step, she planted a small boot in B. J.'s chest and flung him backward to sprawl on the hard ground. "You're a piece of work, B. J.," she sneered. "But that's all done, now, isn't it? Boudreau Jackson Simms, do you 'ave anything to say before the Commonwealth of Australia passes sentence on you?" She raised her gun, straight-armed like a marksman, and set its sight on the black man's skull.

"Hold it!" Logan demanded. "This man's in my custody. Just back off, Agent Blevins!"

Harriet hesitated, glancing around. "My jurisdiction, matey," she purred. "Prime temporal effect determines prime jurisdiction. If this bloke 'ad snuffed ol' Haile, Australia would 'ave wound up a Japanese protectorate by the end of World War Two. AusTEC's got the prior claim."

"Custody supersedes jurisdiction," Logan pointed out. "He's my prisoner, and I'm taking him back to TEC for Timecourt trial."

"You'll take 'im nowhere!" Harriet frowned, still aiming at B. J.'s head. "We're playin' by Aussie rules, 'ere. TEC an' AusTEC may be affiliated, but jurisdiction determines legal code. Check your treaties. Bloke 'ere's 'ad 'is trial, de facto. 'E's mine to sentence!"

"He's a citizen of the United States of America, protected under the Geneva Accords of 1988!"

"Well, it won't be 1988 for fifty-two bloody years yet, will it! And we're in Africa, not the bloody States! Now back off, Yank! This one's mine!"

For an instant their eyes locked, and the instant was all B. J. needed. With a rolling dive, he grabbed the dart and raised it, fumbling for the fuse stud above its spike. Desperation beaded his face. Then he tumbled backward, twitched once, and lay still. The two bullets through his heart—one from a Webley AF-44 and one from an Eagle .45—had sounded as one shot.

Harriet lowered her firearm and crouched beside the dead man. "Now see w'at you've done!" she hissed. "I'll see you on report for this. This man was a convicted temporal felon, in the custody of the Commonwealth of Australia!"

Logan pried the dart from B. J.'s dead fingers and studied it. The plastique charge in it, if the sniper had depressed its fuse, would have leveled every bush and cracked every stone for a hundred yards around. "I shot a criminal in the act of trying to kill us," he said. "If you hadn't interfered, he'd have been before a TEC tribunal right now. They'd have executed him, legally, as a time assassin."

"An' w'at d'you think I was about to do?" Her blue eyes blazed at him. "I'd 'ave saved 'im the trip an' the trial, though. Aussie justice is tidier than yours, Yank."

"Logan," he corrected. "My name is Jack Logan."

"Logan," Harriet said, standing. "TEC's top agent, eh? 'Eard of you, too, mate. Recruited from Metro-Dade, right? Age thirty-three, bootful of commendations an' 'alf a dozen reprimands to match. Expert in 'and-to-'and, qualified with SWAT, an' in line for a gold shield before TEC came along, right?"

"Right," he said. He picked up the big Baldwin sniper rifle and inspected it, shaking his head. Where in the world had B. J. Simms, a New Orleans street thug gone big-time, picked up such a piece of ordnance? "Can't leave this lying around in 1939," he noted. "I'll take it back with me. You wanted B. J. so bad, you can have what's left of him."

"Big bloody deal," she sneered. "You get the 'ardware, I get the blinkin' reports to file! Two bullet 'oles in 'im, and I can't even swear to a proper execution. Don't reckon you'd offer an affidavit of circumstance, Yank?"

"What circumstance?" He glanced at her, his eyes as cold as blue ice. "I had a prisoner in custody, then was forced to kill him because of extrajurisdictional interference. Is that what you want reported?"

"Stone the bleedin' crows," she muttered, her temper flaring. "I 'eard you 'ad a partner once, Logan, but now you're always the loner. Reckon I understand why. 'Best suited to solitary missions,' your file says. Know w'at that means in plain English, cobber? Psychologically unpredictable, is w'at it means. Means you're a loose cannon, Logan! Or at least a bloody nuisance. Personally, I 'ope I never lay eyes on you again."

"Then stay out of my time," Logan growled. He shouldered the big sniper rifle, took a brief look around, and fingered his retrieval bracelet. The air shimmered, and he was gone. But the echo of an angry mutter hung in the air. "Send women to do men's work and what do you get? Women!"

Time Enforcement Commission Headquarters
Washington, D.C.
October 2007

It was three-fifteen when Jack Logan cleared retrieval security and presented himself for debriefing. It was nearly seven-thirty when the last bits of data were fed to ChronComp—TEC's global network of Chronolog Comparison Frames—and Captain Eugene Matuzek coded the data file closed.

The probability ripple, a widening pattern of historical alterations that would have followed the assassination of Haile Selassie in 1936, was erased. As with most temporal corrections, there were lingering traces. The sound of gunfire on a vacant hillside a few miles from the royal landing strip outside Addis Ababa had delayed departure of Selassie's aircraft by ten minutes. As a result, an outbound flight of League of Nations observers was held up for nearly thirty minutes, resulting—among other things—in Sigmund Erhardt missing an appointment to take Mrs. Erhardt to the Grand Theater in Vienna two days later. Because of this, the Erhardts never had a grandson named Philip, and the subsonic reverberator never became a major component in third-generation Rebel Classic music.

And, as usual, Sergeant Grover had a few cutting words to say. The gist of them was that, in Grover's opinion, Logan had not handled the confrontation with the Australian agent very well. "It seems to me Agent Logan lost control of the situation," the sergeant said. "There are forms and procedures for handling jurisdictional disputes between precincts. But, as usual, Agent Logan ignored prescribed procedure. The moment he regained his weapon, he should have established his custody of his prisoner. Instead, he let himself be drawn into an argument with a foreign national."

"That foreign national is a TEC agent!" Matuzek snapped. "AusTEC, but still TEC! She had as much right to be there as Logan had. The TEC and AusTEC warrants were simultaneous. What was he supposed to do, shoot her?"

"We all know—" Grover fixed Logan with a malignant gaze. "—that Agent Logan is seldom inclined to operate by the book."

Pompous ass, Logan thought. But he kept it to himself.

There were blips on the E-warp screens—minor anomalies that would smooth out with time. Some small modifications occurred in the treatment of Addison's disease, S. I. Hayakawa had served an interim term as president of the United States Senate, and the milk goat population in the Himalayas was up by 3 percent.

But there were other blips, too—blips that had not been there when Logan launched for 1936 Ethiopia, and that could not be accounted for by the Simms episode.

"It's almost as though someone else reacted to you and Agent Blevins being there," Dr. Dale Easter mused. "That's one scenario, anyway. These blips could be third-party reactions."

"The problem with history in this job," Amy Fuller complained, "is that I have to keep reprojecting it. Of course, field agents have to relearn it." She tapped a final note into her foldout and closed its case, then stood and stretched luxuriously, momentarily attracting the attention of every man in the room. "Are we through here?" she asked the captain. "My cat's gonna disown me if I don't get home."

"That's it for now." Matuzek nodded. "Remember, we have a situation briefing tomorrow morning. Nine sharp. Historians, technicians, and all available field agents. Routine procedure, no excused absences. Now get out of here, all of you."

Tired and stiff, the debriefing team packed their gear and filed out through the squad room. The night crew had already come on, and the E-warp screen glowed steadily while its dozens of banked monitors scrolled ripple readings and printers ticked out endless streams of calculations. People were at work in about half the cubicles around the squad room.

Over by the tracker banks, a young woman in the distinctive red blast suit of a downtime courier was watching the displays. Idly, Jack Logan wondered why she was still here. Couriers from the future were extremely rare. Logan remembered only one other that he had seen, a TEC cadet who stayed only long enough to deliver a logistics packet to Science and Research, then was gone. But this one had been hanging around the squad room since before five o'clock.

Even from the conference room, Logan had noted her presence. Dark auburn hair, close-cut in a style not quite like any current style, and a slim, graceful bearing that even the grav-padding of a TEC courier's garb couldn't hide . . . he grinned. Across the big, drab squad room beyond the glass partition—the girl smiled back. Then she was hidden, beyond the jumble of debriefers heading out.

Eugene Matuzek watched his team file out, began gathering his own stacks of handwritten notes, and glanced around. At the end of the long conference table, Jack Logan lounged back in a chair, hands behind his head, his booted feet crossed on the scarred tabletop.

"Why are you still here, Logan?" Matuzek rasped. "You've had a long day. Go home and get some sleep."

Logan got to his feet and strolled across the room, but only to the door. He closed it and turned back. "What's up, Gene? Since when is a situation briefing 'standard procedure'? Does it have something to do with the packet from downtime?"

Matuzek sighed. "Noticed the courier, huh? Have you seen today's ripple reports?"

"Glanced through them," Logan said. "Nothing big."

"No, nothing big," the TEC captain agreed. "Nothing above .01. But a whole hell of a lot of blips. Some of them we can assume to be aftereffects of our own closures, and we can credit some more to Timetrust and the Aussies' Pastime Authority operations. But not this many!"

"From the future, then." Logan shrugged. "Who else is there? There are only three real timefields in operation, that we know of. Four, if you count the Kleindast prototype, but it's out of service."

"That's just it." Matuzek nodded. He glanced at the stained poster on his wall: Temporal Technology Is Expensive—Only Governments and Other Large, Unscrupulous Organizations Can Afford It. The poster was there partly as a

reminder, partly as a gag, and partly as a dig at the sometimes pompous politicians who made up TEC's watchdog
group, a secret Senate oversight committee. "We know of
three temporal operations now in existence, but that doesn't
count the hobbyists and the shotgun launches. Hell, time
travel's like atomic energy. The knowledge is out there, and
sometimes somebody comes up with a jackleg launch. Some
of them don't even kill themselves in the process. That's
probably where most of our jumpers come from . . . and
maybe a few from the future."

"Most, but not all." Logan frowned. "Like I said in briefing, this wasn't a blast-shocked B. J. Simms, back there in
Ethiopia. He was from now, and he jumped from a solid,
sophisticated launch system."

"Yeah, he could have been," Matuzek sighed. "Remember the guy Hastings tagged altering the bootleg trade in
1929? He didn't come from downtime. We got fiber-carbon
tests on him. He was from the present. And we know he
didn't slip through the cracks in our own operation." The
captain shook his head. He seemed worried, and very tired.
"Or the one who wanted to kill President Bush. That was
no basement-lab jumper, or somebody slipping past the
future TEC scans. He was in the present time a week ago."

"Not from the future, or from any known present timefield." Logan frowned. "What does that leave?"

"Present, unknown." Matuzek shook his head. Hands
behind his back, he paced across the conference room,
then back again. "We're off-the-record here, Jack. Agreed?"

"Agreed."

"Okay. There is another timefield in operation, Jack.
Right now. And I don't mean a one-shot wormhole, either.
Theoretically, the scientists tell us, a very rich individual—
or maybe a private syndicate—might set up a full warp
field, track and sled and all, in some remote area, and possibly make a few leaps before their energizers melted down.

We know for a fact that it can be done on a one-man–
one-jump basis, using rocket thrusters and a stolen atomic
warhead to power the field. Chancy, but possible. Remember the Nelson brothers? That's what they did."

"Technology is Pandora's box," Logan mused. "Once a
discovery is made, there's no way to keep it from being
used."

"Right. But with those one-shot amateurs, we don't even
need a ripple trace to know they've jumped. We just follow the bang, then the ripples tell us where they went. But
not all of them are like that. Today we recorded fourteen
blips. Times ranging from 1992 all the way back to the
1400s. We think they represent time jumpers from our own
time, not the future. They're blips now, but they might become ripples."

"Might? What does downtime say?"

Matuzek glanced across the squad room. Bob O'Donnelly, one of TEC's best—and weirdest—history logicians,
had homed in on the cute courier like a bat to a juicy bug.
"Horny little bastard," Matuzek muttered. "Bet it's never
crossed his mind that that's somebody's daughter out there."
He turned back to Logan. "Will, then. Some of those blips
will be ripples, and downtime can't handle them." The
captain glanced at the closed door, then came around the
table to sit beside Logan. "This is top secret, Jack. You
don't hear it—any of it—until tomorrow. As of now, TEC
in the near future is shut down. I don't know when it happens, but it does—sometime soon after now. And unless
something alters, TEC will be a besieged fortress by 2010.

"That's when that courier is from. She was the last out.
They even turned off her retrieval bracelet, so I'm stuck
with her."

"Sounds like they're under direct flat-time attack, downtime." Logan frowned. "And all from the blips in our past?

How did ripples that big get by us, to them . . . or I guess it's to us . . . three years from now?"

"Well, it sure as hell isn't coincidence! This is a planned campaign. These blips we've got, they never grew. They just showed as minor anomalies, until early 2010. Then they all erupted. A ripple storm, and TEC 2010 was caught—will be caught—right in the eye of it.

"They don't even have a reliable link beyond this complex. They don't know how much of their system is breached, and they can't take chances. Somebody out there—out there right now—is playing hell with the future by planting time bombs in the past. And we—TEC of three years from now—we never saw it coming."

"But we know about it now."

"Yeah, we've changed that much future history already. But only because the TEC captain in 2010 broke—will break—every rule in the book to get word uptime to us. Couriers are expressly forbidden from making any contact—any at all—with their uptime predecessors, beyond simply delivering their packets and getting the hell back home. But right out there we've got a stranded courier from the future, who just might know things that could affect half the people in this unit. She knows the future, Jack. Maybe not much, but she knows some of it. And I'm stuck with her right here among us."

In the squad room, Sergeant Grover had waded into the crowd around the little courier, scattering her admirers in all directions. "At least the pompous bastard is good for something," Matuzek muttered.

Logan felt a sudden sympathy for his commanding officer. One of the real nightmares of time travel was the possibility of information leaking back. No one really knew how it would affect people, to know in advance what their future would be. "Yeah," he muttered. "Well, maybe she can keep her mouth shut." Then, shifting the subject, "So you think there's another full-grown time machine out there somewhere? In our time?"

"We think so. Lord only knows how. EuroTEC and the Aussies think so, too. That's why the conference. We've been on-line with them. They're flying people in tonight."

"You make it sound big," Logan said.

"It is big." Matuzek sat on the edge of the table and yawned, running his hands through his rumpled hair.

"Time travel is the best-kept secret in the world . . . officially. Nobody outside the Tritemp Treaty knows about TEC, or the timefields here and in Paris and Brisbane. But somebody knows! Somebody's trying to wipe us out, Jack. And they've figured out just how to do it." He sighed, and looked again at his poster. " 'Governments and other large, unscrupulous organizations . . .' Jack, tell me again what B. J. Simms said, about who sent him."

"He didn't say," Logan said. "He was scared half to death. All he said was, 'Don't mess with the viper.' "

"What does that mean? Any ideas?"

"None at all." Logan turned to the door. "We're not getting anywhere with this now, Gene. I need to get some sleep."

"Yeah, I'll bet." Matuzek grinned. "Glenda and the kids are waiting for me, right now. When are you going to settle down, Jack? Man needs a woman, you know."

"I have all the women I need, thanks," Logan snorted.

"Yeah, well, there's having and there's having, you know."

"Just drop it, Gene. Old wounds, okay? By the way, I'll take one problem off your hands for a while."

"Get going, then." Matuzek gestured toward the door. "This conversation never happened, Jack. See you in the morning. Oh, and Jack?"

Logan glanced around.

"This 'problem' you're taking off my hands," the head of TEC operations said. "You know she might be a target."

"I know," Logan told him.

III

Julie's eyes were emerald green, like summer leaves reflecting in deep, clear water. They were a nice complement to her copper-red hair. "I'm not supposed to talk to you," she said. "I'm not cleared to talk to anybody uptime. I might tell them something they'd rather not know."

"Then don't talk." Logan shrugged. "You still need a meal, a bath, and a place to sleep. Come on."

"Where are we going?"

"My place," he said.

In the lot behind the huge, quarter-mile-long sled-track building—the heart of TEC's time-jump complex—Logan led the courier to his private car. Its door opened to the touch of his thumb on its print scanner. "Seal all visuals," he said when the doors were closed. Obediently, metal louvers closed over all of the car's windows. "Full autopilot," Logan said. "Destination, home."

"Not that I could tell anybody anything," Julie resumed as the vehicle's computer took over and the car headed itself out. "They screen courier candidates for any background contact with TEC personnel, and we're trained in isolation. But I guess you already know that."

She's scared, Logan realized. She doesn't know why she's stuck here, or what's going to happen next. "I know," he said. "You'll want to change out of that uniform. What are you, about a size six?"

27

She nodded. "I didn't bring anything with me. Right up to the last minute, I thought I'd be right back. In the briefing, they said I'd deliver my packet and come right back. But then at the sled, they told me on intercom that there was a lockdown and my return was postponed indefinitely. My retrieval bracelet's dead, so I guess that was right."

"Yeah," he said. Nervous as a cat, he told himself. Out of her own time, shut up in a closed car with a stranger . . . she's chattering to keep her nerve.

"Boy, you don't talk much, do you?" She gazed at him. "So what's the story with you, anyway? You're really a nice-looking guy, but the lady in the cross-files section said you live alone. So . . . anybody steady, or anything?"

"It's a good thing you're the quiet type." Logan shrugged. "Otherwise we might get into a conversation."

"Isn't that a fact!" Julie's green eyes went dark with concern. "That was really tough, waiting there in that squad room, with all those nice men all around, and trying not to say anything. Not that I'm much of a talker, usually, but there are limits! I grew up around Mason, Texas, you know. People in the hill country talk a lot. But I tried to just be polite and not really say much to anybody. I really don't want to talk too much."

"Of course not."

"It was nice of that sergeant—what's his name, Grover?— to step in when he did. Everybody was being so friendly, it was really hard to be closemouthed."

The car's computer voice purred, "Destination three minutes."

Logan glanced at the panel clock. It was seven-fifty. "Access TEC logs," he commanded the machine. "Agent Logan, home at eight P.M." He watched the car's communication panel register his command, and a moment later a little light blinked. The message had been sent and received.

Julie looked around the car's interior, acknowledging

the blind windows. "I haven't the vaguest idea where we are," she said. "I don't suppose we could see out, could we? I guess not, though. I suppose, as a TEC agent, it's a secret where you live."

"Insurance," Logan said, and nodded. "Some of the people TEC cops meet aren't people you'd invite to your home."

The car slowed and stopped. "Traffic delay," the computer voice said. "Scanning."

"Estimate delay," Logan said.

There was a pause, then the computer voice said, "Overturned utility vehicle, all accesses blocked. Estimated traffic delay eight minutes."

Logan shrugged and leaned back. "Washington traffic," he sighed, settling back. The girl was starving for a little reassurance. "It could be worse, though. Tell me about yourself, Julie."

She gazed at him, her big, green eyes narrowed. "I'm not supposed to talk to anyone in this time," she reminded him. "That's part of my training. It's TEC policy, too, isn't it? Not to reveal the future to those in the past?"

"By TEC policy, you're not even supposed to be here," he pointed out, "but you are, and I seem to have adopted you for the time being. So you can tell me about yourself. Just don't tell me anything about me, or anybody I might know." He looked her up and down, liking what he saw. In her red blast suit she looked like a cheerleader masquerading as a linebacker. "That TEC pin on your lapel, it's unusual. Something new?"

She glanced down, then touched the jeweled pin with her fingers. "It's pretty, isn't it," she said. "Sergeant Grover gave it to me. He said it will serve as temporary identification until I either get sent back or processed in. Sergeant Grover seems like such a nice man. It must be a pleasure to work with him, like you do."

"Grover's a real prince," Jack muttered. "Texas, huh? When I was a kid I had a baseball signed by Nolan Ryan. I kept it in a glass box on a shelf. I still have it, and one from Roger Blake. I guess some mementos just become part of your life."

"I suppose so." She smiled, like morning sunshine. "You sounded as though you were surprised that you . . . adopted me, as you called it. I wasn't surprised."

Logan's eyes narrowed. "You weren't?"

"No. This evening in the squad room, when all those people came out of conference, several of the men were concerned about where I'd be staying. But somebody said for them to just leave me alone. He said Logan would take me home until they figured out what to do with me."

"Oh? And who said that?"

"Sergeant Grover. He told me just to wait there for you."

"Perceptive of him," Logan muttered, puzzled. He wondered, idly, if they were talking about the same Grover.

A light winked on the drive console and the car's computer voice announced, "Alternate route now open, eleven minutes to destination."

Logan glanced at the coded route-screen by his elbow. Eleven minutes . . . that would be a roundabout approach, across the Potomac, then arriving at his apartment building from the other direction.

"Alternate approved," he said. As the car began to move again, he turned to Julie. "I guess you can watch the scenery now. The route we're taking won't tell you a thing about where we're going." To the car, he said, "Open visuals."

At all the windows, louvered shields opened, and they had a nice view of Washington's evening lights.

They were across the Potomac and heading for the Jefferson bridge when a sudden glare erupted on the skyline directly across the river. A fireball blossomed in the top of a building there, mushrooming outward, carrying debris with it.

Julie gasped. "That's an explosion." She pointed. "Something blew up over there!"

Logan knew instantly what he was seeing. The building was his building, and its top floor was his own apartment. "Course correction," he told the car. "Abandon route plan. Maintain present traffic lane." Twisting around, he grabbed the ornate pin on Julie's uniform lapel, tore it off, and dropped it on the floorboard. His boot heel demolished it. He picked it up, studied the pieces, and broke a dangling loop of fine wire. The wire was attached to a battery barely larger than the head of a pin. Within the shattered case were a half-dozen components, all microminiature electronics.

"Cyber-spy device," he muttered. "This thing read the car's course computer and transmitted our destination and ETA. Whoever was listening knew where we were going and when we'd arrive before we cleared the gates at TEC. Plenty of time to align a plasma charge."

Visibly shaken, Julie stared at the demolished electronics in Logan's hand, then looked out the window again. The fireball across the river was now a raging fire, engulfing several upper stories of the building. "That—" she gasped. "That's where we were going? You—you live there?"

"I used to," he told her. "If it hadn't been for that traffic jam, we'd be in there now. Or whatever was left of us would be."

Julie thought it over, looking very pale. "What do we do now?" she asked finally.

"Somebody wants one of us dead," Logan decided. "So the first thing we do is go to ground." To the car, he said, "Cancel original destination. Code six, read five and six. New destination, logfile nine-BK."

"Destination confirmed," the computer voice responded.

"ETA twenty-seven minutes." Beyond the louvered windows, the vehicle changed its color from gray to black, and its registration tags dropped into concealed slots to be replaced by different tags. Mode-coding was an expensive automotive option, perfected during the nineties but still almost unknown except on high-visibility transports assigned to the Secret Service. It was the first time Jack Logan had ever used it, but he was glad now that he had it.

Bob O'Donnelly's place of residence could hardly be called an apartment. More properly, it was the back half of a loft in an old warehouse building in the Fulbright district—fifteen hundred square feet of contained space crammed with computers, printers, electronic gear, and a few vague pieces of furniture. Everything in the happy jumble seemed to be connected to everything else by great webs of insulated wires and coaxial cables strung all over the place, and most of the computer and electronic equipment was in operation.

The lord and master of all this looked even more distracted and childlike than usual as he stood in the littered entryway, clad in rumpled sweats and battered Nikes, his eyes as big as silver dollars.

"This is Julie," Jack Logan had just advised him, "and she needs a place to sleep."

The young logician stared at the auburn-haired courier, at a loss for words. In addition to being one of TEC's top historians, Bob O'Donnelly was the acknowledged wizard of all computer science in TEC's arsenal. He held doctorates from two universities, and even though he resembled an addle-brained teenager more than a respected scientist, he was considered a ranking authority on probability analysis. At the moment, though, his adoring eyes drinking in the stunning red-uniformed creature before him, he looked like a basket case. It took him all of ten seconds to get his mouth closed and his senses back to communication level. "Outstanding," he said finally. "Terrific!"

Logan grinned and shook his head. "Bob," he said. "You with us, son? Good. You have a bed of some kind in this rat's nest, don't you? Julie can use that. You can sleep on the floor. And behave yourself!"

"Oh," O'Donnelly sighed. "Oh. Well, sure. Okay." He looked around. "Yeah, there's a cot right over . . . well, it's here someplace. Where are you going to be, Logan?"

"I have to see a man about a bomb," Logan said, frowning. "Just take good care of this courier, Bob. Think of her as TEC property. Don't let her out of your sight, and don't tell anybody—repeat, anybody—that she's here. Or that you've seen me. I'll explain it later. Just don't believe everything you hear at TEC tomorrow, and keep quiet!"

"Jack," Julie said as he turned to go, "I'm really sorry about your apartment . . . and your balls. I'm sorry you lost your balls."

Chief Sergeant Wayne Grover had been a policeman for most of his adult life. Recruited by TEC from the Metropolitan Region force at Philadelphia, he was a veteran of the streets and a specialist in detection and surveillance. Thus it was second nature to him to check his backtrail as he made his way along D.C.'s backstreets that night. Traffic was light off the main thoroughfares, and within minutes he had a fix and a scan on every vehicle within three blocks behind him.

There had been three—all innocuous—and then there were four. A block back, another car had turned his direction, cruising along three hundred yards behind. Routinely, he touched his tail-scan and read the data. Fully equipped Gen-Em Trace, black over black. Not exactly a common model, but there were probably a hundred or more like it in and around Washington.

Nonetheless, he kept tabs on it and made a couple of evasive turns to check it out. On the first turn, it was still with him, a hundred yards back and closing slowly. But on his second turn it popped off the screen.

Grover relaxed and returned to his route. Three blocks later there was, again, a Gen-Em Trace behind him. But this one was maroon with silver detailing. He didn't bother evading, this time. It was not the same car, or any car he knew.

Passing the causeway, he glanced to the left. Over there, just a few miles, was the town house that had been his home for nineteen years. But he wouldn't see it again. Tonight the world had changed for Wayne Grover. In a locker at Jefferson station, a locker leased and unused for years, was enough money for a new life in a new place—a life with all the comforts any man could want.

Satisfied that he was not being followed, Grover headed for Jefferson station.

At Jefferson he made his way through the usual crowds, and found the locker. It was a simple, single-lock briefcase vault. Perfect security, he thought, sardonically. The package inside—that's supposed to be inside—has been here for a decade or more. But if I hadn't performed today—if somehow I had missed, and Logan and the courier aren't dead—then it won't be here at all. The wonders of time travel.

Inside the locker was a simple vinyl pouch. Grover scanned it with his pocket proofer, then opened it. Neat bundles of currency lay there—all untraceable used bills, denominations of $50, $100, $1,000. Even without counting it, he knew it was complete. A little scanner lay atop the bills, a CD wafer in place.

He touched the play button, and on the little screen he saw a scene from long ago. In the darkness of an alley he— a much younger version of himself—waited and watched as a 1993 Porsche pulled away from a curb and disappeared around a corner. One man remained there—a Latino with a briefcase. Grover saw himself approach the Latino, saw the flare of his own gunfire, and saw the man fall. Then he saw himself wipe his throwaway gun, drop it on the dirty pavement, and walk away, carrying the briefcase.

No witnesses. The perfect grab. But then—just hours ago—the recording had played for him on his private picturephone, and they had told him what he must do.

He had done it, and now he was repaid. The Verde gang had kept its bargain.

He closed the pouch, hid it in his coat, and turned. He took one step, then looked up and gasped. Directly in front of him, Jack Logan stood, barring his way. The TEC agent displayed no visible weapons, but the pure ice in his gaze was an invitation. Just try something, the eyes said. Please. Grover froze.

"Wayne Grover, you're under arrest," Logan growled. "You have the right to immediate process, and to closed tribunal by Timecourt. If you choose to give up these rights, or to resist arrest, then I have the right to terminate your existence here and now."

TEC headquarters was a subdued place on the morning of the Tritemp situational briefing. No notice had been posted, but within minutes everyone from ThinkTank to the data programmers knew that the Potomac Heights building bombed the previous night was Jack Logan's building, and that Jack Logan had logged home eight minutes before the explosion.

Also missing from the squad room was Sergeant Wayne Grover, but an amended timesheet at the bullpen listed him as on indefinite emergency leave.

Dr. Robert A. O'Donnelly, looking like a misplaced juvenile as he sauntered through the squad room in his usual sweats, sneakers, and go-to-hell cap, paused only for a moment to listen to the circulating rumors and check the timesheet. He looked slightly mystified. But then, he usually did. At his cubicle—a welter of electronics, loose wires, and discarded food containers that had been nicknamed disaster area number nine—he shuffled a jumble of readouts into a file folder and headed for ThinkTank. Captain Eugene Matuzek snagged him en route and herded him into an interview booth.

"Logan's going to remain dead for a while," the captain assured him. "Where's the girl?"

"She's safe," O'Donnelly said. "Right now she's having breakfast with my grandmother in Georgetown. I didn't want to leave her alone at my place, and I didn't know what else to do with her."

"Your grandmother?" Matuzek frowned. "O'Donnelly, that courier is a walking security leak. Everything she knows and anything she says is classified. You know the rules about downtime information."

"It's the best I could come up with," O'Donnelly said, and shrugged. "What could I do, lock her in a closet? They'll enjoy each other's company. Julie can say anything she wants and it won't matter. My grandmother has never in her life stopped talking long enough to listen to anybody else."

"So you had a rogue," Jean-Luc Poulon summarized, cocking his head at Eugene Matuzek. "You have reviewed his origins, of course?"

"All the way back to the first twinkle in his father's eye," Matuzek said, and nodded. "Clean as a hound's tooth, until last night. Just like the two who betrayed your precinct. Do you have any ideas?"

"A suspicion only." TEC's French *préfecteur du temps* shrugged. "Our measurement of historic alteration is the same as yours, of course. We trace ripples in the timestream, by E-warp coordinated to known history. But we found no ripples from other times that related to our criminals. Thus, we conclude that Louis and Pierre were . . . how you say, moles, set in place before there was an E-warp screen. Which means, before Timetrust existed."

"But EuroTEC and Timetrust went into operation just a year after TEC was formed," Matuzek pointed out. "And I know your people were screened further back than that, just as ours were in the U.S. How could anyone that long ago have known that there would be time police? How could anyone sabotage time police before time travel was invented?"

"Obviously," Poulon breathed, "we were not the first."

"Makes a man wonder 'ow many more bleedin' moles there might be," the third man in the quiet-room muttered. Dudley Wilkins was Australia's TEC precinct chief, the counterpart in his land of Matuzek and Poulon.

"There's no way of knowing, unless we find their source," Matuzek said. "The only break we've had is that downtime message from 2010. Except for that, we'd never have even known we have a problem."

"And you are sure of the message itself?" Poulon asked. "There is no question?"

"None at all," Matuzek assured him. "It was a sealed message, tamperproof, and in a code that only I could break."

" 'Ow can you be so certain?" Wilkins asked.

"Because it was from myself," Matuzek said. "Myself, three years from now."

"Mon Dieu!" the Frenchman muttered.

"I suggest a joint investigation," Matuzek told them. "One of my historians, Dr. Amy Fuller, has established a probability curve linking some of our uptime blips to the shutdown of TEC. I suggest a team of agents, people our enemy—whoever he is—can't predict."

"Easy for us," Wilkins said, and nodded. "Pastime's only eighteen months old, an' AusTEC a week younger. Our security is airtight so far, an' Parliament 'asn't meddled. Not too blinkin' likely anybody knows any of our people yet."

"Alas, EuroTEC cannot be so certain," Poulon confessed. "Like America, we know that Europe has moles. The Timetrust penetration proved that."

"We're limited, then," Matuzek said. "But I think I can send an agent no one will expect. And you, Wilkins?"

"Give you the best I've got," the Australian said.

"Fine." Matuzek thumbed his console and glanced at the clock. "I have a situational briefing for my people in five minutes. I have to outline the situation for them, but I'll keep the details need-to-know. Will you gentlemen sit in, since undoubtedly everybody within half a mile already knows you're here? We'll call you observers."

"And it begins now, the joint effort?" Poulon asked.

"It already started," Matuzek said. "Amy has the coordinates on some blips, and our sled's on standby. If we're being observed from some other timefield, let's give 'em a show."

"Did you learn anything at all from your mole?" Wilkins asked.

"Nothing much. He clammed up, wouldn't even talk to the Timecourt. Just two puzzling things, when he was sentenced. He said we 'can't beat the viper.' And something about a Verde—or maybe verity—gang. That name mean anything to either of you?"

Wilkins shook his head, but Poulon paused, thoughtfully. "Are you sure it was a name?" he mused. "Could it have been a word? A common noun? There is a German word, *verteidigung*. It means something like 'defense,' or 'to keep intact.' Odd, though . . ."

"What is?"

"It is a word the *Sûreté* knows. We have found *verteidi-*

gung in European police files several times. Never anything definite, just . . . as you say . . . a mention of it by a variety of felons. Interpol believes it is some sort of criminal ring operating in several countries. A kind of Teutonic Mafia, they suspect, but all they have is a possible linkage— to a man named Emilio Vargas von Steuben. Present whereabouts unknown."

Across the table, Wilkins frowned. "Vargas von Steuben? We've seen that name. One of our historians tagged it, as an anomaly. An old, rebuilt World War Two steamer disappeared off Tierra del Fuego in 1994. The ship, the *Krofft*, had Argentinian registry in the name of Emilio Vargas. It carried a cargo of state-of-the-art electronics, bound for the Antarctic. Lloyd's paid the claim to one E. von Steuben."

"Ships disappear in those waters," Wilkins noted. "What's the anomaly?"

"Simply that *Krofft*'s cargo included high-level electronics," Poulon said. "State of the art for 1994—about the time Hans Kleindast was developing his theories into real time-travel technology. There are no clear records, but the Kleindast notes indicate there was a second bidder for almost every device he required. The 'von Steuben interests.' "

"Now that," Matuzek said, "is interesting. The blip Amy Fuller has coordinated for temporal insertion—a puzzling event in Norway in 1945—has a name. She calls it the von Steuben blip. It coincides with the disappearance of a mid-level Nazi named Helmut von Steuben, from one of Heinrich Himmler's playhouses in Norway."

IV

The field was fully powered and the insertion programmed when Jack Logan climbed into the sled and hit the READY switch. Powerful rocket thrusters rumbled, and the pod trembled like a racehorse at the gate.

Even after dozens of missions into the past, the view down the track was still daunting. A thousand yards of reinforced two-rail track diminished into shadows ahead, dwarfed at the far end by the gigantic arms of the timefield generator—barely half a mile to reach critical velocity, then nothing. At adequate velocity, the projectile sled would enter the wormhole and dematerialize, flinging its contents onward, in a direction that did not exist in the three-dimensional universe.

At Q-velocity, the sled became a launcher into the timefield. But at less than Q-velocity, the sled was only a hurtling sled and the field simply wasn't there at all. There was nothing beyond it but the wall.

Every TEC trainee knew the equations. The timefield was the gaping maw of a wormhole in the time-space continuum—but only if it was encountered at a relative velocity greater than 2,994 feet per second. Over 2,000 miles per hour, with barely half a mile of acceleration! The grav-force on a timesled was tremendous, but it was a walk in the park compared with the psychological stress of gazing down that brief track, through the seemingly empty aperture of the field arms, and seeing that wall.

It had marks on it, little splashes of discoloration fused deep into its substance. There was no margin of error in a time-launch. Sometimes—rarely, but sometimes—they failed. Every stain on that wall was a failed attempt at launch.

By force of will, Logan calmed his reflexes. He slowed his heartbeat to one a second, steadied his breathing, and concentrated on his mission.

Vapors rolled around the sled, igniter jets fired, and the projectile lurched violently and headed down the track. It had gone eighty feet when the launch rockets roared to life. Massive gravity flattened Logan back into his harness. The sled hit the timefield at Q-velocity—2,994 feet per second—and dimensions flexed and gave way. The nothingness of a waiting wormhole loomed ahead.

Krakenfjord
March 1945

Icy rime froze and crackled on his blast suit as Logan climbed from the dark waters of the fjord, pausing only for a moment when he gained the deck of the docked trawler. He was alone. The fishing fleet was in harbor, and the boat rocked slightly among patch-ice floes under a black-velvet sky that spit little snowflakes as hard as grains of sand.

Shaken and shivering, Logan wished fervently that TEC's techs could become a little more precise about landings. Being dropped into an icy Scandinavian fjord was an experience he could have done without. He crossed the vacant fantail silently, and snapped the hatch on the boat's aft cowling. He disappeared into the darkness below, lowering the hatch behind him. His penlight played around vacant crew quarters, and he nodded, contentedly.

Twenty minutes later, a tall man in the flapped cap, woolen sweater, peacoat, and rolled boots of a fisherman climbed the icy slope from the fish docks and approached a lighted gate. He rattled the tall, link portal, and light showed beyond a ten-by-ten guardhouse. A sleepy-looking sentinel in the helmet and greatcoat of *Reichswaffen* regulars stepped out and faced the gate, cradling a short, automatic-fire weapon across his arm. *"Was ist los?"* he demanded, each word a little cloud of steam.

The fisherman drew a sheaf of papers from his coat and stepped forward, offering them. The guard reached to take them. It was his last act.

The sky was darker and the snow heavier when a solitary perimeter guard in an ill-fitting uniform crossed a motor yard full of canopied gray military vehicles and approached the postern gate below Lundsgrofenwerk, the Nazis' Krakenfjord Fabrikenwerk III-SS. In perfect German with a Bavarian brogue, he complained about the weather, then asked the officer of the guard for permission to test his field telephone. The unit at the fishdocks gate, he said, seemed to be out of order.

The guard quarters here were larger, a four-man post in the charge of a tall, sullen, overage SS lieutenant. The officer balked for a moment, then considered the consequences of awakening his superiors at this hour. With a muttered, "Yes, all right," he led the way into the guardpost and the visitor followed, face down and shivering with cold.

It was an SS lieutenant who penetrated the outer compound of Krakenfjord, and a Wehrmacht major who appeared at the armored main-tunnel gate at nine minutes past two that morning, requesting a visitor's pass.

The interview room was a twelve-foot-square cave cut into solid rock just outside the tunnel gate, fronted by a solid wall of sandbags. The interviewer was a tall, rodent-faced Gestapo underling backed by a pair of taciturn SS troopers with submachine guns.

Casually, Logan removed a small, disk-shaped apparatus from his coat pocket and laid it on the interrogator's desk. Then he turned his attention to the SS twins. They never knew what hit them.

Alarms sounded at first light, up and down the slope below the Krakenfjord tunnels. Inside the subterranean complex, deep within the stone of a precipitous crag, no sound carried from outside. But the stamp of marching boots, the shouted commands, and the general bustle of activity near the portal gate told of a general state of alarm.

Among the bystanders deep within the complex, a tall Gestapo officer stood aside as troops passed, then spent a moment studying the map of tunnels displayed on an intersection wall. Satisfied, he strode away along a cross shaft the size of a railroad tunnel.

It was the work of an hour to investigate the disruption beyond the portal gate, then bulky intercom speakers here and there in the complex announced the cause of the disturbance. Saboteurs, they said, had penetrated the exterior yards—Norwegian resistance fanatics masquerading as fishermen. One of them had made it to the Gestapo post outside the main gate, before the bomb he carried exploded. Unfortunately, two guards had been killed with him, and several others in encounters at peripheral security gates. But the incident had done no significant harm. *Heil Hitler!*

And no significant historical alteration, either, Jack Logan mused, squinting through the Gestapo agent's steel-rimmed eyeglasses. Three hours from now Allied bombers would plaster this whole mountain with heavy ordnance. Everybody dead out there will be legitimately dead, then.

"Make no tracks!" Matuzek had warned him. "Remember, this *Verteidigung* gang has historic-ripple tracking as good as ours. If we make ripples, the opposition will know it."

The tunnels were vast, seeming to go on for miles. Logan saw hundreds of people—frock-coated scientists, gray-aproned technicians, brigades of laborers flanked by armed guards, and, everywhere, SS and regular army troops. Hammers and drills rang in side tunnels where slave gangs continued the never-ending task of chiseling, hoisting, and loading stone. Millions of man-hours had gone into the building of these tunnels—and thousands of lives. As with so many "great works" of history, Logan mused, the forgotten resource behind this place was the blood and sweat of enslaved people.

Like nearby Telemark, Hitler's Reich had invested heavily in this facility. Unlike Telemark, though, there were many separate researches under way here. Every harebrained notion that passed muster anywhere else, he thought, must have wound up here.

For a time, he simply explored. There were railways in some of the tunnels, and more bits of coal scattered along the tracks than tender cars might have dropped. He strolled along one set of tracks until a locomotive and string of hopper cars passed. They were carrying coal. Somewhere under this mountain was an electrical generating plant, and Logan judged it must have enormous capacity.

And now the map Amy Fuller had drawn made sense. Historians a few years after this time had speculated about the so-called T-head vault at the north end of the tunnel complex. But no witnesses ever explained what precise research had been done there. Rocket testing of some kind, it was thought. But now, intuitively, Jack Logan knew. A huge, open tunnel nearly four thousand feet in length, with walls scorched by rocket blast. Reinforced bedding down its center, a thing like an enormous catapult base at one end, and the remains of mighty steel beams still bolted into the stone at the other—a time machine! And with a massive generating plant, they had the power to activate a timefield.

There had always been rumors that the Nazis had toyed with fourth-dimension insertion, and now Jack Logan knew it for a fact. Somewhere back there, beyond a dozen *Verboten* signs and checkpoints, was the first time-launcher.

The facility had been dismantled by the time Allied investigators got to it, which meant that the experiment had failed prior to the fall of the Third Reich. But to have failed, it must actually have been tried! Logan decided he definitely wanted to have a look at that thing. But first he had a mission to complete.

It took only minutes to locate the quarters of *Oberkommandeur* Helmut von Steuben. It was an observation room only a few paces from the infirmary. So von Steuben took part in an experiment, Logan deduced.

The corridor was a busy place. Doctors, nurses, attendants, and orderlies scurried here and there among tramping squads of booted troops, and he saw at least three Gestapo types at a glance.

Squaring his shoulders, Logan knocked at von Steuben's door. But it wasn't von Steuben who opened it. The man was a civilian, with the look of authority about him. *"Ja?"* he demanded. Beyond him, through the partly open door, Logan saw others—armed SS guards and at least two more of the civilians. Gestapo, he realized. A special unit. Himmler's personal elite.

"Heil Hitler!" Logan saluted. "Perhaps I have come to the wrong room? I am looking for *Oberkommandeur* Helmut von Steuben."

"This is his room," the man at the door said softly. "Your business?"

"He asked me to join him here," Logan said stiffly. "There was a matter he wished to discuss with me."

For a moment the man eyed him, then his face relaxed in a wide smile. *"Ja,"* he said. *"Sehr gut!"*

Logan felt the sudden, sharp pressure of gun muzzles against his back. The man in the doorway leered at him, then bowed slightly, contemptuously. "How very convenient," he purred. "Just when we have such a puzzle, here is the man who can solve it for us. Here is Herr von Steuben, missing these past four days, and now one comes who has spoken with him." He signaled, and the gun barrels pressed brutally against Logan's back. He was pushed through the door and it closed behind him. A hard fist cracked against his temple, and a gun butt thudded into his side. He was forced to his knees.

"Where is von Steuben?" a hard voice demanded. "Where are the documents? Who are you, and why are you wearing Hans Vogel's uniform?"

Trying to clear his vision, Logan sagged for an instant. Then he twisted, found a grip on a submachine gun, and pivoted, tearing it from the grasp of the soldier who held it. Still on his knees, he plunged forward, going for the knees of the man in front of him . . . rolling and bringing the weapon up.

A rifle butt descended behind his ear, and the world swam around him. "Subdue that man!" a voice thundered, in German. Logan was pummeled, gasping and fighting. Boots, fists, and clubs lashed at him. "To the silent ward!" the distant, swimming voice commanded. "He is to be interrogated!"

Distantly, Logan felt himself half lifted, hard hands dragging him along an echoing corridor. The corridor faded and there was a small, stone-walled cubicle, a dissection table with leather straps . . . and he was on his back, being strapped down. A man in a white smock stood over him, venting an old-fashioned, silver-frame hypodermic needle. Something stung his arm, and his strength seemed to fade away . . . into swirling, relaxing tones and pastels that dispersed gently, leaving nothing where they had been.

Logan opened his eyes, enjoying the gentle touch of soft hands at the restricting, aching places on him. Idly, he pieced together his returning sensations. A nurse, he decided. She was a nurse, and she was relieving the pressure on his arms and wrists, his thighs and ankles. And she had the bluest eyes . . .

Those eyes leaned close to peer at him, and became eyes that he had seen before.

" 'Ello, Yank," she said cheerfully. "You look like you took on 'alf the bloody German army, and lost."

He let it sink in, then sat up, wincing at more aches and pains than he could count. His face and ribs felt as though he had been used for target practice, and his left eye was swollen almost closed.

The room was a simple cubicle cut into mountain stone and partitioned at its open end by a padded, soundproof wall with a heavy, closed door. An electric lamp burned overhead in a shielded cage. Beside the table where he sat, there was an open iron cabinet filled with medical and surgical apparatus and little glass vials.

And there were inert bodies scattered here and there— one wearing a medical smock, two in 1940s civilian suits, and two more in the gray uniforms of SS troopers. None of them were moving. The young woman standing beside him had sunshine curls framing the starched cap on her head. She might have been just a cute little German nurse, but for the Stern-Benning slung over her shoulder, the 9mm Walther tucked into her waistband, and the amused grin on her face. The grin was pure Australian.

"Hello, Harriet," Logan said, his voice distorted by the

swelling bruises and cuts around his mouth. "What did I tell them?"

" 'Oo knows?" She shrugged. "They 'ad you in 'ere for near two hours, on Sodium Pentothal and 'oo knows w'at else. You're probably resistant, but if you'd been of this time you'd 'ave recited your life 'istory to 'em by now, an' tossed in references. Where d'you 'urt the most?"

"Everywhere. Want to kiss it and make it well?"

"Another time, luv." She chuckled. "Right now we've a bit of a pickle. You've lost your retrieval bracelet, and mine's got a 'ole in it." She glanced at the floor, indicating one of the Gestapo agents sprawled there. A 9mm Mauser slug had gone through his hand and the bracelet in it, on its way to his heart.

"Grabby bloke," Harriet muttered.

"Are you telling me we're stuck? In 1945?"

"Stuck in the past," she said, and nodded. "No way for us to get back to our time. I'm afraid we've cashed it in, Yank. There's guards outside that door, and 'alf a regiment between 'ere an' the main gate. They've got an air raid alert. I can't see any way we can get to the front of these tunnels."

"Then let's take a look at the back," Logan said. Stiffly, feeling every ache, he crouched and began stripping the smock off a dead Nazi. It was the one with the needle. The top of the man's head had been blown away by a 9mm slug, but there wasn't much blood on his smock. "How did you get in here?"

"Just Fräulein Joder bringing linens," she said, smiling sadly. "The guards were more interested in searching me than in searching the linens. They let me in."

"Then the guards will be expecting you to come out with an armload of soiled linens," he said.

A few minutes later, two hulking SS guards stepped aside from the soundproofed door, leering as a blond nurse with a bundle of wrinkled, blood-spattered linens stepped out between them and looked both ways along the corridor. She half turned, smiled a dazzling smile at the pair, and stooped, as though to lay her bundle on the floor.

The interesting gap at the top of Harriet's pinafore was the last thing either guard ever saw. One took a spine-shattering knuckle-punch from behind, just below his helmet. The other's skull was broken by the linen-shrouded gun butt that jabbed upward, colliding with the bridge of his nose.

With the bodies stowed in the closed room, Logan pointed to the left. "This way," he said. "Follow me."

The thunder of distant bombs rolled through the Krakenfjord tunnels as Jack Logan and Harriet Blevins crouched in the shadow of a sandbag blast wall, their eyes roving over detail after detail of the first time-travel device. Somewhere on the face of the mountain, Allied bombers were softening up the defenses of Krakenfjord, while U.S. troops and Norwegian partisans assembled on the slopes below, for the ultimate assault. But here, deep within the mountain, two temporal police officers stared at a contraption unlike any they had seen before.

In appearance, it bore little resemblance to the perfected sled tracks and timefield armatures of 2007. But in function, it was basically the same.

The sled was a long, lightweight, and fragile-looking framework of polished wood and stretched canvas, almost like an open canoe resting on a keel that was nothing more than three long runners of nickel-alloy steel with stabilizing cross members at intervals. Inside the "boat" was a long row of webbed leather double seats. The entire contrivance thrust out like a flimsy arrow ahead of a trio of rocket jets, which Logan recognized.

"V-2 launch pods," he growled. "Thirty seconds of controlled, raw explosion. Good God!"

"Best they 'ad," Harriet said, shrugging. "Tachyon drive's a 'alf-dozen decades in the future."

Ahead of the thrusters, the boat was at least a hundred and fifty feet in length. At each webbed bench, a sharply angled baffle of what looked like laminated pine was set, to serve as a windscreen. The entire vehicle, rockets and all, would weigh barely a tenth of the total mass of a TEC or Pastime sled, but the payload capacity was enormous.

The vehicle rested in a trough of grooved, milled steel, which extended away into shadowed distance through a circular, fifty-foot tunnel. In the remote distance, girder towers flanking the track held the frames of a rudimentary field generator almost hidden by banks of transformers, clusters of glass insulators, and huge induction coils.

"That thing couldn't possibly generate a timefield," Harriet said, scowling and peering into the shadowy distance.

"Doesn't look like it," Logan agreed. "But, then, the Wright brothers' airplane didn't look like it would fly, either."

Just across from their hiding place, long rows of bulky, clumsy-looking instruments glowed with dim lights. "Vacuum tubes!" Harriet muttered. "Vacuum tubes and rheostats. Not a single 'ardwired bank or circuit board. Not even any transistors! Lord, 'ow primitive."

"It's state of the art, 1945," Logan reminded her. "Like V-2 boosters. Trace the schematics. Let's see how this thing is controlled."

"That's simple enough," she said. "The boat 'as its own controls—double toggle switches, rear seat. Flip 'em an' pray. Dimensional insertion must be calculated by those four Copernicus-globe things over there. They're calibrated, y'see? An' the timefield 'as a simple enough mechanism. Turn th' bloody thing on an' it'll spark when it hits overload. Trick bein', to 'ave the boat in the field when it sparks."

"Fine," Logan growled. "I didn't ask for a guided tour. Do you think you could trigger a launch?"

Harriet glanced up at him, her blue eyes unreadable. "Sure, like I can fly like a bloody gull, Yank. No easy thing, to launch without somebody at the fixed controls. Guess I might single-lever everything, an' make a gravity contact with a sand delay. Course, those thrusters will wreck the control banks, if we do that. There's no shielding in place, an' nobody to regulate the load. Lord only knows if the banks'd last long enough to generate a timefield."

"It's warmed up and ready." He indicated the glowing tubes across the track. "I'd say somebody was about to do a test when the bombs started falling outside."

Casually, the two crossed a catwalk to the control side. There were sentries there, patrolling the tunnel at intervals, but the first ones they passed only glanced at them. They were used to people in white smocks here, and these two aroused no suspicions.

At the field banks, Harriet studied the calibrated settings. "I know these spatial coordinates," she muttered. "That's Argentina, somewhere around Buenos Aires." The fourth coordinate, though—the temporal one—brought a sigh and a shake of the head. "Doesn't make sense," she said finally. "This looks like it might equate to October 1945. But that's impossible. That's seven months into the future! Time travel can't go futureward!"

"Maybe the Nazis didn't realize time travel is a thing of the past." Logan shrugged. "Can you reset it?"

"Can't," she said. "Bloody thing's locked in."

"Well, we don't have a choice," he decided. "We've both lost our retrieval bracelets. We can't go back to our time, and we can't get out any other way. This thing is our only way out of here."

"But we'd go nowhen," she argued. "That stuff about slingshot effect, that's outmoded theory. Can't compute for the future, so there's no predictable bounce to the past. Wulden thought you could, but that was before quantum theory."

"This technology is so far removed from ours," Logan said, "let's face it, we don't know what those settings mean, for sure." Gripping her hand, he led her to the boat, then crouched there, curious. "Roller bearings riding on a film of oil," he noted. "Ingenious."

"Come on, then!" Harriet snapped. "If we're for it, don't stop an' gawk!"

"You just set up a launch," he said. "Anything you don't understand, fake it. What have we got to lose?"

He helped her rig a delayed-action weight and cross-connect the launch controls to a single lever. Then they climbed into the rear seats, snugged themselves in, and put on the padded leather helmets they found there. Harriet studied the boat's switch panel for a moment, then tripped the first pair. A roar erupted behind them, and waves of intense heat eddied through the tunnels. Somewhere aft, a pair of startled sentries whirled and stared. *"Mein Gott!"* one of them shouted. *"Was ist los? Halt!"*

"Be lucky if we're within fifty years of present time," Harriet declared, "but 'ere goes nothin'." She flicked the remaining switches. Mighty thunder cascaded directly aft, collapsing the sand-wedged control lever beside the bay banks. A huge, spring-tension catapult slammed them forward and the two agents in their stolen time-boat careened down the tunnel. Bone-crunching waves of gravity thrust them back and back into the steel-hard web of their perch. Ahead, approaching impossibly fast, the twin towers grew and lightning spiraled around them. "Spark, dammit!" Logan screamed silently. "Arc across! Give us our wormhole!"

His cheeks rippled with grav-force and his sight dimmed

as the pressure approached blackout threshold. Out of the corner of his eye he saw a flicker, and tried to focus on it. It was a bullet! An 8mm projectile in full flight from the snout of a Mauser 98-K rifle. At point-blank velocity it floated in space a foot from his shoulder. For an instant it kept pace with the sled, then the sled surged past it.

Military-issue 8mm . . . the numbers flashed in Logan's dizzy mind. Muzzle velocity 2,800 feet per second—he strained at the pressure crushing him, willing it onward, toward the magic number—2,994. Q-velocity!

The rockets thundered, the towers grew, lightning flared and sizzled, and a sheet of intense blue flame grew in the interval between the frames. The boat dived into it . . . into black nothingness.

Logan blinked his eyes and spat sand from his bruised lips. Groaning, he raised his head and looked around— directly into the wise, disinterested eyes of a bridled mule.

Just beyond, Harriet Blevins was in earnest conversation with a bandy-legged old man wearing a brass-buttoned coat, gaucho trousers, and sandals. As Logan sat up, they both gazed at him.

"Well, we're 'ere," Harriet said. "Problem bein', 'ere is just up-country from La Plata, forty miles south of Buenos Aires, an' twenty-five years too early. It isn't 1945 anymore, Yank. This, as best Señor Ramos 'ere can reckon, is the year 1920."

Logan stood, looking around. The sun was high in a cool, clear sky over vistas that became hillsides in one direction while sloping in the other toward a distant little town.

"Nineteen twenty," he muttered. Somehow, the vector equations that had seemed to read 1945 had equated to 1920. Wouldn't TEC's scientists find that interesting! "Problem being," he growled at Harriet, "we're stuck here. We have no means of retrieval, and nobody knows where or when we are. I wonder why they had that thing aimed at Argentina."

"That's w'at I meant to tell you, Yank," Harriet said. "Helmut von Steuben disappeared from Krakenfjord four days before you got there. The Gestapo traced 'im to Lisbon, where 'e boarded a ship called *Krofft*, bound for Argentina." She smiled at the old man with the mule, then told Logan, "Señor Ramos says there's a nice inn at La Plata where we can stay while you reckon a way out of this mess."

Krakenfjord
1945

In the smoke-blackened wreckage of the acceleration tunnel, a figure stirred and looked around with dazed eyes. *Herrdoktor* Josef Heindl had no idea what had happened here, except that the time-boat was gone. Its rockets had been triggered, and it had blasted itself into oblivion.

All he had seen, coming through the reinforced portal from his private quarters, was the intense flare of thrusters and the melting down—the fusing—of his beloved control banks. Without blast shields, they had become useless slag.

He got to his feet, staggering, and felt the wet blood running down the front of his smock. Looking down, he saw a foot-long shard of blackened metal protruding from his abdomen—a piece of demolished V-2 rocket, hurled up-tunnel when the boat hit the far end.

He had wanted one final test before disassembly—a simple vector and rebound test, nothing more. It was something von Steuben had suggested. But now the facility was a wreck and there was nothing to test. He walked a few feet, staggered, and fell. And in falling, he knew what the metal sliver had done inside him. He knew he was dying.

There was a boy with him then—a little boy cradling his head, sobbing and weeping, saying over and over, *"Pate Josef! Mein Pate . . . mein Pate!"*

Heindl felt his strength ebbing away with his flowing blood. He looked up at the boy, and tried to smile. "Ah, Hans," he whispered. "Little Hans. You must hide yourself now, Hans, as we practiced. Soon the Americans will be here. They will care for you."

"Nein!" The boy wept. *"Pate Josef,* you keep me—"

"Hide, Hans," the scientist whispered. "And the locked book . . . don't forget the locked book! Keep it safe, Hans. When you have grown to be a man, maybe it will . . ." Blood surged from his mouth, and his eyes went dull. "The book has ideas . . . maybe you will know what to do."

When his godfather was dead, Hans Kleindast crawled into the secret cavern below the accelerator shaft and curled himself up to wait. The cavern was well stocked with provisions and even a few comforts. Josef Heindl had seen the end coming, and provided for his godson the best he could. There was enough here to see the boy through until Allied troops took charge of Krakenfjord, and papers to identify him to the officer in charge.

And in a locked box, beneath the supply shelves, was the book. It was Dr. Josef Heindl's legacy to Hans Kleindast— basic ideas behind the Nazi experiments. Ideas from which viable time-travel technology might one day be developed.

La Plata, Argentina
1920

La Forma wasn't the only hotel in La Plata, but it was the only one with electric lights and a semblance of plumbing. It had a ballroom, a café, and a view of the harbor, and its one vacant guest room was clean, spacious, and airy.

In a hillside transaction, they had traded Harriet's Mauser and ammunition for Señor Ramos's mule. In La Plata's *mercado* they sold the mule, bought a good meal and a leather suitcase, and traded their German clothing for a wardrobe suited to the time and place.

Though the sun was still high, the *plazuela* was beginning to fill with strollers. The music of tango bands floated on a cool breeze, and evening spots around the square enticed trade with garish, electric-light signs and the tangy scents of cooking.

Three ships lay in the main harbor—a Brazilian coastal cruise vessel, an American pleasure steamer, and a newly arrived German passenger liner, still discharging its bilges. Tramp steamers, sailing where their fares took them. They put in here, at little La Plata, to avoid the tariffs at Buenos Aires.

Strolling through the *plazuela*, Harriet glanced toward

the little railroad station at the head of the shipyards. A train was just pulling out, heading for Buenos Aires.

"Lot of people traveling, lot of places," Harriet commented. "A crazy, golden time for those as 'ad the wherewithal."

"Tourists and adventurers," Logan said, and shrugged. "The jet set of the twenties."

For a time they mingled with the crowds, absorbing the atmosphere of the time and place. Fresh-combed, trimmed, and bathed, barbered and curled and splashed with lilac water, and wearing the attire of the time, they fit right in.

They had a meal at a courtyard cantina and listened to a local band inventing new versions of the sensuous, commanding domestic music called tango. Then they walked to La Forma and checked in.

While Harriet inspected their quarters, Logan headed straight for the only bed. He slept for twelve hours, and awakened at dawn. Harriet was curled beside him, her head on his shoulder. He yawned, stretched, and she opened one eye. "Good morning," she purred, her fingers tracing a delicate path down his chest. They paused at a welt of scar tissue just below his ribs. "You've got your share of scars on you, Yank. W'at's this 'ere? Bullet wound?"

"Lead ball," he told her. "Thirty caliber. Do-it-yourself jumper arranged a duel with Aaron Burr over New York City water rights. Our insertion was off by nine seconds and I dropped right between them on the count of twenty."

"So you took a bullet to save Burr?"

"No, it was Burr who shot me. It was a botched jump. A self-correcting anachronism, and I was in the middle. The scars come with the job. How about you, Aussie? Any interesting occupational blemishes worth noting?"

He turned toward her but she pulled away and sat up, wrapping herself in the bedsheet. "There's a bath at the end of the hall," she said. "Nice, cold shower. 'Ave you reckoned 'ow we get out of this mess, yet?"

La Plata was the perfect tourist town, Logan decided. All the sights to be seen—the *puerto*, the *mercado*, the gaudy little *plaza de las flores*, and Mission Santa Maria del Río—could be thoroughly seen in less than an hour, leaving new arrivals plenty of time to catch the train up-river to Buenos Aires. Most of the tourists they could see were waiting for the train.

"I wish Amy Fuller were here," Logan mused, as they sipped Venezuelan coffee in the *plazuela*.

Harriet shot him a sharp glance. "Well, thanks, luv," she said. Morning sunlight glinted on the blond ringlets of her close-coiffed hair and brought out the pastels in the simple flower-print dress she wore. " 'Oo's Amy Fuller?"

"One of our historians," he explained. "She always reads the fine print. She'd know what to look for here."

"W'at's to look for? We're lost, Yank! Get that through your bloody 'ead! We're stuck in a past that we can't get out of, an' we've lost the track to boot. We're twenty-five years too early for w'atever the Nazi chronophage was set for!"

"I'm wondering about that," he said. "The random-future concept is as basic to temporal theory as four-dimensional manipulation. It's part of the basic math. It isn't likely that future-range setting was an ignorant mistake. Maybe it was experimental, but whoever set it probably knew the rebound potential. Maybe even calculated it in, as a backup target."

"So?"

"So, maybe it was an intentional bounce. The spatial co-ordinates were fairly well plotted. At least we didn't materialize underground, or a hundred feet in the air. Maybe the temporal was, too. If that's the case, there's something going on around here, in 1920, that somebody in 1945 Norway was—will be—interested in."

"There's nothing going on 'ere." Harriet waved a hand, indicating the *plazuela* with its rows of little shops, the desultory foot traffic around the square, the half-dozen low-fenced patios where other people sat at other tables, drinking coffee. Along the rutted streets beyond the *plazuela*, drays were delivering produce from the surrounding farms, and in the harbor outbound fishing boats puttered like ants around the silent ships. "It's a sleepy little Latin town going about its business."

"Then we'll look in Buenos Aires," he said. "It's only forty miles."

Above La Plata, the rails ran parallel to a graded road. Traffic there was light, mostly farm carts and haywagons and a few motorcars, but there were horsemen, as well. Harriet watched these with interest. "Gauchos," she said. "Finest 'orsemen in the world, outside the Outback."

Where the rails and the road crossed a miles-long area of rocky breaks, a viaduct was under construction. Hundreds of laborers—whole regiments of dusty, copper-skinned men supervised by armed horsemen—were at work there, moving tons of earth a barrow at a time. On the bench next to Logan, as the train chugged past a nearby squad of workers breaking stone, a *sarape*-clad elder squinted out the window and crossed himself surreptitiously. Out there, fifty yards away, four laborers hung from a suspended rail by their tied wrists while a man with a whip cut bleeding stripes into their backs.

"*Descamisados,*" the old man muttered. "*Ai, los Indios pobres!*"

"Slave laborers," Harriet whispered to Logan. "Notice, they're all Indians."

They were in the outskirts of Buenos Aires when a troop

of twenty riders came from behind, overtaking and passing the train at a gallop. Their bright, woolen *sarapes* flying, hat brims curled by the wind, the gauchos had a wild, fierce look about them. Logan noted that they were all armed, and all wore distinctive green cloths at their necks.

The dust of their passage swept off inland, and in its wake came a motorcar unlike the few they had seen before. It was a long, elegant machine—lemon-yellow panels and bright silver trim, spotless and gleaming even through the dust.

"Deusenberg," Logan said, and pointed. "One hell of a car, for its time or any time." For long moments, the car ran alongside the train, fifty yards away. The goggled face of a liveried chauffeur glanced their way, and the faces of passengers peered from the white-covered salon behind the driver's cockpit. Three people—a gray-haired, middle-aged man, a younger woman, and a dark-eyed girl child. Then the magnificent machine pulled away, following the gauchos.

Logan noticed that other passengers in the railcar had gravitated to the left windows to watch it pass. One group in particular, ahead of him, seemed especially intent upon the vehicle. They were five young men, all dark-suited and quiet. Even from the back, they had the look of Europeans, and as voices drifted back to him he identified them as Germans . . . probably passengers from that same tramp steamer that had vented its bilges in La Plata harbor.

They resumed their seats when the Deusenberg was past, but Logan was puzzled. He had only a glimpse of their faces, but one of them had looked oddly familiar to him. It was a very young face, pale and serious with narrow, disapproving eyes, a pinched nose, almost lipless mouth, and a shock of carefully combed, oiled hair above high-barbered temples. Hardly more than a boy, he noted.

Probably not over twenty, but somehow the face looked old and angry despite its youth.

It was a face he might have seen, but not in this time and not at this age. He puzzled over it, then put it aside as the train's whistle sounded the approach to Estación Bartolomé Mitre, the main rail terminal in Buenos Aires.

Just off the Plaza de Mayo, they saw the Deusenberg again, and out of curiosity Logan led Harriet to a low-walled open-air patio cantina where little wire tables sat on slate tiles and bustling waiters served coffee and sweets. The people from the Deusenberg sat at a long table near the cantina doors.

At least a dozen armed gauchos lounged casually around the place, wide hats shading their watchful eyes. Bodyguards, Logan guessed. Escorts for the steel-haired don, the woman, and the girl at the reserved table.

They found a table and ordered coffee, and Logan asked their waiter who the distinguished gentleman across the way might be.

"Aya son el Señor Vargas y su familia," the waiter said, speaking with reverence. "A very famous man, señor. Don Fernando Vargas is master of Estancia Vargas, and *patrón del puerto* for Río de la Plata district. A very big man, señor. Very powerful. Don Fernando honors us with his presence."

When the waiter turned away, Logan glanced across at Harriet Blevins. "Vargas," he repeated. "Ring any bells for you?"

The family Vargas was served breakfast, then the servants dispersed and the hard-eyed gauchos spread around the *plazuela*, blending into the scenery. As though on cue, a group of young Europeans entered from the cantina and Vargas waved them over. They were the same five from the train.

Harriet was watching them, too. "Germans," she muttered. "A school tour, or something. I heard them talking. They're from Munich." She squinted, shading her eyes from the high, bright sunlight, then tugged at Logan's sleeve. "Look at the first one! Look closely, Yank. Picture 'im older, an' 'oo d'you see?"

Logan shook his head. "I don't place him," he said. "Another one's familiar, though."

"That's Alfred Rosenberg!" Harriet whispered. "I was at Nürnberg when 'e was sentenced in '46. The ideologist, they called him. Author of National Socialism. The first Nazi!"

Logan didn't respond. With her mention of Nazi, it clicked into place. He stared at the third one—the one he had wondered about—and knew who he was. Logan's knuckles whitened slightly and his eyes narrowed. It was him. A younger version, but unquestionably him. "Himmler!" he breathed.

Heinrich Himmler was in Argentina, in 1920!

"That's it," he whispered, "we're looking at our answer, right there. That's why the Krakenfjord field was set for now. It wasn't a mistake. This is where the ripple starts."

"But there won't be a ripple now." Harriet frowned. "We wrecked their launch banks when we took off. There were no blast shields in place, remember?"

"Oh, there's a ripple, all right," Logan growled. "The historians have always wondered where Hitler and his friends got the money for the Munich Putsch. I'll bet we're looking at the source right now. Don Fernando Vargas. A real-time ripple that changed the world."

There was no response, and Logan glanced around. Harriet was gone.

Logan turned slowly, his policeman's eyes sweeping the surroundings. Then he saw her. She stood in the interior door of the cantina, beyond Vargas's table. A tall cocktail glass tilted dangerously in one hand, and the other hand clung to the doorframe for balance. The hand slipped and she staggered forward, awkward on high heels. "Oops," she said, then giggled.

Gauchos materialized all around the Vargas party, hands at their weapons, but Harriet only waved giddily at the nearest one and staggered forward, past him, to collide with the first of the young Germans. Her drink doused his lapels, and she giggled again as he grabbed her shoulders, steadying her.

The scene lasted only a moment, then *sarape*-clad gauchos had Harriet, half carrying her away from their patron's presence. Somewhere near Logan, a man chuckled. *"Turista,"* someone said. *"Tienes a'mas des jovias."*

A pair of somber federal police hurried through the plaza gate, and the gauchos veered toward them, Harriet in tow. With a growl, Logan heaved his weight backward, feeling the fragile leg of his chair buckle as he did. The chair toppled, and he went with it. His thrashing feet, as he fell, kicked over the wire table before him. He twisted, catching his weight on one hand, pivoted, and knocked the legs from under a passing waiter.

It was enough. The instant's commotion had done its work. Logan picked himself up, looking acutely embarrassed. Glancing around, he saw that he had the full attention of the *policías*, the gauchos, and everyone else. Harriet was nowhere in sight. *"Perdóneme,"* he muttered, brushing himself down, then he said it more loudly, turning to assess the damage he had done. He helped the fallen waiter to his feet, then dug a handful of currency from a pocket. *"Permítame, por favor . . ."*

A half hour later, he found her in an art gallery on Avenida Soliz. "That was a dumb stunt," he said. "We're stuck in the past, without retrieval contact or documentation, and you try to get yourself arrested. What the hell—"

"No problem, Yank," she said cheerfully. "I knew you'd think of something." She took a wallet from her purse and handed it to him. "Take a look at this!"

He glanced into it. "Rosenberg," he muttered. "You picked his pocket!"

"Course I did, luv. Keep looking. Their names are all there, and a list of their travel documents. You were right. The kid with the rat nose is Heinrich Himmler. But there's more. There's a letter of introduction in there, from Reinhard Krupp to Don Fernando Vargas, introducing Herr Rosenberg and his associates as representatives of the *Verteidigung Innung Provozieren Rache*. The letter is countersigned by Adolf Hitler 'imself."

"Verteidigung . . . Innung . . . " Logan pronounced the words slowly, puzzling over the intentional vagueness of their meaning.

"It's a bit obscure," Harriet said, and nodded, "but a rough translation might be Defense Guild for the Initiation of Retribution. It's got a nice, fascist ring to it, doesn't it?"

"More than that," he said. "There's that word, *verteidigung*. The word the jumpers used. And look at this— V-I-P-R. Viper! I've got to get this to ThinkTank, Aussie."

" 'Ow 'bout sending 'em a letter?" She shrugged. "Maybe the United States Postal Service would keep a dead letter for eighty-seven years, then deliver it."

"Maybe pigs can fly, too." He paused, thoughtfully, then thumbed through more of the papers in the Nazi's wallet. "They're booked at the Villa Córdoba," he noted.

"Herr Rosenberg will be missing 'is wallet," Harriet pointed out. "Best if an ordinary thief took it, don't you think?"

"Absolutely." Logan thumbed through the remaining papers, memorizing a few names and numbers, then removed all the currency from it. He thrust this into one pocket, the wallet into another. "Meet me across from Villa

Córdoba," he said. Without waiting for an answer, he turned and strode away, back toward the *plazuela*.

The wallet would be found within the hour, hidden beneath ornamental shrubs just off the plaza, all the cash removed, everything else intact. The predictable work of any casual pickpocket in any big city.

Villa Córdoba was a three-story stone structure, a haven for *turistas*, near the Parque de Retiro. A brief investigation located the Nazis' suite at third floor rear, overlooking Avenida des Aires with its Ascension observation tower.

Logan rented a room on the second floor, and left Harriet there. He crossed Avenida des Aires and headed into the nearest *Porteño* section, where wrought-iron fences hid the dwellings of the city's natives and protected the windows of their shops. Here, beyond the *plaza grande* and the grand edifices by which Buenos Aires proclaimed itself to the world, beyond even the night-crawling buffer zone where *turistas* and *Porteños* mingled in the gaiety of the city's dance halls and dark-hours cafés, was where the real Buenos Aires lived.

He was back in an hour, his arms full of linen-wrapped packages. In their room, he spread his acquisitions on the bed for inspection and assembly. In separate parcels he had a pair of box-magazine Krag rifles, a box of ammunition, two sniper barrel rests—one with a pedestal stand and one with folding bipod legs—a full-bore sight calibrator, and two long-tube four-X telescope sights with mounting lugs and rings.

"Are you familiar with the Krag?" he asked Harriet.

"I've qualified with military bolt-actions, same as you," she said. "W'at's all this for?"

"I paced the distance from the Ascension Tower to the rear wall of this place," he told Harriet. "It's an easy shot, a hundred and eighty yards. Angle about fifteen degrees lateral, eight to ten vertical."

She stared at the assemblage, mystified. "So w'at do you aim to do, Yank? Go to war?"

"I've 'reckoned' a way to get us out of this mess, as you said." He grinned. "All we have to do is get TEC's attention, and they'll send a ride for us."

"Get their attention? 'Ow?"

"We'll give them an E-warp ripple they can't miss. We're going to kill Heinrich Himmler."

The old Ascension Tower was nearly a hundred feet tall, with a walled walkway at eighty feet. Built in 1811 as a lookout point against Spanish invasion, the old tower had become a fading monument to Argentinian independence. As recently as 1905, it had served as an observation point for sightseers. But now it was rarely climbed.

By moonlight, Jack Logan and Harriet Blevins deposited their burdens on the narrow floor of the parapet and looked down at the quiet streets below. Two avenues crossed at the base of the tower, and someone had built a little triangle garden there. Beyond rose the buildings that fronted on the *plaza grande*. The nearest one, the Villa Córdoba, had little balconies at each suite, and electric lights in the rooms.

"Third floor, third balcony from the left." Logan pointed. "It's a three-room suite. All five of them should be there. They have a couple of girls with them, so there should be some activity." He extracted the pedestal rest and positioned it on the stone parapet. "This should be about right," he muttered. Fitting a scope onto one of the Krags, he loaded its magazine, put a round in the chamber, and set its forestock on the cushioned rest. Kneeling, he peered through the sight, aligning the rifle. "Ah, yes," he said. "Quite a picture."

Harriet raised the other sight and held it like a spyglass.

She gazed through it for a moment, then lowered it. "God!" she said. "Those 'orrible pigs! That's disgusting!"

"Little Heinrich does have some bizarre tastes, doesn't he?" Logan agreed. "He's acting out his sexual-sadistic fantasies. Well, at least he's in full view of the window. Any further reservations about committing assassination?"

"That's not a 'uman being." Harriet's voice was deep with disgust. "That's a monster. And the rest no better. Still, I'm a cop, Logan. By Pastime regs I'm rated for execution. Assassination's not the same thing. I just wish I could face the bastard an' give 'im 'is rights. Then blow 'is brains out."

At his you-know-better-than-that glance, she picked up the second Krag. "I know, I know," she muttered. "If it doesn't 'appen, nobody will come to keep it from 'appening."

As expertly as Logan had, Harriet assembled the rifle, placed its scope and sniper rest, and knelt to the sight. " 'Ow d'you want to play this, Yank?"

"Staggered shots, a second apart," he said. "You first, count of two, I'll fire on three. Center on Himmler and shoot to kill. The glass may deflect the first bullet, but not the second one."

There was no need to explain. Once they opened fire, the grounds below the tower would be alive with police in a matter of seconds. There would be no way down. And to miss would be to fail. Himmler still alive, even Himmler wounded, might not change history enough to cause a ripple in the timestream. When the first bullet flew, the Germans in that lighted room would dive for cover. It had to be a sure kill, first shot.

It was hit or miss, all or nothing. They looked at each other in the moonlight—the tall, somber TEC agent and the small, blond Pastime agent—and knew what failure would mean.

"Now?" Harriet steadied herself against the parapet, snugging the Krag's stock into the hollow of her shoulder. Beside her, Logan did the same. He peered through his sight, praying that his sight and trajectory bore calculations were exact. In his sight, two young Nazis, naked as jaybirds, were holding down a dark-haired girl on a couch, pretending bondage while a third, the young Himmler, toyed with her. It was only sick play, but the ice pick and pliers in Himmler's hands matched the ecstasy in his eyes. Logan set his crosshairs at the notch of Himmler's collarbones and touched his trigger. "Count," he said.

"One . . . two . . ." Harriet's Krag discharged, loud and sharp in the quiet night. The window glass exploded, and Himmler's head jerked up.

"Three!" Logan squeezed the trigger. The Krag bucked against his shoulder, its roar blending with the other shot. He saw the bullet strike, saw it enter the base of Himmler's throat, saw the young Nazi's arms flap like grotesque wings as his spine was shattered by 170 grains of lead moving at a velocity of more than 2,500 feet per second.

Logan set his crosshairs at the base of Himmler's neck and touched his trigger. "Count," he said.

Beside him, Harriet steadied down to fire. "One!" she said. "T—"

Behind them there was a thud, a grunt, and a steely, angry voice said, "Freeze or you're dead!"

An instant from firing, Harriet eased off on her trigger and raised her head from the scope sight. Beside her, Jack Logan loosed his grip on his own rifle and turned, slowly. "Do you really mean that, Gene?" he drawled.

A long second passed, then Captain Eugene Matuzek— upside down against the low parapet wall behind them— lowered the deadly stitcher machine gun in his hands and untangled himself from his own arms and legs. He clambered to his feet. "You!" he hissed. "What in God's name? . . ."

"Only way we could think of to get your attention." Logan grinned. "Must have been a hell of a ripple, to bring you out on a mission, Gene. Who's minding the store at TEC?"

"You don't know how much of a ripple." Matuzek looked pale, even in the moonlight. "No sooner did we have it on the screen than a jumper with a black mask and a pair of Uzis materialized . . . right in the TEC squad room! With a EuroTEC agent right behind him. It sounded like Bull Run there for a minute." His eyes narrowed. "Somebody didn't like what you were doing here! I lost two people in the cross fire. Brady's dead, and Cassini. The jumper and the EuroTEC agent, too. Some other injuries, but I couldn't wait for the counts. I was the only trained sled-jockey available."

"Then VIPR picked up the reading, too," Logan said. "They saw the significance, and went for the source. Euro-TEC must have reacted sometime in the future."

"Yeah, they—Viper? What's Viper?"

"V-I-P-R. *Verteidigung Innung Provozieren Rache.* We've got a handle on our enemy, Captain. But we need a hitch back to base."

In the lighted suite on the third floor of Villa Córdoba the party continued, uninterrupted. Five young men who would soon help initiate one of history's abominations, in a Munich beer hall, continued their fun with a pair of *Porteño* prostitutes, oblivious to the guns that had been pointed their way a minute before.

The alternate probability sequence generated by the assassination of young Heinrich Himmler would never occur. On three known timestream screens—and somewhere on a sinister, hidden fourth one—a full level-eight ripple blipped out of existence as the two TEC policemen and the Pastime Authority agent linked hands and entered retrieval.

EuroTEC Headquarters, Timetrust Research Complex
Paris, France
2007

Jean-Luc Poulon, inspector of the French *Sûreté* and chief executive of TEC's European precinct, watched through the three-inch-thick glass of Timetrust's launch control as the wormhole field a half mile down the track shimmered and a timesled appeared, erupting into substance like a big, incoming missile. He could almost feel the reverse Gs as the sled decelerated thunderously, hurtling toward the launch platform, slowing as it came to finally creep into its completion position between the embarkation stanchions.

The hatch slid open and two field agents climbed out. Emery Brooks was an Englishman and Pieter VanDoorn was Dutch. Their ongoing competitions with each other—over everything from women to marksmanship to who wore the best shoes—were legendary, but they had been partners since the beginning of Timetrust and were the best field team Poulon had.

The two glanced toward the observation window, saluted solemnly, and stooped to lift an inert, muffled form from the sled's cockpit. Brooks keyed the sled's control mike and said, "This bundled gentleman is Mr. Kepram Singh, a citizen of India, currently resident in Nepal. But he took a little holiday to 1964 Cuba, to fire one of Fidel Castro's intermediate-range warheads. It wiped out most of South Carolina, and touched off a nasty little atomic war."

Poulon took the control-vault mike. "Why?" he asked.

VanDoorn grinned. "The little fart had bought out three U.S. shipyards," he said. "They were insured by Prudential International, with no act-of-war exclusion."

Poulon sighed. No such events existed, either in his memory or in historical record. But he had no doubt they had occurred . . . in another probability sequence, reversed by his policemen. Debriefing would clarify it all.

The two agents dragged the unconscious man across the loading dock and dumped him onto a motorized dolly. Emery Brooks peeled back the hood of Singh's heavy parka, revealing a dark brown face with a trickle of blood at the chin. "Mr. Singh resisted arrest," he explained. "Even when we had him cold, he put a bullet in my flak vest and tried to launch his missile. Pieter had to give him a rap to calm him down."

Poulon left the vault and met them at the locks, accompanied by Felipe Cardenas. "This man is wearing full arctic gear," Poulon pointed out. "Why was he wearing this, in Cuba?"

"We didn't actually have a chance to ask him that, sir." Brooks shrugged. "Thought you might find it interesting, though." With a grimace, he pressed a hand to his aching ribs. A vest would stop a .38 slug, but not its impact.

"I think this one will talk to us, sir," the head of Indo-European history for Timetrust—Europe's cooperative time research venture—told Poulon, while Singh was being transferred to interrogation. "Kepram Singh is a man without a history. He just emerged on the international criminal scene a few years back, after Hong Kong reverted to Chinese rule. He has no family, no records, and no real ties except his business associates. He's been a major player in the hashish market, and Interpol wants him on white slavery and arms smuggling."

"The viper can't reach him, then?"

"I imagine Mr. Singh is more worried about the Chinese

cartels," the historian said. "He recently diverted eighteen million pounds sterling out of a Swiss account that was supposed to be only for drug-trade expenses. It's likely that his insurance scheme was supposed to cover his tracks."

Poulon nodded. He was truly curious about a time-jumper who arrived at the scene of his crime dressed in parka, mittens, and thermal mukluks. Where had he jumped from, that such clothing was necessary?

The head of EuroTEC bowed his head in thought, fingering his short, Vandyke beard. "Let us have a private debriefing on this one," he decided. "My ears only, if you please. Then I'll want a secure black-ops channel to Matuzek in Washington. Set it up."

Washington, D.C.
2007

At TEC headquarters, Matuzek hurried Jack Logan and Harriet Blevins through a secure corridor to a back exit. "You're both officially dead," the captain told them. "Let's keep it that way for a while. It might come in handy."

"How's the squad room?" Logan asked. "Did you—"

"All normal," Matuzek assured him. "Brady and Cassini are there, doing reports. You didn't kill Himmler, so the ripple never happened, so there wasn't any attack. So, we'll never know just how that scenario played out, because it never did."

At the rear of the compound, he led them down two flights of stairs to an underground parking area. In a secluded stall, Logan's private car sat waiting. It was royal blue now, with neon detailing, and carried Michigan tags.

Logan cocked a thumb at Harriet. "What about her?" he asked Matuzek.

"Take her with you." Matuzek shrugged. "You're partners for the time being."

"Like hell!" Logan's eyes narrowed. "I don't work well with partners, Gene. You know that!"

Harriet bristled. "An' 'oo was it saved your bloody bacon back there in that Nazi interrogation room, Yank?"

"Cool it!" the captain snapped. "Both of you! Agent Blevins is your partner until further notice, Agent Logan. The two of you work it out for yourselves, or not. But that's the way it is."

Matuzek gave them a Georgetown safe-house address, told them to stay out of sight, and disappeared, back up the stairs.

Logan looked down at Harriet, still dressed like a 1920 Argentinian tourist, and sighed. "Why aren't you on your way back to Australia?"

He gave the car a command, and gestured as its hatch opened. "Oh, well," he said. "Get in."

The safe house was a tiny, boxlike building on secluded acreage, in the outskirts of Georgetown. It might once have been a gardener's shed with a potting room above. But it had been converted. Now it was a one-car garage with a tiny apartment above—a twelve-by-twelve room, a utility kitchen, and a small bath.

Logan put the car away, checked and secured all the locks, and led the way upstairs. As he opened the door to the apartment and turned on the lights, Harriet squeezed past him. Then she stopped, angry fists planted firmly on her hips.

"I might 'ave known," she said. "One bed, again."

"We'll just have to make the best of it, luv." Logan stifled a grin and took off the pin-striped coat he had worn in Buenos Aires. Tossing it aside, he kicked off his shoes and fumbled with his belt buckle.

"Like 'ell we will!" Harriet snapped. "This time the bed is mine!"

" 'Cordin' to your exchange file, you've 'ad a partner or two," Harriet said drowsily. "W'at 'appened?"

Moonlight through a high window fell across the pillows, the only illumination now in the little room. A decent enough safe house, she decided. The closet was well stocked with a variety of men's and women's clothing, the little pantry and the refrigerator were provisioned, and there were plenty of clean towels, blankets, and fresh linens.

" 'Ow very American," she had commented, when they first arrived. "All the comforts of 'ome. 'Oo does your department's catering, Yank? 'Idey-'Oles, Incorporated?"

Not a bad place to hide, she thought, present company excepted. From their very first meeting, in 1936 Ethiopia, and then thrown together in a Nazi installation in 1945, and in 1920 Argentina, she and Logan had impacted each other like flint and steel. Sparks flew, it seemed, every time they so much as looked at each other.

He could be so infuriating!

She could feel his presence behind her, only inches away, his back to her emphasizing the determined silence from across the bed. "You're not sleepin', Logan," she snapped. "W'at's the story on past partners? W'at 'appened?"

"I only had one regular partner," he muttered. "Temporal accident. I worked with another cop for a while, but not really partners. That one's dead. Shut up and go to sleep."

Sparks. Just like that, always sparks! Moths and flames. "I just wondered," she said. "I'm not any 'appier about bein' 'ere than you are, Yank. There's crocks in th' Outback I'd rather be cooped with. But 'ere we are. Both loners, an' we ought to know why. You tell me your story an' I'll tell you mine."

The bed rocked slightly as he turned on his back. "No

story," he growled. "Temporal accident. It happens, I guess. The other one . . . well, I never was sure. Might have been a flaw in the booster. The sled didn't make Q-velocity. Splat, another spot on the wall. I should have been there."

"Feelin' guilty, eh? You should've been there? To do w'at, Yank? You can't shortstop a launch." She sighed and shook her head. "So that's why you don't work team. You lost a couple of friends an' you blame yourself."

Silence, then his voice, deep and angry. "No, dammit, I don't blame myself! I just don't know why it happened. I don't know why she took off alone!"

She? Harriet caught her breath. So that was it, she thought. That's where the sparks come from. Logan had lost more than a partner in the service of TEC. He had loved someone, and lost her, too. Long moments passed. Then she whispered, "Sorry, Yank. It wasn't any business of mine."

Moonlight slanted through the high window, creeping across the carpet, invading the night shadows there. She ignored the nearness of him, tried to erase the image of his dark eyes gazing down at her, his strong hand holding hers in the moment of retrieval from Argentina.

Best not to dwell, she told herself. He's a good cop. Nothing more. Maybe as good as me, but nothing more. Nothing more.

Again the bed trembled, and she felt his breath, above her.

He rested on one elbow, brushing back his untidy hair. "So," he said, "what's your story?"

It was three days before Eugene Matuzek contacted them, and when he did the instructions were brief.

They closed the apartment, got the car out, and headed into Washington. But not to TEC headquarters this time. Their destination was the White House, third floor west.

* * *

It was a big, solemn room, with a small, solemn crowd.

"Nothing leaves this room," the president of the United States repeated. "The files before you remain on this table, the discussion is for your ears only. If I did not have your oaths on this, upon your honor, and you mine, this meeting would not be convened. As it is, when each of you leaves this room today, this conference never happened." He let it soak in for a long moment, then leaned back. "You may begin, Charlie."

If Charles Graham had an official title, it was never mentioned. As chief of National Science Security Agency's black-ops branch, no title was required.

Graham stood, and in a darkened corner, patterns of light swirled and danced. It was a screen, a hologram, an exercise in virtual reality. Graham pointed toward it as pictures of words appeared. Four words in German, repeating—in a handwritten scrawl on a torn piece of paper, in the museum-preserved text of a speech by Adolf Hitler, ink-stamped on the side of a wooden packing crate, highlighted on pages of legal transcript, as devices in a tattoo on the arm of a corpse . . . The same four words, over and over again.

"*Verteidigung, Innung, Provozieren, Rache.*" Graham pronounced them, slowly. "Random appearances of those four words, collected by Interpol over a span of more than fifty years. *Verteidigung, Innung, Provozieren, Rache.* The Defense, the Guild, the Provocation, the Retribution. V-I-P-R. Viper!

"The occurrences have centered in Europe, South America, and the United Kingdom, but have not been limited to those areas. In recent years, VIPR has been noted in virtually every section of the globe. The clues form a pattern. A secret organization, a criminal organization by any legal or moral standard accepted in any country or culture on Earth. Very old, very big, very real.

"We know now that VIPR has time-travel capability,

and a study of pretemporal anachronisms—oddities of recent history that already existed before our first E-warp scan was programmed—suggests that it predates our own technology. It appears now that VIPR has the ability to manipulate history, and sells its services to the highest bidder. It also has the ability—and has demonstrated its willingness—to dominate or destroy any person, any group, or any nation that gets in its way."

The diagrams on the screen faded to a shadowy photograph—a dark-browed, middle-aged man in evening clothes. A man who—except for the affectation of an old-fashioned spade beard—might go unnoticed in any urban crowd, anywhere. Then the scene split, and the same face appeared, this time in close-up, and from almost straight ahead. And now the face was notable. Piercing, dark eyes blazed from the face of a man whose word was law, whose every command must be followed to the letter. Seen without the mask of civility, it was a face one would not forget. And the eyes . . . those eyes seemed to see everything and fear nothing.

"Emilio Vargas von Steuben," Charles Graham said. "The son of *Oberkommandeur* Helmut von Steuben, an officer in Hitler's armed forces, and Elena Maria Vargas, the daughter of Don Fernando Vargas, patron of Estancia Vargas, which includes sizable parts of several districts in Argentina." On the screen, other photographs appeared for a moment, then the twin views of the bearded man returned.

"These are the only known likenesses of Emilio von Steuben. He is believed to be the primary executive—and possibly the originator—of VIPR."

"How, Charlie, if it's that old?" the president asked.

"A legacy," Graham said. "The memoirs of Dr. Hans Kleindast, inventor of time travel, refer to some ideas of a Dr. Josef Heindl during World War Two, at a place called

Krakenfjord, Norway. As a child, Kleindast was rescued from a secret Nazi installation there, by Allied troops.

"It's obvious now that the Nazis succeeded in their experiments, without knowing it. But apparently someone there knew it. Interpol investigated a missing steamship in 1994—the SS *Krofft*, which departed Punta Arenas on the Strait of Magellan laden with state-of-the-art electronics. Those electronics were insured to one E. von Steuben. The transactions by which they were acquired involved crude-smelted gold ingots that have been positively identified. They were part of the cargo of the Spanish galleon *Santa Ysabela*, lost at sea in the year 1534 while transporting Inca treasures to Spain.

"SS *Krofft* sailed on schedule from Tierra del Fuego. Sailings are meticulously recorded there because of the latitude's extreme tidal variations. She was noted by a weather plane out of the Falklands, steaming southward. It was never reported again. The Argentine weather station at Laurie Island did not confirm the sighting.

"E. Von Steuben is Emilio, son of Helmut von Steuben— the same Helmut von Steuben who took part in Nazi temporal experiments at Krakenfjord. Emilio traded the Inca gold for modern electronics, which disappeared at sea off Tierra del Fuego in 1994. Off the southern tip of South America!

"Finally, we have the testimony of a criminal time traveler, given before the Cour du Temps in Paris. Under examination, the defendant revealed that his contact point for temporal launch was a remote airfield near a village called Estrellita in the Patagonian highlands of south Argentina. He boarded a cargo plane there, on instructions delivered over a speaker, and was sealed into a small compartment. He saw no one he can identify. Men with machine guns and ski masks. Within minutes after the plane took off, he went to sleep, and didn't awaken until he found himself at the controls of an IRBM silo in Cuba. There were dead Cuban soldiers all around him, killed— he noticed—by automatic-weapon fire.

"The date was September 12, 1964. The missile was aimed at Charleston, South Carolina. It was what he had requested, and what he paid six million pounds sterling for.

"Under voluntary hypnosis, the defendant, Mr. Singh, revealed trace memories of a frozen landscape—snow and ice as far as he could see, and extremely low atmospheric temperature. He recalled impressions of a white tunnel. An ice tunnel. People around him—gangs of workers, guards with masks and machine guns. And of himself being bundled into arctic clothing. Also, oddly enough, he recalled rail trucks laden with coal.

"One other rather vivid impression came through under hypnosis. Mr. Singh is certain that he was looking up at a night sky at one point—a sky where the major constellation was the Southern Cross.

"Thus, a polar environment, a subterranean location, a time launch.

"Mr. Singh is presently in maximum security custody in central Europe. Our logicians have interviewed him extensively, and have extrapolated a location from the images he recalls subconsciously. They speculate that the launch point might have been somewhere in the Horlick Mountains, above Byrd Station. Byrd Station, Mr. President, is located at south latitude eighty degrees, west longitude one hundred twenty degrees, in the interior of the continent of Antarctica."

The president waited while the muttering died down. Then he said, "We have the situation before us. I have been in direct contact with Eurocord and UKAustralia. I have issued orders declaring a state of executive emergency, effective thirty minutes ago. Total covert. I ask de facto ratification here and now."

The chairman of the Senate's black-ops oversight committee tapped a thumb on the tabletop, then turned. "What are the alternatives, Mr. President?"

"There are none, Bill. The enemy we face has an unprecedented capability—the ability to reverse, retroactively to any point he chooses, any situational control we have. There are hundreds of ways—thousands of ways—for him to make what we are doing at this moment never to have occurred."

"VIPR can change our history at virtually any point, in any way he chooses," Graham pointed out. "He can make us not even exist. Our only hope is to find him and nullify his threat, before he realizes that he has cause for concern."

"I propose a task force," the president said. "A task force insulated from every alternate reality that could occur. Grade-ten covert, self-contained and self-perpetuating. It is absolutely necessary that this force be insulated from all possible alternate histories, and that means no one—not even us in this room—knows about it."

"Chances are—" Graham shrugged. "—we actually won't know about it. Let the background of any one of us here be altered, and history as we know it will change. Only our task force, operating under tight security, will have any chance of maintaining continuity."

In a private conference room on the third floor, Eugene Matuzek briefed Jack Logan and Harriet Blevins on the gist of NSA's findings, and the decision made.

"It's a search-and-destroy mission," he told them. "An international strike force, total insulation, total blackout. We have orders, but we can't assume those orders exist anywhere else. TEC is in point position on this, and VIPR is the target."

"Then am I assigned to TEC?" Harriet asked. "Or do I still answer to AusTEC?"

"Neither," Matuzek reminded her. "You're dead, remember? Both of you are. But for practical purposes, you're TEC's resource. Your orders to that effect are word of mouth only, from Wilkins to me to you, with the authentication code Angel."

"So, we don't exist." Logan nodded. "Nonexistent players in a game that maybe never was. We need a starting point."

"Not simple." Matuzek shrugged. "Interpol, NSA, Chron-Comp, and the Joint Chiefs of Staff agree that VIPR's base is too well hidden to be found by any current technical means. A subterranean complex somewhere in West Antarctica—a hidden, camouflaged hole in the ground somewhere in an area half the size of Brazil, in the most hostile land environment on earth.

"It has to be found in the past. A timesled complex is a big thing, you know. At some point, it had to be visible from the surface."

"Presatellites," Logan mused.

"Also, we have to assume that VIPR has enough data from its moles to identify every living temporal police agent, and the surveillance technology to keep track of their movements."

"In other words," Harriet said, "nobody alive is going to find the blokes."

"Right," Matuzek said. "So it's up to a couple of dead people to locate the viper's nest. TEC headquarters is sealed as of this moment. EuroTEC and AusTEC will cover our ripples, as long as they can, using the Timetrust and Pastime fields. We have ChronComp and the E-warp system, and we have the sled field. I'm robbing ThinkTank for a team of historians . . ."

"Amy Fuller," Logan said. "We'll need her intuition. And Bob O'Donnelly."

"Done." Matuzek nodded. "I've already briefed Dr.

Easter, so those three will be our team. We'll use Harriet's code: Angel. I'll handle the techs and the security. Where do you want to start?"

"This Amy Fuller." Harriet frowned. "Is she that good?"

"The best," Logan said.

"Then let's start with some profiles on 'istoric connections—Nazi Germany, Argentina, South Polar exploration—"

"People, first," Logan interrupted. "I want to see a pedigree on Emilio Vargas von Steuben. Everything Chron-Comp can come up with."

"Dale Easter is already working on that," Matuzek said.

Logan grunted. "Easter's a bean counter. He'll give us a family tree and label all the twigs. I want to know what makes VIPR tick, Gene. Put Amy Fuller on it."

VII

TEC headquarters, seen from the world outside, remained just as it had been—invisible. To all appearances, the site was a drab complex of old office buildings and connected warehouses. Some of the streetfront spaces were actually in use for a variety of marginal enterprises—a video vendor, a mill outlet fabric loft, a CPA's office—and some were simply boarded up.

All of that was camouflage, though—a shell surrounding the real occupant—the Time Enforcement Commission of the United States of America. Nowhere in the nation was there tighter security or more ironclad secrecy than around TEC. Fewer than a hundred people, outside the TEC itself, knew or even suspected that time travel was a reality in this, the year 2007. Fewer yet knew that a policing agency existed, and only the president, a few select senators, and a handful of executive staff knew the truth about TEC.

And now, its perimeters sealed by executive order, TEC was an island within a vault.

It was eerie, Amy Fuller thought, how vacant the place seemed now, with only a few techs here and there logging control data, and ThinkTank and the squad room down to fewer than a dozen people. The only noncritical personnel present now were a scientist-observer from S and R—a brusque, blond woman named Claire Hemmings—and two S and R techs assisting her. So far, they had managed to stay out of everyone's hair.

It must have been like this twelve years ago, when the ChronComp went on-line, the E-warp screens came alive, the timefield's capacitors received their initial charge, and Captain Eugene Matuzek—freshly recruited from D.C. Metro—introduced himself to that first new squad of time police. Even then, though, there was outside contact—communication coming in and going out, people reporting for duty . . . Now there was nothing. TEC was sealed. The central headquarters was as penetration-proof, as anachronism-proof as anyone knew how to make it.

Bob O'Donnelly had noticed the eeriness, too. "What goes around comes around," he said, dredging up vernacular from his early childhood. "The most dangerous enemies are those with time on their hands."

They were gathered in the briefing room now, and Amy looked around at them. Seven familiar faces and one not so familiar. Despite her professionalism, Amy had mixed emotions about the Australian assignee, Harriet Blevins. Agent Blevins was a good cop, she knew. One of the best, and Amy had no doubts about her determined loyalty to her job and her teammates. Still, she had seen how the Aussie sometimes glanced at Jack Logan—shielded, concerned glances when nobody was looking.

And, she had to admit to herself, the little blonde from Down Under was a knockout. It wasn't in Amy's nature to hate another woman for her looks, but there were moments when she almost wished it was.

"Emilio Vargas von Steuben," she began now, focusing her thoughts as the screen on the briefing room wall displayed a pair of photographs, side by side. "Born November 8, 1952, at Estancia Vargas, Argentina. The third of three children of Helmut Krupp von Steuben and Elena Maria Vargas. The father—" The screen changed. "—was a former field-grade officer in the German regular army. He served with Rommel's Afrika Korps through most of World War Two, then was transferred to Lundsgrofenwerk in Norway, top secret orders. There are no existing records of him after that, until he surfaced in Argentina in October 1945."

"A Prussian," Dr. Dale Easter noted. "You can see it in his features. Probably eighth- or tenth-generation career soldier."

"Tenth." Amy nodded. "He had ancestors in every European war since 1740, and in several other conflicts including the American Revolution. He might have made general, but for Hitler's politics. The von Steuben name was 'old army' in a 'new guard' order." Again the screen changed, picturing a dark-haired, aristocratic woman wearing a mantilla. "This is Emilio's mother, Elena Maria Vargas. She was the only legitimate child of Don Fernando Vargas, founder of Estancia Vargas and a known supporter of fascist causes. Her mother died in childbirth. When Don Fernando and his mistress were assassinated, during the Patrias del Sol riots, Elena—and through her, von Steuben—fell heir to the entire Vargas fortune."

"Nearly a fifth of the real estate in Argentina," Bob O'Donnelly clarified. "Not to mention mines, a shipping company, a railroad, several blocks of New York City property, and voting interest in two Zürich banks. And, of course, a cattle and wheat empire."

"Assassinated?" Eugene Matuzek asked. "By whom?"

"Officially, Peronista radicals," Amy explained. "That's questionable. A lot of people in Argentina didn't like Don Fernando. The *descamisados*, the labor party, and the Indians. Rumor had it that he built his empire with slave labor, mostly Indians from the lower slopes of the Andes. But ChronComp doesn't have any real data. There aren't any records."

The screen went dark. "No more photographs," Amy said. "And not much information. Elena Maria died in 1983, in Buenos Aires. Congestive heart failure. Helmut von Steuben simply disappeared, about 1985. Emilio's sisters, Consuela and Antonita, died in a hotel fire in Bogotá at about the same time. Both were unmarried. Which leaves Emilio."

" 'Deed it does," Harriet muttered.

Amy glanced at the Australian, then continued. "Emilio Vargas von Steuben. A mystery and a legend. There are no real records of him, anywhere, that ChronComp can find, yet his name appears repeatedly in police reports around the world, connecting him vaguely with at least three international criminal empires. Flagged cross-reference items include confirmed connections with the disappearance of an old steamship, the *Krofft*, off Tierra del Fuego, and unconfirmed connections with a covert instrumentality known variously as *Verteidigung*, V, and Viper.

"As to background, we know that Emilio attended the *escuela de artes* in Buenos Aires, and was an exchange student to Harvard University in 1972. He also studied briefly—1973 and 1974—at the Sorbonne, read for letters at Oxford, and appeared briefly at MIT. There are conjectures that he may have attended one or more lectures by Albert Einstein in New Jersey, and that he may have been in some way acquainted with Dwight Holcomb, before Holcomb became secretary of state.

"And here's something ChronComp dug out of old Interpol files: At the age of twelve, Emilio disappeared. He was gone, without trace, for a year and a half. From October 9, 1964, to April 17 or 18, 1966. It was first reported as a kidnapping, then the reports were withdrawn. It seems he had been on an excursion with his father, and they neglected to tell anyone they were going."

"Ah, the whims of the idle rich." Dale Easter chuckled.

Jack Logan glanced at the head of ThinkTank, then made a note in a pocket pad. Glancing over his shoulder, Harriet read: "NASA '66." She leaned close to him, her hand on his shoulder. Nice ears, she thought, idly. Whoever heard of a man having nice ears? Grinning at her own silliness, she whispered, "Spy-in-the-sky research, Yank? Could be."

Logan turned, his cheek brushing hers. "I don't go partners, Aussie," he whispered. "List your own leads."

"Leads, is it?" She nuzzled his ear, teasingly, while she noted the other scrawls he had made. At the top of his list was a puzzling note: "Slave labor . . . sources???"

Amy Fuller saw the exchange, and turned away, quickly. "That's about all we have on Emilio," she said, and shrugged. "All the data is here in the printouts if you want more detail. No record of where he is now, or what he's doing. No records of any kind, in fact, since 1993. He'll be fifty-five years old now, if he's still alive, and whatever he's doing, he's in complete and sole charge of it. My guess is, this is a man who'll commit no small crimes."

Matuzek looked around him. "Any questions?"

"Yeah," Bob O'Donnelly muttered. "When do we eat?"

Matuzek ignored him. "Then I guess we have at least a couple of starting points," he said.

Punta Arenas, in the Strait of Magellan
September 1994

Captain Voigt himself welcomed the stranger aboard SS *Krofft* and conducted his tour of the cargo holds. The inspection was an inconvenience, but considering the value of *Krofft*'s cargo it came as no real surprise that Lloyd's should send a man to check the inventory.

The insurance agent, Emery Brooks, was a sandy-haired young man in his thirties, with impeccable credentials and incipient frostbite. The captain glanced at him in amusement as they descended into the forward hold. "You are not accustomed to this cold weather, eh?" Voigt chuckled.

"Hardly." The agent shrugged. The word made a little cloud around his face, as frosty as his clipped, British accent. "My usual turf is Rio de Janeiro. This is Justin's territory, down here, but he's on holiday so they sent me."

At the foot of the cargo ladder a pair of large, ski-masked men with semiautomatic weapons looked them over, then stepped aside. Brooks glanced back at them as they passed. "You . . . ah . . . seem to have a large and well-armed crew, Captain," he noted. "I've seen a dozen of those masked gentlemen since I came aboard."

"The goon squad?" Voigt shrugged. "They're not crew. Guard complement for the cargo, put here by the owner. Don't know him, myself, but I gather he's a wealthy eccentric of some kind."

"Certainly ought to deter the timid," Brooks observed. "May I see your bill of lading, Captain, if you please?"

"Of course." Voigt watched as Brooks stood under a caged cargo light, methodically thumbing pages in the sheaf of lists, comparing them against an encrypted list of his own. The Lloyd's man squinted, then took a little flashlight from his coat pocket and scanned the pages with it, reading by its light. "There are two delivery ports shown here," he said. "Laurie Island . . . that's in the Antarctic, isn't it?"

"A weather station," Voigt said, and nodded. "The cargo is electronics, computerware, and tractor parts."

"Yes, I see. And Bouvet?"

"Another island. A research facility of some kind. The rest of the electronics off-load there."

"Then it's on to Cape Town for you, right?" Brooks finished his survey of the list, put away his penlight, and handed the papers back. "Really quite valuable cargo to

consign to such an old vessel, isn't it? How old is this ship?
Fifty years?"

"The hull, yes," Voigt said defensively. "Pre–World War
Two vintage. But she's completely refitted. I'll show you
around, if you like. *Krofft* is quite modern, and perfectly
sound."

"That won't be necessary," Brooks conceded. "It's all
in the policy file. And these ladings seem to be in order."
He turned, peering down the stacked rows of stowed
cargo. "Now, if we could just have a look at a few of these
crates . . ."

TEC Headquarters
2007

The message was obviously at least twelve years old.
The oaken conference table in the briefing room had been
there since 1995, and the message was etched into a small,
innocuous brass plate set into the polished surface of it—
like a maker's trademark always present but seldom noticed. It had obviously been there since the table was
installed, just at the edge of the tabletop, directly in front
of the TEC captain's usual seat.

No one had ever given it a second glance, until now. It
was just a label on a product, nothing more. Eugene Matuzek noticed it now, though. He noticed it because in the
twelve years that it had been under his nose, only sublimi-
nally noticed, the engraving on the brass had read:

Royal Oak Superior Furnishings
Baltimore, MD

Yet, now, it didn't say that anymore.
Eugene Matuzek stared at the message and grinned.

"Poulon," he breathed. "Leave it to the Frenchman to find a way to get a message into a temporally sealed facility." Pushing aside the probability charts he had been studying, he leaned close, reading the little characters carefully.

EM—
#Kft-ptars91594-cgcp*cp*EW
+ga+sirbmct-cds/cpH
bch—j-lp

A simple, consonant-phonetic code. Matuzek didn't even need his codebook to read it.

Eugene Matuzek—
    SS *Krofft*—Punta Arenas 9-15-94—Cargo complete*** repeat complete***E-warp—Also ground-to-air and strategic intermediate range ballistic missile components—Course due south Cape Horn
            Bonne chance—Jean-Luc Poulon

Good luck to you, too, Jean-Luc, Matuzek thought. Then he headed for his chief tech's cubbyhole. Craig Holloway should be able to estimate the time involved in delivery and assembly of an E-warp system, factoring in a guesstimate of access time to an interior Antarctic location at that time of year. Then they'd have some idea, at least, of the temporal range of Viper's spy system.

The South Atlantic, off the Coast of Uruguay
October 1945

"Don't make tracks," Harriet Blevins reminded herself as she brought the little sailboat into the wind, letting its two triangles of fabric luff and go limp. "Do nothing that will show on an event chart."

It was the admonition Eugene Matuzek had repeated to her as he helped her strap into the timesled in the nearly empty complex of Time Enforcement Commission headquarters. The admonition was an axiom of temporal police work, but knowing that the bad guys had E-warp tracking capability gave it new importance. It had become a watchword for everyone involved, in the past few days.

Don't make tracks!

With TEC sealed under maximum security—no one in and no one out, and the best-trained security guards at every door, gate, and passageway—the complex was reasonably secure from penetration, either from the outside or by temporal jump from the future. The guards were all volunteers, chosen at random from a dozen federal services, with explicit orders to shoot to kill, and TEC had become a self-contained island to itself.

History might change beyond the TEC gates, but until those gates were opened, those inside were insulated from anachronisms. And without communications, there was no way for anyone outside TEC to know what was happening inside.

Nevertheless, though VIPR might be blind, it still had its sting, and it still had its E-warp screens. Any slightest modification in history, resulting from TEC's activities, might be noted by VIPR.

"We have to catch them off guard." Amy Fuller had spelled it out. "The slightest hint that we're tracking their installation, and they'll come down on us with enough anachronisms to make us never have existed."

"Imagine," Bob O'Donnelly agreed. "If Dwight Eisenhower hadn't been there for the Normandy offensive, there wouldn't have been any GIs to rescue Hans Kleindast at

Krakenfjord. If either of two key senators had missed the Morgan briefing in 1993, there never would have been a Time Enforcement Commission. And if Charles Graham hadn't been at NSA, we'd have closed up shop after the first botched launch."

"If Captain Matuzek's father had never met his mother . . . ," Dale Easter chimed in.

"That's enough!" Matuzek growled. "We get the picture."

"The point is—" Craig Holloway turned from his beloved quadralizer console. "—what we have here is kind of like World War Three, only quieter. And we're not soldiers, we're just cops."

"I said, that's enough!" Matuzek slapped a large palm down on the planning table. "The point is, this is a police operation. Surveillance, detection, investigation, and pursuit of evidence. Basic, standard police procedure! What we're doing is what we're best at. Field investigation and the compiling of data. Police work! Maybe this is World War Three, but—"

"World War T," Bob O'Donnelly corrected. "We're dealing with temporality here, more than geography."

"World War T, then!" Matuzek glared at him. "The point is, we are the point! The military has plenty of resources to blow VIPR right out of existence, if they can catch him by surprise. All we have to do is find the son of a bitch, and not make tracks doing it."

Don't make tracks! Harriet heard the words over and over in her mind as the little sailboat rose and fell on the steady waves of the open sea. Well, so far, so good, she told herself. The disappearance of a little bay sailer from its berth at Montevideo would hardly register on a time-field chart, nor would a casual rescue at sea by a passing freighter.

She scanned the horizon. There was no sign of land, anywhere. A full night's sailing, generally eastward with the Southern Cross off her starboard beam, had brought the little boat into the offshore shipping lanes that came down from Brazil's Punta Estera. In the early hours she had glimpsed occasional lights, fishermen trawling the shallows. But this far out at sea, there was no sign of anything on the horizon except that little plume of smoke growing slowly in the north. Setting up her ranging scope in the boat's bow, she adjusted its electronic enhancers and studied the approaching ship.

It was still twenty-two miles away, its superstructure just clearing the curvature of the horizon. But in the enhanced image of a twenty-first-century scanner, its details already were clear. Two smokestacks trailed dark horsetails of coal smoke above the Swiss-registry ensign flying from its spanker boom. And now she could see its name, emblazoned on its bow: SS *Krofft*.

"Bingo!" Harriet muttered. " 'Ello, *Oberkommandeur* von Steuben!"

The steamer was good for twelve knots, she estimated. An hour and a half, then. Taking her time, she lowered the mainsail and let its fabric drag over the starboard rail, floating on the sea like a tangled carpet. She cracked the petcock and let six inches of water into the sloshing bilge. The boat sat deeper now, rolling sluggishly on the waves.

Then, methodically, she tore rips in the long skirt and peasant blouse she wore, and checked her appearance. The dark bruise on her left cheekbone was real, and only two days old. She grinned wryly at the memory of it. Of all the men in the TEC task force—even the pragmatic Captain Matuzek—not one had been willing to provide her with a battle scar. But the pretty historian, Amy Fuller, had obliged.

Feisty sheba, that, Harriet told herself. She actually enjoyed it. Pulled on a leather glove to protect her dainty fingers, all proper an' ladylike, then stepped up an' near knocked me stupid. Can't complain, though. It was my own idea. But did she 'ave to enjoy it so much?

The bruise had to be real to be convincing, just like the plaster cast on Harriet's left forearm. The cast looked as real as the dark bruise, and it hid some essentials—including the retrieval bracelet on her wrist.

When the approaching steamer was within ten miles of her, and still coming on, she dismantled her ranging scope and enhancers and dumped them over the side. Then she crawled to the stern of the little boat and sat back to wait. An image of Jack Logan formed itself in her mind.

Tall and lithe, graceful as a stalking cat—and every bit as unpredictable—his shadow dominated the undulating horizon before her, and those piercing blue eyes seemed to look right through her. Unreadable eyes, she thought. Eyes full of secrets and surprises. Eyes sometimes far away and sometimes incredibly intense—as they had been when he said, "We're going to kill Himmler."

Yet each time she tried to look into those eyes, to see what lurked behind them, the gaze shifted and all she found was the distant, empty sky.

"So all right, we're not partners, Logan," she said to herself, feeling the subtropical sun on her face. " 'Ave it your way, then, Yank. We're not bloody partners! But we're still workin' side by side."

Side by side, she thought, ironically. 'Ere I am, back then, an' there you are, back when. Oh, well . . . maybe time will tell.

When *Krofft* was a mile away she opened the petcock again. The little boat listed on the rolling swells. Harriet stood in the sinking stern, waving frantically—a pretty, blond girl adrift at sea on a dying sailboat. Not even the darkest of ships, the coldest of villains, could resist such a plea.

VIII

Puerto Deseado, South Argentina
1964

"There were always the Indians in those days," the old man said. "They lived in the mountains, around Mato Armilla and Villa Esquel. When I was a child in San Patris I saw their little boats, coming down the River of Desire. They came to trade at the markets. Camino Andesitas then was called Paso de los Indios, because there were so many. Half a million, the census said, just in the Escadrella alone. Half a million *Indios*, bringing the colored corn and the bright *sarapes* to trade. But they are gone now."

More than fifty people had gathered at the embarcadero above the boat docks as the morning sun climbed high in a cool, cloudless sky. A huge crowd, for the little village on the cliffside port. Like most places in southern Patagonia, Puerto Deseado clung precariously to the thin strip of stormy seacoast that was Argentina's Atlantic shield. Here storm-sheared cliffs dropped from cold, arid desert to a muddy beach that existed only when the tide was out.

Strangers were rare in Puerto Deseado—the port named Desire—except on those occasions when there were ships at anchor here, or when the trains came through. Today was a day of both events, and the travelers almost equaled the number of families living here. Most of the strangers were simply waiting—either waiting for the northbound train from Río Gallegos or waiting to board one of the steamships at anchor in the distance, off Cabo Blanco. Four ships were visible from the top of the sea cliffs—a tramp steamer, a big seagoing yacht, a freighter loading wool and hides bound for United States ports, and an Argentine Navy frigate on patrol at least five miles out.

Benches of wind-bleached rough lumber were provided at the sentry gate, outside the *oficina del puerto*, where a gravel veranda with low walls gave a break from the constant, chilling desert wind. Some of the waiting men—a dozen or so watchful, dark-suited bodyguards waiting for the arrival of a dignitary, and a pair of uniformed federal officers—had taken over the front office of the *oficina* building, to wait in comfort. Others had wandered off to the cantina across the square, but there were still enough men to fill the benches. They were a variety of travelers and townspeople, a few in business suits but most in work clothing. Jack Logan blended in easily. His boots hid the fact that his pants were too short, and the worn, sheepskin coat snugged at his neck hid the condition of the old shirt he had found. A stained, wide-brimmed hat and a wool scarf completed the attire. He had been in this time and place for only a few hours, but he had used the time well, scouting the area.

Two days ago, the boy named Emilio Vargas von Steuben had left his home at Estancia Vargas, in the company of his father. Today, they would both disappear from historical record, leaving no trace of their whereabouts for the next two years. It was what Logan had come to see. Now he sat at ease on a fence rail near the little tool-horse and barrow where the old leather-worker plied his trade, and waited.

It was difficult to believe, watching the old craftsman's hands, that he was blind. His gnarled fingers seemed to dance in the sunlight as he tapped intricate patterns into the oiled leather of a pair of fine botas—old fingers weaving a magic that his blind eyes would never see.

Scents of cooking drifted from some of the low, wind-sturdy houses that made up the little village between the desert and the sea. Seabirds wheeled and circled in a rare cloudless sky, the perennial dust-haze of the Patagonian desert was barely evident, and out beyond the mudflats a populace of penguins dotted the shoreline. The old craftsman turned a bota in his hand, traced its pattern with his fingertips, and set it back in place on his wooden anvil.

"Where did they go?" Jack Logan asked casually. "All those Indians . . . what became of them?"

"Quién sabe?" The old man shrugged. "The hunters come, with many gauchos from the north. They go into the hills. Then at night they come back, with *Indios*. Men and women. Children, but no old people. The hands are tied, the faces covered with bags, and they are herded like sheep down to the sea. Many times it occurred. I am only a muchacho then. Sometimes I hide in the brush and watch them pass. But who knows where the dark boats go? No one speaks of it, señor."

Dark geese winged high overhead and the old man turned his blind eyes toward them. "The geese and the penguins," he mused. "They all come here in season. Then when the season changes they go away. Maybe that is where the *Indios* have gone, señor. Maybe they go where the penguins go."

Nearby, a burly man wearing a business suit and an air of importance—a man of the town, not a traveler—shot a frown at the oldster. "Crazy old man," he growled. "Pay no attention to poor Chako, señor. His mind is as clouded as his eyes. He lives in dreams."

The busy fingers hesitated for an instant. "I can tell a dream from a memory," Chako muttered. "I know what I saw, when I could see. The poor *Indios*, the gauchos—I saw them all, a long time ago."

"You saw nothing but sheep milling in the night, Chako," the man growled. "One without eyes should be careful what he says. Someone might be offended by the words of an old dreamer and take his tongue, as well."

Jack Logan felt his hackles rise. Every culture has its bullies, he thought. This bully was demonstrating his importance, by shaming a harmless old blind man. Yet Logan's instinct told him there was something more here, as though the old man were dancing around the edges of some code of silence, and Mr. Important didn't like it. The man's words were casually abusive, but in their tone there was a veiled threat.

But the old saddler wasn't impressed. He turned sightless eyes toward his tormentor. "I am still a man, Felipe!" he spat. "I speak when I want to. Those were not sheep I saw driven down to the sea. And the men driving them were not shepherds. I saw the guns they carried. The whips and the cattle prods. Slave-herders without faces. *Enmascarados!* And with them the gauchos. And I saw an automobile, too! *Un automóvil grande!* I would never dream such an automobile!"

Felipe's glare, wasted on the sightless oldster, now held real warning. "You talk too much, Chakito," he said. Heavy shoulders bulged the seams of his gray topcoat.

Logan tried to stay out of it. "Make no tracks!" he whispered to himself. But when the local bully's sneer turned toward him, Logan had had enough. "I don't mind listening," he said in precise Spanish. "Let the man speak." He rose to his feet, tall and languid, steady eyes piercing the bully. In his manner there was nothing to suggest a threat, but his blue eyes, boring into the burly man, had a message of their own. "I am enjoying a quiet conversation with an amigo, señor," he said. "Is there a reason that you interrupt us, or are you simply impolite?"

For a moment, quick anger darkened the burly man's features. His hands balled themselves into big fists as he glared at Logan. So much for being unobtrusive, the agent thought grimly. So much for not making tracks. But then, thinking better of it, Felipe shrugged. "As you wish, señor," he growled. Again he glared at the old leather-worker, a threat and a promise that went unseen. Then he turned, striding away across the plaza.

Chako sighed and went back to his work. *"Gracias, señor,"* he said. "Felipe Reyes is a lout. He forgets that I knew him when he was nothing but a dirty muchacho playing in the street. I think now he owes too much to *el patrón*. His words are not his own, since he became *un importante*."

"He will give you grief, *tío*." Logan took a quick look around, then seated himself again. "He didn't like what you were saying."

The oldster grinned. "Maybe it is not wise to speak of the past," he said. "But I am old, and have no family. What can anyone do to me that I would care about? Today the sun shines on me and I do not feel like being wise."

"You were telling me about *los Indios*," Logan prompted. "You said you saw a car . . . *un automóvil grande*?"

"Muy grande," Chako said. "Very big, very important. It was as yellow as ripe lemons, señor, with polished silver everywhere. It was a Deusenberg. In my whole life, I have seen only one Deusenberg automobile."

A Deusenberg! Logan felt his hackles rise again, as pieces of a puzzle fell into place. *"Dígame, señor . . .* in those times you spoke about, what would someone do with all those Indians?"

The blind eyes turned toward him, as though they could see his soul. "You are not what you pretend, señor," Chako said. "The blind see what others miss. That coat you wear hung in the shearing barns this morning, and your breeches are for a smaller man. Your Spanish is good, but it is not your native tongue and not of this place. You wear boots, but they are not of any leather I know. I think they are plastic, instead. I smell the gun in your pocket as clearly as I smell Mama Rosa Obregon's laundry soap on the shirt you wear. You are more than a traveler, señor. And my ears tell me that you have no casual curiosity.

"But Felipe Reyes is a lout, so I will tell you what I think. To the south there are mines, señor. Coal mines and other mines, as well. I think that is where the *Indios* of the Patagones went. I think they went into the mines, and never came back."

The quiet village seemed to be waking up now. In the distance, a train whistle carried across the wind. And a few hundred yards away, in a fenced enclave obviously set aside for the comfort of visiting *ricos*, a dusty black custom limousine appeared from a side street and pulled to a stop. The big car looked garish and conspicuous here, totally out of place in these humble surroundings.

People gathered at the car, then trooped into the comparative warmth of a slate-roofed building with a patio overlooking the best docks and a paved ramp leading down to the waterfront below. Signal flags climbed a halyard above the building, and in the distance the big, private yacht responded with signals of its own. As though on cue, the *oficina* door opened and the squadron of business suits filed out, heading for that enclave.

"One thing more, señor," Chako added. "Felipe does not fear the old stories. When I saw the *Indios* being brought down from the mountains . . . that was a long time ago. Maybe fifty years ago. But now it has begun again. That is what *el patrón*'s people do not want discussed. Ships come in the night, señor, when the tide is high. They come in close, then they leave with their holds full of *Indio* slaves.

No one speaks of it, but it happens. In Chile, across the passes, and maybe in the pampas to the north, the *Indios* have a voice in the law. Here they do not. Here they are only *Indios*.

"The coal mines of Río Turbio are worked by *Porteños* now, but still someone collects *Indio* slaves from the mountains. *Enmascarados* bring them from their villages, they say. They do not go to Río Gallegos now, but still they go south. Always they go south."

A speedboat had put out from the yacht, and Logan tagged along as a handful of curious observers made their way down the path to watch it put in at the enclave dock. A short, chain-link fence blocked the path at its base, and a pair of business suits had stationed themselves there, barring entry to the enclave.

Logan eased away from the throng of bystanders and slipped into the shadows of a vacant boathouse. Inside, he took out a pocket scanner and unfolded it. Fully opened, it was a little twin-prism ranging scope with an enhancer the size of a coin. From the shadowed doorway he scanned the distant yacht, and whistled silently.

That was no ordinary yacht out there. It was big—at least a hundred twenty feet in length—and in the enhancer's close image the fresh white paint didn't quite hide the pattern of scrapes flanking the knifelike, underslung prow of the hull. Recognizing the distinctive silhouette, Logan could guess what lay belowdecks. Paired tandems of big diesels were concealed there, probably driving twin sixteen-foot screws. Power enough to maneuver anything afloat! *Extempor* may have looked like an oceangoing pleasure palace—a rich man's toy—but she was something else entirely.

"An icebreaker," he breathed. "A floating tractor disguised as a pleasure vessel."

Along the inshore rails, dark-clad men waited—men with automatic weapons, and ski masks covering their faces. *Enmascarados,* Chako had said. Now Logan knew what the word meant.

The incoming speedboat slowed and sidled up to a floating pier at the foot of the enclave ramps. People were gathering there. Several of the business suits clustered around a tall, snowy-haired man who held the hand of a young boy. Logan focused on them, and muscles rippled in his jaws. He knew that pair. He had seen photos of them—the man at a younger age and the boy many years older. The old man still had the proud, stiff bearing of a career soldier. The boy would change much in appearance in coming years, but his eyes would not change. It was the eyes that Logan recognized immediately, from photographs in another time—piercing, dark eyes that seemed to see everything and fear nothing.

Beyond the two, porters wheeled carts of luggage from the limousine, down to a second pier where a weathered cargo lighter waited, already piled high with bales and crates.

As the speedboat was snugged into place, the business suits filed aboard, seating themselves amidships, leaving the best seats open. The last to board were the white-haired man and the boy—Helmut von Steuben and his twelve-year-old son, Emilio Vargas von Steuben.

Logan watched the speedboat head back toward its waiting mother ship, then he climbed the path to the village and went in search of Felipe Reyes.

The TEC agent was under orders to avoid making tracks if possible. But now the subjects of his surveillance were gone, and Puerto Deseado was just what it always was—a small, unimportant dot on the landscape of one of Earth's most remote and least attractive areas.

It wouldn't make much of a ripple in the timestream if

the town bully of such a place were subjected to a few raps on the skull and a lecture on common courtesy. And it just might ease the remaining years for an old blind man too proud to be bullied into silence.

"Don't make tracks!" Logan reminded himself again as he cut his way out of a bale of antarctic garments in the aft hold of the icebreaker *Extempor*. Getting aboard the yacht had been a simple matter. The Vargas von Steuben people had a showy security system—a lot of highly visible guards with mean-looking guns. But like most celebrity-security systems, this one was focused on keeping unauthorized persons away.

Hardly anybody ever bothered to inspect inbound cargo and luggage.

Now Logan prowled the bowels of *Extempor*, memorizing its layout, contents, and personnel. The cargo was particularly interesting—a pair of big, quad-drive tractors like tall Sno-Cats with insulated cabs; several tons of dried meat, freeze-dried vegetables, powdered carbohydrates, and other preserved foodstuffs; bales of thermal wear—mukluk boots, parkas, mittens, masks, and insulated undergarments; and crates of tools; drums of diesel fuel . . .

Extempor's big engines came to life while Logan was inventorying the cargo. He heard the muffled thrum of them, and a few minutes later—faintly through the hatches of the hold—Klaxons and whistles signaled crew stations.

Logan had a general idea of where the ship was bound, but it wasn't enough. South of Cape Horn, buried under a mile or more of solid ice, lay the most hostile land area on earth—an unpopulated continent three times the size of Europe. *Extempor* was bound for Antarctica. But where in Antarctica?

Logan completed his scouting of the hold, then settled in to wait.

* * *

Extempor sailed with the evening tide, in the lingering twilight of subantarctic dusk. Her course was southeast, but five hours out she altered course to fall in with a convoy of three containerships bound southwest from the Falkland Islands. At this season, against strong west winds and the prevailing Drake Passage current, navigation of Cape Horn would have taken a week. But *Extempor* and her flock altered course again off Wollaston Island, to head due south.

The convoy was nearing the Antarctic Circle, with *Extempor* in the lead, when two of the *enmascarados* entered the aft hold to break out parkas and thermal gear for those aboard. Within moments, they found traces of a stowaway, and separated to search the hold stack by stack.

The one who went left had gone no more than ten paces when he rounded a webbing-secured pallet and found a hammock strung across a loading lane. Beside it, Jack Logan leaned against a frost-rimed packing crate, smiling benignly.

"We can do this the easy way, or the hard way," the TEC cop said. "I really don't want to kill you."

With a muttered oath, the masked man raised his weapon and pointed it. His finger tightened on the trigger, and Logan dropped and rolled. His boot smashed into the man's kneecap, and as he toppled Logan came up behind him. "Well, I tried," he growled. It was the last thing the *enmascarado* ever heard. Strong hands gripped him from behind, lifting him and bending him backward. A hard palm cut off his breath. A knee to the kidney paralyzed him, and a quick, expert twist broke his neck.

It was too bad, Logan thought. We could have done it the easy way. But now we can't.

Logan eased the body down to the decking, then went hunting for the second man.

It was over in less than a minute. Logan peeled the ski masks and dark sweaters off the bodies, and looked them over. Both were big men, one lean and bearded, the other bald and muscled like a weight lifter. And both had tattoos.

"Mercenaries," Logan noted. "Soldiers for hire."

In the short darkness between twilights, he carried the bodies aloft, one at a time, and dumped them over the stern rail. "Sorry, boys," he whispered as the second of them disappeared into *Extempor*'s ice-frothed wake. "You'll just have to settle for 'missing at sea,' if anybody cares. I can't afford to leave tracks in the timestream."

They wouldn't be missed, historically. But they would be missed soon enough, aboard this ship. Then there would be a search.

Crouching in the shadows of the afterdeck, Logan looked out across the icy sea, wondering if TEC would ever again have the advantage that he had right now—the ability, if he chose, to make a decisive first strike against the insidious enemy that would threaten all of history within forty years.

They don't know I'm here, he told himself. They don't even know, down there in my time, that I'm alive. I could behead the viper right now, before it ever comes of age . . . if that boy is in fact the viper. But is he? Is he all of it? Or would I only make a bad situation worse, by setting off a ripple that VIPR couldn't possibly misunderstand?

Dear Harriet, he thought wryly, having a wonderful time, wish you were here. Things are simpler by Aussie rules— whack the blighter an' 'ave done with it. Problem being, that isn't how we play it at TEC.

Moonlight on the sea sparkled on the drifting ice floes that dipped and tilted in *Extempor*'s wake . . . sparkled like the sparkle of taunting blue eyes in a tough-as-nails honey-doll face.

"Why the devil am I thinking about Harriet?" he muttered to himself. "I've got better things to do."

Clad now in dark woolens and a ski mask, he went scouting. The two *enmascarados* would be missed soon, and it would be time to terminate the jump—to retrieve himself back to TEC. Somewhere ahead, he was certain, VIPR's timesled field was being created at this moment . . . somewhere ahead, somewhere on the western half of a virtually unexplored continent. He wouldn't find the location on this trip, and until it was found—certainly found—it would be deadly to make tracks in the timestream.

Twice around the ship—in full view this time, passing as an *enmascarado* mercenary—and he had all he was likely to get. He had a present course, that aimed southward toward the Bellinghausen Sea west of the Antarctic Peninsula. Beyond lay the Amundsen Sea and West Antarctica. Somewhere inland there lay Byrd Station, and beyond it the Horlick Mountains and the South Pole. He had an inventory of goods and a count of trailing vessels. And he had stood within ten feet of Emilio Vargas von Steuben and his father, on the prow of the icebreaker.

Once again out of sight below deck, Logan activated the retrieval bracelet on his wrist and disappeared into the wormhole of recovery.

Behind him, in the "empty" hold, shadows stirred. Two men in white blast suits—heavier, better armored, and more intricate than the trim TEC launch suits—stepped out from between stacks of supplies. The one in the lead was a tall, middle-aged man with a spade beard and piercing, intense dark eyes—eyes that seemed to see everything, to fear nothing. The second was a giant.

The first gazed thoughtfully at the spot where Logan had disappeared. "It is true, then," he mused. "The Heindl principle was somehow passed along. They do have time travel, developed in secret. And, of course, there are time policemen. It was predictable."

"It is as you said, jefe," the giant said, and nodded. "This explains the failure and disappearance of Weintraub . . . and of Simms, and Marat Jahud and of Singh and the rest. Time police, of course! But how could they know of us, jefe?"

"I suspect it is their own future they fear," the bearded man said. "There is no way they could know of VIPR, at least not at our time. But a little later they might. This agent's presence aboard *Extempor* means they—those of his time—know something. So we must find them, and neutralize them."

"Find them? How, jefe? Their secrecy must be very tight."

The bearded one turned, glaring in abrupt anger. "Must I do all the thinking, Kurt? Are you an idiot? *Mein Gott,* don't I pay well enough to expect some basic intelligence in return? Police mean government, *estúpido*! Governments with all their secrecy have few real secrets. Governments are penetrable! You saw that man's retrieval device. Such subminiature electronics do not exist before the 1990s— our own time. So we return. We find the people in high places who have answers. We find the temporal capability, and we place moles. Then we act on what we learn!"

"There is more immediate work to be done," another voice said.

The two time travelers turned. Just at the foot of the aft ladder, the gray-haired man stepped to the hold's deck, then stood aside to make room for his young son. The boy clambered down and turned, gazing thoughtfully at the spade-bearded man. "So you're me, when I'm older." He frowned. "The time machine is completed, then?"

"We're here, aren't we?"

"And you are me? You're Emilio Vargas von Steuben?"

"Of course he is, Emilio," the old man snapped. "It is as I told you."

The boy ignored him, stepping forward.

"Not too close," Helmut von Steuben warned. "You must not touch him. He is you."

"Then does he remember seeing me—his younger self— here aboard this ship when he was my age?" The boy Emilio fixed his older self with a demanding stare. "Well, do you?"

"No, I do not," the older Emilio sneered. "This meeting changes time. It did not happen . . . but now it has." He raised his stare, to his father. "Teach him—me, then— about anachronisms, old man. Explain to him how you will remember—thirty years from now—this moment which never occurred until a moment ago. But first, what did you mean, 'more immediate work to be done'?"

"Have you forgotten what I taught you of sequences, Emilio?" Von Steuben raised a scolding brow. "In English, it is the five Ws. Who, what, when, where, and why. It is always so. The time policeman who boarded us was— as you deduced—from a future in which we have been discovered. He came to this place and time knowing who we are, possibly what we are doing, and definitely when we are doing it. His question is where. Fortunately, he learned nothing more precise than that we are bound for West Antarctica.

"But there was another, I think, who traveled further back, seeking other answers. A young woman. I was much younger then, and only wondered at the coincidence of finding a young woman adrift in the open Atlantic—a woman who knew too many questions to ask. I suggest, Emilio," he said to the older Emilio, "that you make it so that coincidence never occurred."

"Kill her," the child Emilio said coldly.

His older self gazed at him with a mixture of surprise

and contempt. "Was I really so stupid when I was twelve? Well, you will outgrow it soon enough." He turned. "Are we ready to retrieve, Kurt?"

The giant nodded. "Yes, jefe."

"Very well." Emilio Vargas von Steuben looked from one to the other of the past selves—himself and his father, of thirty years before. "Give the enterprise a name," he commanded. "The name is V-I-P-R: *Verteidigung Innung Provozieren Rache*. Let those outside have that to puzzle over."

"V-I-P-R." The boy Emilio frowned at the letters. "Viper? Is that supposed to mean something?"

"It will," the bearded Emilio assured him. "It will mean many things in coming years."

"*V-I-P-R Über Alles!*" Kurt the giant rumbled. "*Und* Viper always!"

The bearded Emilio glanced at his hulking servant, contemptuously. "There will be a polar cyclone, starting the ninth day of October," he told his father. "The first of the winter season. Byrd Station's relief ship will be frozen in, just off Thurston Island. Go around it, out of sight, then take the tractors inland. There will be a six-day calm on the high slopes. You'll have cloud cover and clear visibility from the eleventh through the seventeenth. Have the lair secured and covered before the high clouds disperse."

Taking Kurt's wrist in his hand, he opened a breast flap on his own blast suit and tapped a code into a miniature keyboard there. The air around the two of them seemed to flow, to coagulate for an instant—a distorting lens of refraction—then it shimmered and the two visitors were gone.

"What difference is cloud cover?" the young Emilio wondered.

Helmut von Steuben shrugged. "You will grow up a tyrant," he muttered. "It is not a bad thing to be. Just do not forget—then or now—who your father is. There are weather

planes from the Falklands. But they won't fly an Antarctic
storm. No aircraft of this time can go high enough to get
inside a polar cyclone."

IX

"Bobby could have had his pick of jobs," Claudia O'Donnelly chattered. "Lordy, with his credentials he could have been rich and famous. Maybe a professor at Harvard, or at least a vice president at Comtech. I always said that boy could be a millionaire by the time he's twenty-five. If he wanted to. He's a genius, you know. I knew it the minute I first saw him. I told his mother, 'Elizabeth, that baby is a genius if ever I saw one.' "

Julie Price managed an interested smile. "He seems a very nice young—"

"But, oh, no," Claudia pressed on, "my daughter-in-law could never see her own son as anything but an ordinary child. 'Extraordinary,' she admitted, but sort of ordinary extraordinary. They don't do child guidance anymore. That's probably why Bobby didn't go into law or something, instead of history. Of course, Bobby always was one to go his own way. More tea, dear?"

"Yes, ma'am, thank you." Julie shrugged. "I think your grandson is very—"

"Of course, far be it from me to tell a person how to live his or her own life," Claudia said. "It just seems such a shame, sometimes. Did you know Bobby could recite the

113

names of the entire First Continental Congress when he was barely two? And now where is he?" She spread her hands in a gesture of futility. "Working for the government, of all things! Oh, well, I expect he'll find his calling eventually. In the meantime I'm sure President Hudson can make good use of his talents. Lord knows the poor man doesn't have any of his own. Bobby may not actually do very much, he's so preoccupied with reading about the past, but whatever he does must be something useful. Of course, you know all about that. You work together, don't you?"

"Well, not exactly," Julie said. "We just—"

"You're his secretary, or something? Well, I just know how much you must enjoy working with Bobby. He's really a sweet boy . . ."

It was past eleven o'clock before Bobby O'Donnelly's grandmother yawned, conducted her household evening inspection, and went off to bed. Julie waited until she heard the old lady's door close, then turned her exhausted green eyes upward. "Thank you, God," she whispered.

Claudia O'Donnelly didn't have a set time to go to bed. The end of the day, for her, generally occurred when she ran out of either someone to talk to or something to say. Julie Price had about decided—after two days of nonstop observations, opinions, and recollections—that the latter possibility was unlikely. Dr. Bob O'Donnelly's grandmother would have something to say about her own funeral.

The TEC courier had undergone a ceaseless barrage of chatter during these two days of being a guest in Mrs. O'Donnelly's home. Julie had heard more about world affairs of the past sixty-five years, about taxes, hairstyles, propriety, and human imperfection, than she would be able to digest in a year. She knew—or at least had received—a vast assortment of trivia about Mrs. O'Donnelly's family, her neighbors, their neighbors, the state of the economy, the deterioration of moral fiber, and the foibles of a galaxy of recognized celebrities. In two days of listening, Julie Price had gone from confused to dazed to numb. She was bordering on burnout.

She had heard nothing from Bob O'Donnelly, or from Jack Logan or Eugene Matuzek or anybody with TEC, and she was worried. She had no idea how—or even whether—she was to get back to her own time. But she did know that something very big and very dangerous was going on.

In the guest bedroom she touched on the AV and flipped through some of the entertainment options: a couple of old movies, an FM bicast of *Redneck Revival III*, a vocal-control 3-D cribbage game, a subcam exploration of the Pacific Trench . . . With a sigh, she settled for the hourly TTS news.

There was the usual panoply of disasters. A thirty-three-car pileup on a Denver highway. Breakthrough discoveries in MS treatment. Cargo bay linkups on space station *Periguard*. Julie stripped off her plaid hypermart wrap and stepped into the shower, still listening curiously. It was a new experience for her, being upstream in time. The displacement was slight—only three years—but still there were the subliminal surprises of time travel. The news she was hearing was old news, to her. Three-year-old-up-to-the-moment coverage. History served hot. More and more, she understood the necessity of absolute secrecy surrounding everything TEC did—surrounding TEC itself.

Time travel. It could be a blessing, or a curse. And like most advances, it probably was both.

Over the sound of the shower, a commentator was reviewing President Hudson's executive orders regarding the takeover of Kazakhstan by an international cartel. Abruptly, Julie turned off the water and listened closely. "That's not right," she muttered. "That isn't how it was!"

Pulling on a fresh wrap, Julie hurried across the bedroom and picked up the phone. She tapped in the code number for TEC, heard the scrabble of routing clicks and the ringing of a phone somewhere. It was about to ring again when she hissed through her teeth and slapped the handset down, breaking the connection. "Dummy!" she told herself. "It's 2007, remember? This is a residential line. An unsecured line! In 2007 there were limited shields on caller ID."

The newscast was still on, a local piece about the discovery of an old Underground Railroad tunnel under an abandoned mall in the Fifth District, but now she ignored it. Julie knew enough about the Time Enforcement Commission, from her training, to know that its whole purpose centered on catching historical alterations before they happened, to keep them from happening. Once a ripple passed, it was history, and only those insulated by temporal transit would ever remember the alternate history it had replaced.

"This isn't right," she told herself again. "It must have happened since I launched from 2010. They must have missed it, but they need to know!"

Harold Hudson was the president of the United States. But he had not been president in the 2007 Julie Price remembered. In her history, Harold Hudson had died in 2006, of a congenital disorder that led to heart failure.

In a closet, Julie found jogging sweats and a pair of scuffed Nikes two sizes too large for her. She put these on, pulled her auburn hair into a ponytail, and slipped out into the quiet Georgetown street. Three blocks south and two west, she found a lighted Uniserve island and slid into a vacant booth.

There were the usual conveniences—universal ATM, a pay phone, soft drink dispensary, and a bank of vending machines. Lifting the phone, Julie dropped a token into the slot and tapped in the code number again.

"Fenton Imports," the mechanical voice said. "Our office hours are eight to five . . ."

She waited while the message played itself out, then hit *4 and repeated the access code. This time a real voice responded. "ID number and classification," the man said.

"ID 328, C-14," Julie told him.

"Three-two-eight," the man repeated. A moment's hesitation, then he said, "Please enter that number on your keypad. It doesn't seem to register . . ."

Julie hung up. Of course her number didn't register. There wasn't any such number. She wouldn't be assigned a number for another two years. By now her call—correct access code followed by a nonexistent ID—was setting off alarms all over the Department of Justice.

She could already hear the sirens when she ducked out of the Uniserve booth and scurried into the park beyond. "God!" she breathed. "First I'm officially dead, now I'm a fugitive." Two streets over, she found a jogging path and headed back toward Claudia O'Donnelly's brownstone house.

"Think, dammit!" she told herself as the house came in sight. "Be resourceful! TEC recruits are resourceful!"

She could go on hiding, and simply wait, but then TEC might never know that history had been changed. How would they know, those who were caught up in the change? The only shield against temporal adjustment is temporal dislocation.

"I have to tell them," she muttered. "But how?" The answer came in a memory—a vague memory from three years in the future. "The tunnel!" She almost shouted it. "Yes! The old Underground Railroad tunnel."

Letting herself into Mrs. O'Donnelly's house, Julie retrieved her red blast suit, put it on, then went through the kitchen and let herself out the back door. Her mind whirled with jumbled memories of two days' worth of Claudia O'Donnelly dissertation. Bob O'Donnelly, "Little Bobby," had always loved his motorbike. Even now he came over sometimes to clean it, fire it up, and ride around the park.

Behind the house, in a fenced shed, Julie found the bike. "Thank you, Mrs. O'Donnelly," she whispered fervently. Vaguely, from maps she had seen on arrival in Washington, she knew where the Fifth District lay. Somewhere in that district was an abandoned shopping mall and the entrance to a hundred-and-fifty-year-old tunnel.

TEC guards intercepted the courier as she broke through a crumbling old wall of antebellum brick and emerged into the now-vacated inductees' quarters beneath TEC headquarters. It was a smudged, stained, and apologetic Julie Price who was escorted upstairs and turned over to Captain Eugene Matuzek.

"I'm sorry," she said. "I guess I changed history a little. It caused quite a ruckus here when the D.C. Public Works people punched through that old wall down there, three years from now. But I guess it won't happen now, will it?"

At the door of the debriefing room, Bob O'Donnelly gawked at the girl. "I hope you didn't bring Grandma with you," he said.

It took more than an hour for the historians to debrief Julie Price. Relentlessly but carefully, they interrogated her, eliciting her memories of "history" as she recalled it, patching those memories into a significant pattern, and feeding the data to ChronComp. And for every item of data they fed the computer, it pulled up a hundred more from its own banks—facts, probabilities, and predictable sequences dancing on the various consoles as it worked.

The task was to match Julie's news to a point of time-field interruption and a significant alternate-history result coinciding with what they knew of VIPR. A second question was why the E-warp had not registered at least a level-seven ripple, for an alteration as profound as presidential history.

"I think we've got it here." Amy Fuller indicated her ChronComp link, then put it on mainscreen. "Probable cause, probability 83 percent. Following the death of President Harold Hudson, in Miss Price's remembered history, Vice President Franklin Forsythe was sworn into office. Within a few months, he fulfilled a campaign promise going back to his first election to the Senate. ChronComp verifies Forsythe's platform."

"Okay." Dale Easter nodded. "My equations confirm that. What was the promise?"

"He abrogated the 1959 Antarctic Treaty," Amy explained. "Under that treaty and its later amendments, all territorial claims in Antarctica were put on hold, indefinitely. The region named Marie Byrd Land, in West Antarctica, was unclaimed and set aside as a scientific preserve, with Byrd Station as its base. As president of the United States, Forsythe apparently ignored the treaty. He began negotiations with international cartels to open the entire region to private exploration and exploitation of mineral deposits in the Horlick Mountains."

"That's where VIPR is, then." Matuzek called up a satellite-photo map on the geoscreen. "Somewhere in there. It has to be. But how did they prevent the death of Harold Hudson? He died of natural causes. Congenital heart failure happens."

"No, it doesn't."

They looked around. The little courier, Julie Price, sat quietly in a corner of the room. But now she was shaking her head. "Not in 2010, it doesn't," she said. "There's a preventive. It's a vaccine stabilized from tuberculin bacteria. It was developed in 2009 at Johns Hopkins, after the president died of that heart condition. They even named the condition for him—Hudson's syndrome. My father had the same condition, but the vaccine saved him. He's still alive . . . will be still alive in 2010 . . . because of it."

"But Hudson died in 2006 . . . in the original history. Three years before there was a vaccine."

"So VIPR used 2010 technology to protect its hidey-hole." Bob O'Donnelly shrugged. "So what else is new?"

"It still doesn't jell." Matuzek frowned. "Say a VIPR agent immunized a president, to change history. Why didn't E-warp reflect a ripple?"

"It did." Amy sighed, accessing a new file on her console. "Remember the blips, Captain? We suspected they were time bombs. Well, this was one of them. It was only a blip, because it was fifty years ago and insignificant. A little boy with a broken arm, treated and released at Lincoln Hospital in Springfield, Illinois. That boy was Harold Hudson. They reached him while he was in that hospital. He grew up immune to the kind of heart failure that otherwise killed him, because he had been immunized as a child."

"Viper strikes, maybe you don't even know it," a quiet voice said, in the stunned silence of the briefing room. Jack Logan stood in the doorway, still wearing an old-style military parka over his blast suit. "Isn't that what B. J. Simms said? Now we know what he meant."

Logan looked around the room, nodded at Amy and Julie, then cocked a brow at Matuzek. "Where's the Aussie?" he asked. "Her sled's in. What did she learn in '45?"

"She isn't here, Jack," Matuzek said. He opened a bulging envelope, tilted it, and dumped its contents on the table. "The sled came back, but this is all it had in it."

Logan stared at the things on the table. There was a plaster cast, open now to reveal its secret hinges, latch, and the little cavity inside. And a retrieval bracelet. Harriet's bracelet.

"They got her, Jack," Matuzek said. "They made her and they took her, and this is their way of telling us so."

"I'll spend one hour in debrief," Logan growled. "Start in five minutes. One hour, Gene! Then I want a sled."

"Look, Jack . . ."

Logan's eyes were pure ice. "You heard me, Captain. A sled. You have the coordinates. Have it ready for me."

He turned, heading for the washroom.

"Goodness," Julie Price whispered. "Is he—is he angry?"

"He gets like that, sometimes," Amy advised. "I'd hate to be the perp he's going after."

Eugene Matuzek shook his head. "Just for the record, I've already cleared his sled for power-up. It doesn't matter. There's no arguing with him when he's like this. Whether he admits it or not, that's his partner out there. He's going after her."

"Then who does that leave us," Dale Easter demanded, "to narrow down a location on VIPR?"

Matuzek looked from one to another of them, then his eyes fixed on Julie. "It might be time for your graduation, Agent Price," he said.

Argentina
1945

West of Buenos Aires, the great pampas seemed to go on forever, vast seas of grass riding the undulations of the rising land—a sprawling, brooding land sparsely settled, laced by little ribbons of forest along the waterways and dotted by scrub thickets. A land where vast fields of wheat seemed swallowed up in the broader expanses of grassland, where great herds of cattle grazed, tended by gauchos on horseback.

But for the occasional groups of ostrichlike rheas in the distance, the scurrying of banded armadillos, the burrows of viscachas, and sometimes a glimpse of huge, graceful condors circling above, each vista might have been a scene in the North American Great Plains, or in central Siberia, or the Ganges River valley, or the wide plateaus of Mongolia.

But it was none of these. This was the humid pampas, the great heart of Argentina.

Estancia Vargas lay to the west and south of Buenos Aires—a million sprawling acres of expanded grants owned and dominated by the family Vargas. Don Pedro Vargas had been one of the "Three Hundred" original *patrónes*, with an *estancia* extending from Bahía Blanca on the seacoast to Villa Patica on the upper Río Colorado. Through a campaign of successful crowding, aided by the judicious marriages of three daughters, Don Pedro extended the Vargas holdings beyond the Salado slough as far as Arroyo Azul, and acquired *anexidades* far to the south, from the White Andes across Patagonia to Puerto Deseado.

All this Don Pedro had left to Don Francisco Vargas, whose name among the common people sometimes was *Diablito*. Don Francisco saw new opportunities for profit. His sinister *enmascarados*—gangs of masked men, mostly European immigrants who went by starlight to do the patron's work—were instrumental in providing the labor force to build the mining of coal and precious metals into a profitable enterprise. That labor force, rarely noticed and never mentioned in conversation, was a ready supply of *Indios* from the Patagonian highlands.

Don Francisco's *enmascarados* harvested Indians the way his gauchos harvested wild cattle—where they found them, then rounded them up, branded them, and delivered them to the patron's use.

And what Pedro Vargas acquired, and Francisco Vargas exploited, the current patron, Don Fernando Vargas, had developed into a tidy international empire during those years of confusion and opportunity—World War II.

The pampas, in 1945, were a vast, semiarid land held in fee by a few landlords like Don Fernando, held profitable by burgeoning international markets, and held together by railroads.

The Saturday train to Estancia Vargas had five public passenger coaches, crammed with people of all descriptions and various destinations. It also pulled two private cars with the Vargas crest emblazoned on their panels and armed gauchos riding the platforms. At Pergamino most of the passengers—tenant farmers returning from market and by-the-week workers coming home from Buenos Aires—got off, carrying their packages and their suitcases. At Santa Rosa, most of the rest disembarked. When the train pulled out for Cresta, only a few farmers and the silent *Norteamericano* remained aboard three of the five public passenger coaches. The other two carried green-banded tenant workers and gauchos bound for Estancia Vargas.

Cresta was a tiny village where two roads crossed the rails. The train eased to a stop at a little depot building, and trainmen came through the public cars. "All out," they ordered in Spanish. "All out for Cresta. Only Vargas personnel and guests from this point."

The cars were emptied. Standing outside the little depot, Jack Logan could see heavy barbed-wire fence a hundred yards ahead, and an iron gate across the track. The men guarding the gate carried rifles and wore the green bandannas of Estancia Vargas.

A weathered, pink-cheeked old man approached Logan,

singling him out as the only stranger in the crowd. "Taxi, señor?" he asked, pulling off his hat. "Sean McGinty, *a sus órdenes*." With a grin, he switched to English. "If yer bound anywhere from here, mate, ye'll be needin' a taxi. Unless you're a guest of the patron, o'course. But then, if you was goin' to Casa Vargas, ye'd not be standin' here now, right?"

"Right," Jack agreed, watching the two private cars just ahead of the caboose. They remained closed, and armed gauchos lounged near their doors.

He glanced across the little street, at the dusty old Chevrolet standing alone there. McGinty's taxi. "Where's the nearest café and bed, from here?"

"That'd be Monty's place, just down the road." McGinty pointed eastward. " 'Bout fifteen miles."

Up ahead, the engine emitted little clouds of steam as its crew was changed and the new engineer tested his boilers. The smoke from the broad-bellied stack was a sedate plume swept away on the wind. Jack sniffed the air. The engine burned high-grade bituminous coal. Maybe even anthracite. "Where does the coal come from?" he asked. "For the engine?"

"The Patagones, I s'pose." McGinty shrugged. "Somewhere south. I've seen the barges come in at Buenos Aires."

Guards were flanking the train now, working along and through the public coaches, checking credentials of all passengers beyond this point. It was a thorough inspection, of all but the private cars. Estancia Vargas obviously valued its privacy and did not encourage strangers. Logan looked east, along the gravel road the taxi driver had indicated. It disappeared in the distance, paralleling the five-strand barbed-wire fence of Vargas land. "Do you suppose your friend Monty stocks Irish whiskey?" he asked.

The driver grinned. "Best ye ever tasted," he said.

"Then let's go." Logan strode across the sandy street, followed by McGinty, and climbed aboard the old Chevrolet.

Barbed-wire fence rolled past on the right as the car headed east, barely outrunning its own plume of dust. They had gone a mile or so when Logan saw what he had been watching for. Beyond the fence, in the shelter of a little cluster of scrub trees, several gauchos idled while their saddled horses grazed nearby. Beyond them, scattered across a grassy swale in the rolling land, hundreds of beef cattle cropped at the sparse grass.

Logan leaned forward to offer a gold coin to his driver. "I've changed my mind, McGinty," he said, "but I need a favor."

"Name it, yer honor." McGinty took the coin, glanced at it lovingly, then made it disappear into his vest. "If I can do it, consider it done."

"Slow down a bit just past that rise ahead," Logan said. "Then drive on to Monty's place and have a drink for me."

"My pure pleasure, sir." The driver chuckled. "Word of advice? If ye make it past the gauchos, look out for the *enmascarados*. They're the ones ye need to worry about. An' whatever it is ye're peddlin', sir, I hope Don Fernando buys a gross of them from you."

Past the rise the old car slowed, and McGinty heard the rear door open and close. When he glanced in his mirror, all he saw was the plume of dust behind him. Shifting gears, he headed east for Monty's place, grinning to himself. "Cocksure gent, that," he muttered. "But a real gentleman for all of it."

The gold coin in his vest was more wealth than he would see in a month of ordinary fares.

X

The sun quartered above the northwest horizon when Logan left the train at the gates of Estancia Vargas. It was sinking into the far clouds over the Andes when he crept into cover at the base of a scrub quebracho and bellied under its branches for a look beyond.

Three gauchos wearing green bandannas sat in the shelter of a cutbank, keeping desultory watch on the cattle beyond, while a fourth stood atop a little rise, shading his eyes to peer after the dwindling dust of McGinty's eastbound taxi. Four fine saddle mounts grazed nearby on leads that were looped to a reata stretched between scrub oaks. Logan sighed, eased out of his cover, and strolled up to the seated men.

Even as they turned toward him, he stooped, grabbed the rifle of the nearest one, and jacked its lever. "*Cuidado, señores,*" he said. "*Los manos, por favor!*"

The one on the rise turned, gaped at him, and Logan gestured. "*Aquí, pronto!*" he ordered.

Within moments the outraged gauchos sat tied, back-to-back, with their own riatas and bolo cords. The largest among them was stripped to his BVDs, and Logan was wearing his clothes.

He chose the best of the horses, a long-legged sorrel with Arabian ancestors, and snubbed its reins to a limb while he stripped saddles and headstalls from the rest and chased them away.

In the distance, its wail eerie on the fitful wind, the train to Estancia Vargas whistled. Logan swung aboard the sorrel, turned it, and glanced back. *"Gracias, muchachos,"* he told the four gauchos. Then he pulled down the short brim of his stolen flat-crowned hat, put heels to the horse, and thundered away. He headed straight south, until he was among the grazing cattle.

Swinging a bolo, he charged among the beasts and gave the horse its head. It was said, in the twentieth century, that the gauchos of the pampas were the best cowboys in the world. True or not, their horses were unquestionably the best cow ponies alive. Responding to the insistent heels of its rider, the sorrel picked out a fat steer and set it running—then another and another. The graze became a stampede, spilling out on both sides yet picking up beef as it went. Within moments, at least fifty head of prime Vargas beef arrowed westward across the open pampas, angling south of west as a copse of scrub trees and a stubby rail trestle came into view ahead. Off to his right, barely visible, Logan saw the drifting plume of the engine's smokestack as the train trundled through the Estancia Vargas gate, heading south.

Just at sunset, the train came over the crest above Salado slough, slowed, and wailed its whistle. There were cattle on the tracks ahead.

Nearing the first trestle, the engineer slowed to a crawl, scattering beasts ahead of the big engine's snout. Slowly, the cattle parted, and the train passed through. Beyond the trestle it picked up speed again as the Andean dusk crept over the high pampas. But now it had another passenger. On the roof of the third passenger coach, Jack Logan eased around the ventilation casement and sprinted rearward, crouching and alert as a stalking puma.

From car to car he scouted, peering downward through the cased, open skylights of the coaches. The passenger coaches held people he had seen previously, on the ride up from Buenos Aires. But at the forward private coach he paused, whistling under his breath. More than a dozen men lounged below him, in the glittering comfort of a rich man's coach.

The men wore civilian clothing, double-breasted suits of the finest cut and fabric, but about many of them there was the distinct air of military, in their close-cropped hair, in their bearing as they moved, even in their quiet voices drifting up through the vent. These were travelers, businessmen abroad, but he could almost see the uniforms they had so recently abandoned.

He wished he had Amy Fuller's grasp of profiles and histories. He knew he would have recognized some of those below him. They were fugitives—expatriates. And among them were some who would be hunted down, eventually—by international police, by Allied military intelligence, and most ominously, by a small, dedicated corps of Israeli volunteers who would never give up no matter how long it took.

These were Nazis who had evaded capture. These were the ones who would not see Nürnberg in this decade— although in future years some would.

Escape from retribution, escape from trial and retribution for their war crimes, escape to a new life in a new country where a patron would sponsor them in exchange for what they had pillaged in Europe. And this, Logan surmised, was how Helmut von Steuben had acquired the SS *Krofft*. He had made the deals in Argentina, for those who suspected they would have to flee.

The train traveled now across a broad, shadowed land where starlight grew in a fading purple sky. Logan crept rearward, looked down at the covered platforms where armed gauchos rode guard, then backed away, took three running steps, and leapt across to the last coach.

Darkened brass trim bordered three cased skylights. The forward one was closed—thick glass obscuring the shadowed cubicle below. Logan crouched above it, squinting through cupped hands, then jerked back as a light went on below. The cubicle was a lavatory, elegant with polished wood cabinets, a floor of fine ceramic tile, and spotless porcelain fixtures trimmed in gold.

The man who had entered was tall, his close-cropped blond hair only a few inches from the skylight glass. He raised the lid on the commode, opened his breeches, and glanced upward, casually. In the darkness above, Logan frowned, recognizing the face—*Oberkommandeur* Helmut von Steuben, recently of Adolf Hitler's proud Wehrmacht. The von Steuben of this time, of 1945.

The long, multipaned skylight in the center of the coach revealed several men relaxing in an elaborate, ornate salon—a palace on wheels, complete with a bar, gaming tables, and a five-piece string band playing Argentine guitars, a mandolin, a cello, and bowl drums. Silent, dark-clad men with masked faces stood guard at each end of the salon. "Watch out for the *enmascarados*," Logan whispered to himself, echoing the warning of the taxi driver, McGinty.

Logan finally found what he was looking for, beneath the small rear skylight. A tiny, closed sleeping room lay below, a compartment with folding bunks and a luggage rack. One bunk was occupied. The small form of Harriet Blevins sprawled there, clad only in a silk nightgown. She stirred slightly when he rapped at the closed pane above, but did not open her eyes.

Even in the dim light of a single small lamp, Logan could see the blood at her lips, the livid bruise on her cheek.

Her wrists were bare, her cast and retrieval bracelet gone.

So they had already found her out. Now they were taking her to the Vargas stronghold. For questioning? Or for bait?

There was really no question in his mind. Harriet lay below him, as though on display. The open skylight, the lighted lamp . . . "Bastards," he muttered.

Voices drifted back to him on the wind—hushed, urgent voices—and something rapped against a ladder riser just ahead, the click of metal on metal. In the afterglow of deepening dusk, Logan saw a gun tip waver above the coach's roof ladder, then the crown of a hat as someone climbed into view.

It was a trap! The engine's wail from up ahead seemed to confirm it. Instinctively, Logan's hand dived toward the concealed gun at his waist, then he hesitated. "Don't make tracks," Matuzek's urgent voice rang in his mind. "For God's sake, keep this covert as long as you can!"

With a muttered oath, Logan rolled away from the skylight, clung for an instant to the edge of the moving roof, then threw himself over into the racing darkness beyond.

From both ends of the car, men swarmed onto the roof—gaucho guards first, then dark-clad men with covered faces and ready machine guns. Lantern light bobbed here and there, and voices called out.

They had expected an intruder. They had known just where he would be, and when. Yet they found no one. Crouching and searching, they inspected the skylights, hung lanterns over the sides of the car, and peered into the night.

Clinging precariously to the brace rails just ahead of the rear truck, where iron wheels clattered and sang on each side while the gravel and timbers of the roadbed whisked past, six inches from his face, Logan squinted against the stinging sand thrown up from the rails, and counted his heartbeats.

Lanterns were dropped on leads fore and aft, giving a

murky glow to the underside of the coach, and Logan saw upside-down faces peering beneath, searching for him. The dancing patterns of flashlight beams waved here and there. The searching faces withdrew, and he braced himself for the shock of brakes, but the train didn't slow.

Three minutes passed, then five, and through the din of wind and sand and drumming wheels he heard the engine's whistle, signaling down-track. A brightness appeared ahead, between the ranked wheels of the train—the glow of perimeter floodlights coming on.

Estancia Vargas lay just ahead, and the signal had been to Don Fernando's security forces. Straining every muscle, gasping with the effort, Logan let loose his grip with one hand and flipped to the side, facing upward. Inch by straining inch he hauled himself forward, clinging upside down just above the battering ties that blurred past him. Past the wheels, he edged aside for a glance down the track. Just ahead sprawled a fortress—high, whitewashed brick walls lined with blinding floodlights. A wide, iron-bound gate was swinging open, and the train track led through that opening.

Fortress Vargas! The train plunged toward the gates, and Klaxons sounded the alert.

Logan ducked back beneath the undercarriage as horsemen came out of the blinding light to converge on the train. Beams of light played along the footings of each car. "Bring the train in!" a voice shouted, in Spanish. "Clear the gate! Riders ready! We will search every car, inside and out!"

Clinging to a single tie rail, Logan hugged the shadows. Brakes were set, nearly shaking him loose, and the train slowed. As the brakes were tightened, sparks flew from beneath the skidding wheels.

Through the floor of the coach, he heard thumps and

crashes. "I'll bet this wakes her up," he muttered between his teeth.

Floodlights glared, coming overhead, and Logan waited, counting his pulse beats. Just a few feet away, a horse ran alongside the coach. From beneath the edge, Logan could see flying hooves, rippling muscles, and the rider's boots thudding at the animal's sides.

The floodlights passed overhead, high walls loomed, and for a moment there was darkness. With a hiss, Logan pivoted his legs outward, swung himself forward, and heaved the tie rail from him. Feetfirst, he flew directly under the horse's chest, body-blocking its forelegs. With a shrill scream, the animal stumbled, pitched forward, and rolled, throwing its rider over its head. The horse went down, rolled, and came up, and it had a new rider. Clinging like a leech, Logan found the reins and hauled the animal around. In an instant he was through the gate and under the floodlights again, booting the horse into a belly-down run toward the darkness beyond.

He heard gunfire, and felt the sting of a shock wave as a bullet clipped past his ear.

Three hundred yards . . . four hundred and he was in night shadow beyond the lighted perimeter. Without slowing the horse, he swung a leg over and leapt, folding his arms and legs, burying his head in his arms. The impact of landing on the hard ground almost knocked him dizzy, but he hit and rolled, absorbing the impact with his whole body, easing the fall.

For just a moment he lay motionless, clearing his head and getting his bearings. His riderless horse was still running, its hoofbeats drumming off into the night. And now mounted gauchos came at a gallop, in full pursuit. Crouching in the shadows, Jack Logan let them pass him by—a dozen or so of them in a bunch, then several more, then a few stragglers. He waited for the last one, crouching and tensing like a puma awaiting prey.

When the last rider came abreast, Logan sprang. A moment later he veered the horse off to the left, dumped the inert body of its unconscious rider into a scrub thicket, then followed where the rest of the gauchos had gone.

The riders returned to the fortress leading a lathered horse, but with no clue as to what had become of its rider. Inside the gates, a few of the riders headed for the stables off to the east, where there were pasture gates. Others spread around the great compound, curious. The train from Buenos Aires sat now at the end of the rail, still steaming, while iron-bound gates were closed behind it.

There were men everywhere, with lights and guns, searching the entire length of the train. Passengers in the public coaches were let off one by one, their identities verified by a guard commander in the dark uniform of the *enmascarados*. Headlights approaching along a curved drive entered the light and became limousines—an even half-dozen glittering Rolls-Royce Silver Ghost phaetons coming out from the main house, a huge, low building several hundred yards away, at the rear of the compound.

Casa Vargas, nerve center of Estancia Vargas—the home and headquarters of Don Fernando Vargas—was welcoming its guests.

Leading his horse, a gaucho among gauchos in the murky darkness away from the train, Logan blended into the shadows beneath a watchtower and kept his eyes on the bustle of activity in the lighted compound. The train had come to rest in a cleared, swept-gravel yard inside the walled compound. Its headlight showed fifty yards of track beyond the engine, stopping at a milled-lumber service platform. Beyond, surrounded by bent-grass lawns and tended gardens, lay the main house.

Barns, sheds, stables, corrals, and barracks buildings completed the assemblage within the walled compound—a self-contained little village the size of a Pennsylvania farm, enclosed by high brick walls.

All of this he saw peripherally. His concentration was on the train, where the passengers were disembarking now from the private cars. Even at this distance, Logan recognized some of the faces, putting names to them. Moder, Krebb, Waldhausen, Kohl, Braunheisen . . . the list was almost a roster of the *Reichskampf* of Adolf Hitler's National Socialist Party. Banker, industrialist, labor organizer . . . Logan shook his head, disgusted.

By fours and sixes, the fugitives were escorted to limousines for the short drive back to the main house.

The last to leave the big Vargas coach was Helmut von Steuben, accompanied by a gang of dark-clad *enmascarados*. Two of them were limping badly, and one was bleeding from a broken nose. Two others stepped off, bringing—almost carrying—Harriet Blevins. She sagged between them, hurt and bleeding from a cut lip. Logan's eyes went narrow and cold at the sight. She had fought them. Barely half the size of most of the masked men, still she had made them pay for her indignity.

He saw them enter the last car, and worked his way toward it—leading his horse on short rein, letting its shadow hide him from the lights of the yard.

The doors were just closing on the Rolls phaeton when Logan appeared beside it and held out the reins of his horse to the green-bandanna gaucho just stepping up onto the car's running board. "Hold this!" he commanded, in precise Spanish.

Instinctively, the man reached out and gripped the reins. As his fingers closed, Logan flipped a loop over the man's wrist, pulled it tight, and turned, delivering a sharp slap to the horse's rump. The animal reared, dragging the gaucho from his perch, then bolted across the compound.

The Rolls purred to life and Logan stepped onto its footboard, turning to glance at the diminishing pandemonium behind, where a surprised gaucho fought to control a panicked horse.

"You could have avoided some of this . . . this inconvenience," Helmut von Steuben said, as the limousine started toward the main house. Facing back in the car's elegant sedan seats, the Nazi gazed at the blond girl seated between two masked escorts. There was blood on her chin, blood on the skimpy silk gown she wore, and her left eye was swollen almost shut. "It is a pity, really," von Steuben said, and shrugged. "You were a handsome woman. Truly a beauty! But now I suspect you will not be handsome again. Emilio—my Emilio who is not yet even conceived, but is here nonetheless, proving my theory—will have questions for you. But of course, you will resist giving him answers. A pity."

"You go straight to 'ell, bozo," Harriet snapped. Her foot shot out, aimed at von Steuben's kneecap, but one of the *enmascarados* blocked her kick. The other slapped her, a backhand slap that made her head rock.

Behind von Steuben, the liveried chauffeur turned to glance back. " '*Sta bien, señor?*" he asked.

"Mind your driving!" von Steuben said. "It is not your concern." With a muttered curse, he rolled up the heavy glass separating the passenger compartment from the driver's seat. As the glass closed, it cut off the sound of the driver's gasp as he was cross-punched, lifted from his seat, and flung out into the dark gardens.

Von Steuben's first inkling of trouble came when the big car swerved crazily, bounded across a rose bed, knocked down a picket fence, and headed for the distant stables, its tires spitting gravel as it accelerated.

Logan gunned the Rolls and felt its big engine respond. Distantly, from the enclosed passenger compartment behind him, he heard shouts and curses. The glass behind him lowered several inches and the snout of a Wehrmacht Luger poked through. Driving with one hand, Logan found the driver's-side window crank and turned it, hard. Behind him someone howled with pain as finger bones crunched. He swerved left, then hard right, throwing his passengers from side to side. A coach door flew open and a masked man tumbled out, onto the racing gravel.

Just ahead now were several gauchos, leading their horses to the stables. Logan scattered them like quail as he gunned through, praying that there were pasture gates beyond.

The Rolls skidded around the corner of a hay barn, roared toward the gap between stables and barracks . . . and something very big blocked its way. Like a trundling mammoth, a panzer poked its long gun through the splintering barn wall, then followed it out into the path of the Rolls.

The limousine swerved, skidded sideways, and slammed against the tank's big treads. Before Logan could change gears to bolt away, the driver's door was thrown open and a hand the size of a ham closed on his shoulder. Like a rag doll he was lifted, hauled out of the car, and flung to the ground, dazed. Standing over him, grinning, was the biggest man Logan had ever seen.

The giant backed away a step, still grinning, and raised a booted foot. But a voice stopped him. "Kurt! *Cuidado, Idioten!*" the dry voice commanded, in a patois of German and Spanish. "Do not kill him just yet. First let us at least have a look at him."

A limousine door opened, and Helmut von Steuben—

the Helmut von Steuben of this time, a man in his prime, gray-coated and every inch the perfect Prussian soldier—looked down angrily. His eyes were narrow with pain, and he cradled his misshapen right hand on his left arm. "Is this the one, Emilio?" he asked. "This is the time-travel policeman you expected?"

"This is him." Emilio Vargas von Steuben—the Emilio of 2007—nodded. "A TEC timecop! I knew they would take the bait. Now let's see who he is."

XI

Two *enmascarados*, a gaucho vaquero, and a passing farmhand pinned Logan down, held his arms, and took his gun. Emilio turned the twenty-first-century weapon over in his hand, looking at it casually, then handed it to Kurt, who thrust it into his belt.

They dragged the TEC agent around in front of the Rolls and stood him up in the glare of the headlights. Emilio stared at him, pointing an accusing finger. "You're Logan!" he rasped. "Jack Logan! But how can you be? You're dead!"

With his arms pinned behind him and an *enmascarado*'s biceps on his windpipe, it was all Logan could do to respond. "I made a quick recovery," he managed. " 'Best laid plans,' Emilio—" The punishing crush of the *enmascarado*'s arm tightened, silencing him. He felt his retrieval bracelet being ripped from his wrist.

"Enough," Emilio stated. "We won't learn anything more. But this time he will stay dead. Adios, Jack Logan."

The pressure increased on Logan's neck, but he braced himself against it. "And goodbye to you, Viper," he hissed. "You really didn't expect to leave this time, did you?"

Emilio raised a hand. "Wait," he told the *enmascarado*. Stepping close to Logan, he stared into his eyes. "What do you mean by that?"

"I mean your base may not be there for you to return to." Logan grinned at him. "The Horlick Mountains, Viper?

Inland from Byrd Station, Antarctica? Ring any bells for you?"

"You're guessing!" Emilio snapped. "It is only a bluff. You surmise the region, but not the site."

"Think so?" His mind racing, Logan pictured a map of the Antarctic continent. In memory he placed grid patterns and cartographers' dots. West Antarctica was a land the size of Spain, and the VIPR base might be anywhere in it. But it was worth a shot. "Coordinates," he said. "Eighty-four degrees south latitude, one-twenty-nine west longitude."

Emilio's face relaxed. "You missed, timecop." He smiled.

"How did he know, so close?" von Steuben muttered. "Only two degrees off—"

"Shut up!" Emilio snapped at the man who would be his father. "He was guessing! A good bluff, but only a bluff." He stepped back, turning away. "Kill him, Guido," he ordered.

The brutal arm tightened again around Logan's throat, cutting off arterial circulation. He felt the *enmascarado*'s free hand placing itself under his ear, for a neck-breaking twist. The world dimming around him, he relaxed every muscle in his body and collapsed, becoming deadweight.

Guido's hold slipped, just a fraction, and in that instant Logan uncoiled like a broken mainspring. Dangling from the grips that held his arms, he swung—a savage pendulum lashing out with both feet. One thudded into the solar plexus of the giant, Kurt. The other crushed the kneecap of the man on his left. As that one collapsed, Logan used his momentum to haul the gaucho on his right around in front of him. Skulls cracked and all four in the tumble collapsed. Guido lost his grip, twisted, fell, and the heel of Logan's hand took him under the chin. He sagged, cursed, and pulled a knife.

The bark of a gunshot seemed to freeze everyone there,

for an instant. Guido raised his knife to strike, then toppled, already dead as he fell, a 9mm bullet in his heart.

Again the gun spoke in the shadows, and the one gaucho still holding Logan spun away, blood spurting from his shoulder.

" 'Old it!" a high, commanding voice shouted. "You blokes jus' back off, now!"

Past the glare of the Rolls's headlights, Logan glimpsed one of the loveliest sights he had ever seen—a bruised angel in bloodstained silk, wielding a Wehrmacht Luger semiautomatic pistol.

Logan scrambled to his feet. "You heard?" he asked.

"Course I 'eard," Harriet snapped. "Now get us out of 'ere."

Logan crouched over the dead *enmascarado*. He found his retrieval bracelet in a pocket of the man's wool sweater, and stood, staying out of her line of fire. All around, from every direction, came the sounds of running feet—men alerted by the gunfire.

Holding the retrieve in his hand, Logan stepped toward Harriet, and at the edge of the light a voice commanded, "Kurt, now!"

From shadows the giant Kurt launched himself at Harriet, his huge arms closing. She ducked, dodged aside, and rapped him on the skull with the butt of the Luger. He hurtled past her, turning, shaking his head to clear it.

But the diversion was all Emilio Vargas von Steuben had needed. Like a cat he landed on Logan's back, clinging there, triggering his own retrieval device even as Logan reacted.

Logan had only an instant. In desperation, he flung his retrieval bracelet in Harriet's direction and shouted, "Use it, Aussie."

Then a wormhole opened and he tumbled into nothingness, Emilio Vargas von Steuben still clinging to him.

Something impacted with his temple, and even the wormhole in time disappeared.

Harriet snagged Logan's retrieval bracelet out of the air, saw the TEC agent and the VIPR leader disappear, and muttered, "Bloody Yank!"

Men were converging on her now from all around. She saw the glint of guns, felt fingers tightening on triggers. "Eighty-four south, one-twenty-nine west," she told herself. "All right, Yank. 'Ere we go."

The retrieve pulsed, and the world around her distorted itself in more directions than it had. In an instant she was inside a timesled materializing around her as it plummeted backward, decelerating up a long double rail . . . reversing, unwinding its own previous acceleration to Q-velocity of 2,994 feet per second.

VIPR's Nest
Antarctica
January 2007

The place was enormous—a huge, vaulted cavern whose main dome extended nearly half a mile in any direction. Three of its walls were sheer faces of solid, striated black rock, plunging downward from the divided dome of roof, into vertiginous depths where tiny people and toy machines moved busily here and there. On the fourth side, the cavern pitched away, angling downward into shrouded distance.

Overhead was a great, stone ledge far above, sweeping outward from the black walls to blend into gray, then white substance that entirely roofed the great space, into the declining distance. Stone and ice, Logan mused, his eyes sweeping the enormity around him as the open tram purred along a wide veranda of polished stone. An enormous cavern in a mountainside entirely hidden by perennial ice. The overhang was a stone ledge, disappearing into the mountain's immense overburden of solid, glowing, translucent ice.

Coming up from the tunnel that housed VIPR's timesled and timefield, the vista had opened before them—a great, subterranean world of ice and stone, the heart of VIPR.

"Remarkable, isn't it?" Emilio Vargas von Steuben waved a casual hand, indicating the panorama of VIPR's Nest the way a tour guide might point out a mountain range. "It's mostly natural formation, you know. This was an embedded glacier, in prehistoric times. It either melted or simply wore away, leaving its empty socket in the mountainside. It was my father's great project, to hollow out the accumulated rime and create this cavern. He used fire, of course— nearly thirty years of constant, subterranean flame fed by high-grade bituminous coal." He pointed at the nearest edge of the distant floor, where massive sheet-metal heating ducts rose above immense banks of furnaces. "We still heat the cavern with coal. Endless heating, an endless water supply from the melt, irrigation for our crops, steam for our generators, lights and power . . ."

"Snug." Jack Logan nodded. "All you need is plenty of coal." His wrists cuffed behind him, ankles chain-shackled, the TEC agent still maintained an air of casual interest as the tram rode along a wide, railed catwalk eighty feet above the cavern floor. A pair of grim *enmascarados* with Uzis sat just behind them, never taking their mask-framed eyes off Logan. In the back of the tram, the giant Kurt guided the vehicle with controls that seemed tiny in his hands.

Emilio is enjoying this, Logan thought. He's enjoying the chance to brag. The VIPR chief chatted happily as they moved along, giving Logan the grand tour the way a vindictive child shows off its toys to a resented neighbor. And VIPR's Nest was nothing if not impressive—virtually a self-contained city hidden beneath the Antarctic ice, invisible from outside but capable of striking out at anyone, anywhere, anywhen.

The man's an egomaniac, Logan noted. All this at his command, and still he gloats in showing it off to a captive. He wants me to see it, to be impressed by it—to realize the magnitude of it before I die.

Emilio Vargas von Steuben chuckled, his eyes boring into Logan. "Plenty of coal? How much is plenty, Agent Logan? Enough to last a thousand years? Maybe two? What do you think this place is built on?" He waved an arm, indicating the lustrous, striated walls that supported the great cavern's roof. "Those walls are not obsidian. Those black bands are solid anthracite, a tapering seam that runs for miles. The roof up there is granite over slate and shale, all of it sealed under almost a mile of ice. The entire natural cavern—everything beneath the stone roof—is anthracite, down to the Eocene layer, and under that is bituminous coal. A coal bed nearly three hundred feet thick! Enough coal to supply the world for centuries, Logan. And it is ours."

"Which explains the high-grade coal imports to Buenos Aires," Logan said, and nodded.

"Vargas coal." Emilio smiled. "The Vargas mines in Patagonia are worthless pits. They always were. Lignite. Brown coal! But no one ever asks the owner of coal mines where his coal comes from. The Patagones pits were always a cover. The real coal comes from here. We operate drift mines further down the slope. The coal is pumped as slag under the ice pack, and recovered at sea. The factory ships are drilling rigs off the Shetlands, and our hopper barges are a fleet of service boats."

"And your miners are Indian slaves," Logan said.

"Of course they are! Most of our laborers here are Indians. Generations of them. They belong to us. Did you know, Logan, that there were more than a million savages in southern Argentina in 1880? East of the Andes and south of Salado, a hundred or more tribes! Today they are almost gone. Yet hardly anyone ever asks, 'Where did the Indians go?' I am the product of genius, Logan. You should know that . . . before you die."

Logan only gazed at him, not responding. The silence seemed to infuriate Emilio. "Genius!" he snapped, turning to face his captive. "Do you know who really discovered Antarctica, Logan? It was not Bransfield, or Amundsen or Scott. It was a German seal hunter, Gunther Braun. In 1812 he made landing on the mainland coast of Ellsworth Land. He found this continent, he claimed it for himself, and he attacked and sank four other vessels to keep the secret of it. He was my ancestor, Logan! The great-great-grandfather of my father, Helmut von Steuben. His son discovered this coal bed, and his son initiated the alliance with the first Vargas patron. And so an empire was born!"

"Quite a lineage," Logan said quietly. "Murderers, thieves, pirates, slavers, and crackpots. You have an interesting family, Emilio Vargas von Steuben."

Like a furious, striking viper, Emilio hissed and slapped Logan across the face, bringing blood. He half drew a side arm, then controlled himself with an effort. "You goad me, Logan?" he growled. "You dare me to kill you? It will not be so quick for you, Logan. Nor nearly so easy."

He turned away as the tram moved on, chattering as though nothing had occurred. The *enmascarados* behind Logan relaxed just a bit, lowering their guns into their laps—though they remained aimed at the captive.

"Genius," Emilio mused. "A dynasty of genius. Braun provided the stage, Karl Moder the place—he found the coal here—and Helmut von Steuben the means, by stealing from the Third Reich its greatest discovery—the technology to travel through time. All this—" He indicated the verandas, the catwalks, the entire man-made city beneath the ice. "—is financed by clients who want to change history here and there. We provide them the means, for a price. And, of course, we have the eventuality device to assure that what they do does not affect VIPR."

"E-warp," Logan said. "We call it E-warp."

Emilio ignored the interruption. "The Vargases provided the structure and the manpower, and I have resurrected the organization. VIPR was nothing, Logan—the original VIPR. Common criminals and fanatics. Imbeciles existing on petty larcenies. But I have reformed VIPR. I have made it the instrument of destiny. VIPR is unstoppable, Logan. Nothing can keep us from our goal."

"Your goal," Logan drawled. "I'll just bet I know what that is. You want to rule the world."

"Of course." Emilio shrugged. "What else?"

"Now, how did I know that?" Logan muttered. "This is really a fascinating discussion, Emilio. I will hate to see it end."

"I expect you will." Emilio smiled. "You know that when I tire of this tour, you will be killed."

"It crossed my mind," Logan said, nodding.

"And of course, you are right." Emilio's smile became a cruel grin. "I rather think I might conduct an entertainment for some of my other guests. Your agonies might be an inspiration to them! You have been quite a nuisance, Logan. And not only to me. You have deeply offended my friend Kurt. That female time traveler that we apprehended . . . I promised Kurt that he could have her for himself after questioning. But now she is gone."

He turned to the giant. "This man robbed you, Kurt. Shall I give him to you, for your pleasure?"

Kurt grinned. Muscles rippled in his massive shoulders,

bulging the too-small sweater he wore. "Yeah . . . yeah, I'd like that," he said.

"Then that is how it will be," Emilio announced. "Kurt will not make it quick, Logan. I think he will kill you a little bit at a time. In the meantime, ponder on this: We did not know that there were timefields other than ours. We did not know of your Time Enforcement Commission. But we know now. Do you know how we know, Logan? You yourself told us, when you appeared on board my father's icebreaker, all those years ago. I was only a boy then. But I was there also as I am now. It was your presence that started our extermination of TEC.

"If you wonder who betrayed the Time Enforcement Commission, Logan, it was you. You, yourself."

With a shock, Logan realized what he had already surmised—why the eyes of Emilio Vargas von Steuben were so remarkable, why they radiated such intensity, even in photographs. They were the eyes of a madman.

The cell was a simple cubicle delved from the ubiquitous anthracite—twelve by twelve by eight feet with several crude cots, a bucket of rimed water, a sewage drain, a screened overhead light, and sheet steel enclosing its open side. It was one of many such cells flanking a cold corridor in the lower regions. Logan shared it with four blank-eyed, emaciated Indians. They sat huddled and hooded, withdrawn and miserable, wrapped in filthy blankets.

"Rest yourself, Logan," Emilio had said with a smirk as the *enmascarados* took him away. "Enjoy VIPR's hospitality. I have clients to entertain, matters of state to plan . . . launches to supervise. When I find the leisure for entertainment, then we will dispose of you."

"How do your clients get here?" Logan asked casually. "We're three hundred miles from the nearest sea."

"Oh?" Emilio grinned that cruel grin. "You've been calculating vectors, have you? Eighty-four south, one-twenty-seven west? Surely you don't consider my father a fool, do you? If you expect your little friend to rescue you, forget it. Those are the coordinates of an abandoned provision camp set up by Amundsen, almost a century ago. It is a long way from here."

Logan was free of his cuffs within minutes after being locked into the cell. The little pick he extracted from the heel of his boot was no larger than a toothpick, but he knew how to use it. With his hands and feet free, though, there was still no way out except the way he had come in—a barred iron door with *enmascarado* guards beyond.

One of the Indians—a young-old man with a scarred face—watched him furtively. The rest ignored him, lost in their own misery. When Logan began scraping at the lustrous black wall, using his leg manacles as tools, the scarred man whispered, *"Qué pasó?"*

Logan looked at him, studying his eyes. "Amigo?" he asked.

The man shrugged. "I am only a slave," he said, in rough Spanish. "Slaves are no one's friends."

A moment later, though, when Logan continued scraping at the wall, the man was beside him, using the other cuff, helping. "My name was Kise, when I had a name," he whispered.

An hour or more of scraping produced a double handful of black dust. Logan removed his shirt, tore the back from it, and tied corners of the fabric to the screen below the single overhead lamp. Then he scooped the coal powder into the little fabric hammock and looked around, to find Kise disassembling one of the bare cots. The Indian came up with a stiff wire two feet long, and Logan took it. He crouched by the barred door until he heard footsteps in the corridor beyond, then told Kise, "Tell your friends to wrap themselves in their blankets and protect their eyes."

Kise muttered to the other Indians, who did as they were told. One of his own blankets he handed to Logan. *"Y usted, señor,"* he said. He covered himself and turned away.

Draping the old blanket over his head, Logan stepped under the light, poked an inch of wire through the screen, braced his feet, and lowered his head, letting the blanket cover his face. In a single movement, then, he slapped the bag of coal dust upward, creating a black cloud around the light, and thrust the wire into the lamp above the screen.

The shattering of the globe was muffled by the explosion that followed it. Powdery coal dust, mixing with the air, ignited by the spark of the broken bulb, erupted into fire and thunder.

It lasted only for an instant. Logan raised his head and tossed off the blanket. Somewhere nearby, a muffled voice whispered, *"Madre de Dios!"* The cubicle was pitch dark now, and filled with the acrid scent of anthracite smoke. Beyond the doorway there were shouts, and the sound of boots on stone. As an explosive, Logan's coal dust had been little more than smoke and noise. But it was enough.

The first *enmascarado* through the door ran headlong into Logan's boot. The second tried to dodge aside, to get his gun up, then toppled as the TEC agent's knuckles crushed his larynx. A third guard, outside, wheeled to raise the alarm, but stumbled and fell as Kise landed on his back with both knees. The Indian swung Logan's discarded chain shackle and looped it around the *enmascarado*'s neck. Then, methodically and with the strength of one who has labored in coal pits, he tightened it, twisted it, and heaved. There was the unmistakable sound of a neck being broken.

Kise stood, crossed himself, and turned toward Logan. *"Gracias,"* he said hesitantly. *"Gracias . . . amigo."*

The other Indians peered around, wide-eyed. Then one of them picked up a fallen Uzi. Without a word, they started along the corridor, opening the slave cells as they went.

* * *

Dressed now in the dark sweater and mask of an *enmascarado*, Logan headed for VIPR's timefield cavern. The hardware of VIPR's sled, track, and armatures, though similar in function, was far different in design from TEC's. VIPR's long, flimsy-seeming sleds, its trough track, and its timefield collar were similar in appearance to the Nazi prototype Logan had found at 1945 Krakenfjord.

Some modifications had been made, but they had not paralleled the Kleindast technology. Logan was not at all sure he would be able to operate VIPR's device. But if he couldn't use it, he reasoned, he might at least be able to ruin it, to put VIPR out of business for a while.

He didn't have the chance to find out, though. Rounding a corner in the remote tunnel leading to the timefield, he stopped, and ducked back into shadows. VIPR had known that he would make for the timefield. At first alarm, the entire area had been sealed off—massive portals closed and locked—and dozens of armed guards on nervous alert at every turn.

Bullets stitched the steel-hard ice ahead of him as he ducked and ran, back the way he had come. Ducking through a frosty doorway, he found himself in a place like a subterranean warehouse—a series of high caverns stacked with provisions of every kind. And at the far end, several hundred yards away, were screw-operated double doors covered with frost and inches-thick ice.

In the distance, he heard the sounds of pursuit. They knew where he was, and they would find him if he stayed. He had only one choice now.

Emilio Vargas von Steuben received the message at his penthouse quarters high in the anthracite towers that backed VIPR's Nest. The prisoner, Jack Logan, had escaped in the slave riots that spread across the fields and the pits. He had not penetrated the temporal-launch cavern, but had evaded pursuit in the supply depots. Now he was gone . . . outside! A tractor expedition was being formed to go out and hunt him down.

Emilio glared at the intercom banks, then sighed. Outside were the Horlick Mountains of West Antarctica. Even though it was January—summer in this hemisphere—still this was Antarctica. The most hostile environment on earth. Outside, beyond the Nest's portals, the ambient temperature was minus four degrees Fahrenheit, with a twenty-knot upslope wind. The elevation was more than twenty thousand feet. It was nearly three hundred miles to the sea, and at least a hundred miles to the nearest camp, station, weather observatory, or explorer's hut.

No living thing, not even the winter-nesting emperor penguins of the ice packs, survived on land in these inland heights a few degrees from the South Pole. Only lichen deep in the crevasses and the high-flying skua, wheeling aloft on the cold thermals, survived such conditions.

"Let him go," Emilio said. "The policeman has chosen his own way to die." He turned away, thoughtfully. "This time-policing agency, this TEC, it has become a nuisance. Don't you agree, Kurt?"

The giant had been dozing on a leather upholstered couch, while a tiny Indian woman manicured his thick nails. At the sound of his name, he sat up, scrambled to his feet—upsetting a lamp and the manicurist's table—and nodded.

"Of course you agree, imbecile," Emilio growled. "You always agree, with whatever I say." To the little Indian woman he snapped, "Clean up that mess and get out!" He pressed a button on the intercom and said, "Send in Jamail."

Within moments, a tapestried door opened and a man entered, bowing as he stepped forward. He was an *enmascarado*, one of Emilio's chosen mercenaries, but now he wore no mask. Swarthy and lean, he had deep-set, dark eyes and a hook nose. The little skullcap on his head was framed by unkempt black hair. "Sir?" he said.

"I have work for you, Jamail," Emilio told him. "Are you ready?"

"Yes, sir." Jamail's wide grin displayed strong, yellow teeth like those of a big rodent.

"Be at the launch chamber in one hour, then," Emilio ordered. "I will instruct you there."

XII

NASA Imaging Center
Clear Lake, Texas
1968

Building security was tight in the restricted-data wing of NASA's new Houston complex. It was here that secrets were kept—highly sensitive material ranging from specialized photography contracted to certain covert agencies, to images from space that might have military application.

The images collected here for overlay and review came from more orbiting sensors—with more capabilities—than were generally known. This was spy-in-the-sky turf. Some of what was compiled here would go to the Pentagon, even more to a secluded estate in Virginia, and a lot of it would never reappear.

Every practical measure of security had been taken here, to keep unauthorized people out. But for those already inside, the security measures were soft. High-profile security is a hindrance to progress, where many people are at work on many projects.

Behind glass partitions, ballroom-size computer banks hummed busily, a montage of bright lights, stainless-steel panels, and big, spinning reels of electromagnetic tape. The beehive cubicles surrounding the banks, literally hundreds of little walled stalls, filled a floor area the size of a coliseum. There were always people at work here, and most of them had little idea what any of the rest were doing.

But in fourteen hours of intensive research here, Julie Price had collected at least one admirer. He came again now, tapping at the cubicle's frame before sticking his head in. "Hi," he said.

Julie looked up from a jumbled spread of data printouts, photo reproductions, and charts. "Oh, hi, Jeff." She smiled a tired smile. "I thought you were making your rounds."

"That was three hours ago," the young security guard said. "Don't you ever knock off?"

"Lot to do," she said, shrugging. "Uh, did they verify my badge?"

He shook his head. "It's a snafu. Happens sometimes. They'll clear it in the morning. Anything I can do for you? Cup of coffee or anything? God, you look exhausted. How about we kick back for a while, and see if the cafeteria's open? I'm due for break."

"Thanks." She smiled. "I'd like that. Maybe later, okay? I still have some readouts to correlate."

"Must be some hot project," Jeff said. He took a short step forward, turning to glance at her viewscreen, but she raised a file folder, blocking his view.

"Top secret," she said, and grinned.

"Yeah." He nodded and backed off, smiling ironically. "Like they'd ever let you and me see anything above level two. Oh, well. How 'bout I check with you next round? Maybe buy you a sandwich, or something?"

"Maybe," Julie sighed. "See you."

When he was gone, Julie got back to her documents. Several of them bore warning labels: TOP SECRET, LEVEL SIX AND ABOVE ONLY.

Orbital satellite data was still a very new thing in this year of 1968. In just over a decade, since *Sputnik I*, science had leapfrogged from fundamental rocketry to variable orbits and slingshot trajectories. The earth had become a "little blue ball" subjected to intense scrutiny, the moon had been reached, and technology was exploding in a dozen related fields.

Telemetry could identify a Volkswagen from fixed orbit, and TV images from *Tiros* had surveyed weather patterns across the globe. Millions of people had watched *Telstar* glide across the firmament. And in places like this, people were just beginning to understand some of what the eyes and spies in the skies could see.

Vast amounts of data would be lost in the process—images set aside as having no immediate relevance, then buried under the crush of new data. Much of this would not be available in 2007, which was why Julie Price had been launched upstream to 1968.

Amy Fuller, Dale Easter, and Bob O'Donnelly had told her what to look for, and now it was up to her to find it. "It" was everything she could find relative to Antarctica, every image that might suggest anomalies there, and every bit of analysis data of those images. In short, she was looking for something—anything—that might indicate the geographic location of VIPR's time-launch facility, in the area between Byrd Station and the South Pole.

ChronComp gave a low probability to the coordinates Harriet Blevins had brought back, but a high probability to the site being somewhere in those frozen mountains.

The pickings were scarce. Spy satellites rarely had their apertures focused on so remote a place as West Antarctica, and a majority of the natural-light images that did exist were obscured by clouds. It was in the infrared that Julie found her best results—a few images showing heat sources beneath the icecap. Meteorological overlays ruled out some of these, and surveys of known volcanic activity eliminated most of the rest.

Julie was getting discouraged by the time she reached the esoteric ranges of gas chromatography and stratospheric surveys. But then she found the anomalies—a visible shift from one year to the next in the O-ring, and an unexplained convection over the Horlicks with persistent traces of CH_4.

These joined the other notes she had made in her belt-pack recorder, just as unusual sounds came from the entry bay beyond the cubicles. Voices were raised in command, and there was the unmistakable stamping of sentry boots.

Carefully, Julie peered over the top rim of her cubicle, then ducked out of sight. "Uh-oh!" she muttered.

It was Bob O'Donnelly who had told her what to watch for. Somewhere in some dusty duty manual he had learned that a part of the surveillance routine for sensitive information centers in the 1960s was the spot inspection of premises. These came at random times, but—in keeping with good military habit—within regular intervals. Sometime within twenty-four hours, Bob had told Julie, she would have to "shag ass out of there on the double."

The time, obviously, was at hand.

She was straightening up the piles of documents in her borrowed cubicle—placing them all in one orderly stack—when her new friend Jeff stuck his head in. "It's sweep-and-peek time," he said, grinning. "Hope your ticket's in order."

"Yeah," she said. "Me, too."

He turned away, to take his guard station at the next aisle, then decided to try one more time. "How about if I get us both some coffee and bring it here?" he asked.

There was no answer. Jeff looked into the cubicle, blinked, and looked again. Julie wasn't there. The girl was nowhere around. There was not the slightest sign that anyone had been there at all, except for a single slip of paper with a cryptic, pencil-scrawled note: "Thanks, Uncle J. See you."

TEC Headquarters
2007

"Detailed images from *Discoverer 13*, with analyses!" Amy Fuller marveled. "A lot of these weren't even in existence when the TEC history banks were compiled, in the nineties. Let's get them on scan and see what ChronComp makes of them."

"*Discoverer 13,*" Dale Easter expounded, thumbing through some of the photos Julie Price had brought back from 1968. "The first really successful reconnaissance satellite. Launched from Canaveral on August 10, 1960. It was the grandfather of U.S. military surveillance satellites. Most of what it sent back disappeared into the Pentagon, and a lot of it never surfaced again. *D-13*'s reentry pod was the first man-made object ever recovered from space—"

"We know, Dale," Bob O'Donnelly drawled. "Boy, ask some people what time it is, they'll tell you how to build a clock." He had only glanced at the pictures and data printouts in the packet. Most of his attention, since Julie's return, had been concentrated on Julie. "Tell us what all this means, Julie," he asked now. "What did you see, that made you choose all these to bring back?"

"ChronComp will give us correlations and significance," Easter said, frowning. "Julie's just a courier, after all."

"Well, she's the courier who scanned NASA's libraries to find clues for us, and these are what she chose!"

Harriet Blevins, bruised and bandaged, came in from tending her wounds. "Yeah," she said, "I'd like to know, too. Tell us about it, ducky."

"I don't really know." Julie blushed slightly. "I was just looking for something . . . anything that looked interesting . . ."

"Good, scientific approach," Dale Easter muttered. "Random intuition."

The rest ignored him.

"Like this," Julie continued, stepping forward to spread satellite photos on the conference table. She picked out a group of four, aligning them side by side. "See this cloud formation here?" She pointed. "It looks kind of like a doughnut. And here it is three more times, on successive orbits. It changes, see? It drifts eastward—"

"Prevailing winds." Easter shrugged.

"Yes, but see how the doughnut sort of drags out, a little more each time, all except for the hole. It acts like it's snagged on something, right here."

"A thermal updraft, maybe." Bob O'Donnelly frowned. "Warmer air rising through a drifting cloud pattern. What else do you have?"

"Well," Julie pressed on, "I got to looking at the red-range images, and there seems to be a consistent heat source just about the same area—where the doughnut's hole snagged."

"Vulcanism, possibly." Easter tapped codes into a keyboard. "We'll compare it to volcanic activity patterns. There would be a natural thermal convection in that area."

Captain Eugene Matuzek shook his head. "Doesn't sound very conclusive. What else do we have?"

"Maybe nothing, sir." Julie shrugged. "But after I noticed the doughnut hole I went back through a lot of other stuff, to see if anything else showed peculiarities at that same location. The first thing I found was this." She spread out an old-fashioned tractor-feed print, page after page of numbers. "There was some interest in stratospheric ozone back then. Something about the O-ring, or a hole in the ozone . . ."

"That's right." Amy Fuller nodded. "It was a big political issue, the hole in the ozone layer. First time anyone had seen it, so they assumed it was something new. The Save the Whales people loved it. Political campaigns, new fund-raising veins to tap, a lot of industrial and economic vandalism in the name of environmental purity. The ozone hole was one of the classic Chicken Little episodes in history."

"They did a lot of research on that hole," Julie said. "And I noticed this. Every chart shows a bulge or wobble in the O-ring, directly above that same area. So I brought these readings along."

"Pretty good." O'Donnelly grinned. "That gives us a triple overlay with anomalies corresponding at a single point."

"And finally I found one other thing," Julie concluded. "When they were testing geostationary orbits in the early sixties, they played around with a lot of different scans. This chart here is called a gas chromatography survey. What I noticed about it was this." She pointed at a column of numbers. "It's like there was an invisible plume of rising gases, that stays pretty much the same from one reading to the next. There are a lot of those plumes, all over the world, but this is the only one I found above Antarctica with a high CH_4 component."

"What does that mean?" Matuzek growled. "What's CH_4?"

"Methane." O'Donnelly's grin had widened as Julie talked. "Methane gas, Captain. It comes from forests, feed-lots, and coal mines. Last I heard, Antarctica is severely lacking in either forests or feedlots."

Grudgingly, Dale Easter stared at the printouts, then at Julie Price. "I withdraw my comment about 'just a courier,' " he said. "Where did you learn about hydrocarbons, Julie?"

"Texas A&M," the girl said.

As one, they gathered around the displayed photographs.

"There are our coordinates." Amy gestured. "At least 80 percent probability, I'd say."

Bob O'Donnelly brought composite scans up on his screens, and extended coordinates. "Eighty-three degrees, four minutes south," he read. "One-zero-eight degrees, one minute west." He turned to Matuzek. "VIPR's Nest?"

"So you gonna send in th' bloody troops, or w'at?" Harriet demanded.

"It isn't quite as easy as that," the captain said. "We're police, not military. Let's see how ChronComp reads all this."

Amy Fuller nodded, then glanced up at the Dome of History, the big, overhead E-warp display. "Look," she said. At the edge of the screen a swirling pattern had formed, extending toward the center. The rest of them stared at it, and Dale Easter whispered, "A five, at least!"

Bob O'Donnelly was already tapping codes into a keyboard. "September 11, 1939," he announced. "Do we go for it, Captain?"

Matuzek strode across to the co-ord banks and studied the symbols scrolling across a screen there. "EuroTEC doesn't show it as a five," he said. "To them it's a three." He moved to another screen. "AusTEC the same. Except for them it's barely a one. So its primary effect is here."

Amy was feeding queries to ChronComp, while Dale Easter decoded the output. "Lot going on that day," he said. "President Roosevelt was speaking at a conference of ambassadors, German troops were entering Warsaw, the USSR was invading Finland, William O. Douglas took his seat on the U.S. Supreme Court, Igor Sikorsky tested the first practical American helicopter, Calvin Graham had all the bells in Boston rung to announce his wife's pregnancy, Macy's introduced nylon stockings in New York, sellout crowds for midwest premieres of *The Wizard of*—"

"Hold it!" Bob O'Donnelly yelled. "Back up! I think that's it!"

"What?" Easter turned. "*The Wizard of Oz*?"

"No! Calvin Graham. That's it. The probability matches, exactly. Calvin Graham was Charles Graham's father!"

Harriet stared at one and then the other of them. " 'Oo's Graham?" she asked.

Matuzek's cheeks seemed to pale under the stubble of two days' growth of whiskers. "Graham," he muttered. "Our Charles Graham?" He glanced at the meaningless duty roster, out of habit, then looked away. With TEC sealed, there were no spare agents. He sighed. "I need a volunteer," he said.

Julie Price was already heading for the launching bay, picking up a blast suit and firearm as she went. "You have one," she said, over her shoulder. "And I don't want to hear a single word about inexperience!"

"Now hold on—" Matuzek started, but stopped when Harriet raised her hand.

"Let the kid go," the Australian said. "She's ready to win her wings." When Julie was gone, strapping in aboard the waiting timesled while ThinkTank fed coordinates to the techs, Harriet got down a blast suit of her own. "I expect it's a trap," she told Matuzek. "But maybe we can lay a little trap of our own, aye?"

83°4' S, 108°1' W
2007

A skua sat on Jack Logan's chest. It flapped its wings lazily, cocked beady eyes this way and that. Like a big, ugly seagull claiming a dead fish, it scored his forehead with the talons on its webbed feet, flapped its wide wings again, and began to bite off pieces of his ears with a sharp, rending beak.

The increasing, nagging pain in his ears brought him out of deep sleep, dragging the dream with him. He cried out, tried to swat at the skua with numb hands, and woke up. There was no skua, only a dream. He lay curled in a close, dark hole where the only light came dimly through a tiny vent kept open by his frosty breath. The pain in his ears, and across his forehead, was creeping frostbite— bitterly cold air seeping through his wraps to burn the skin beneath.

Again he heard the flapping of wings, and knew what the sound was. It was erratic wind, rattling the taut fabric of the little antarctic tent above him, covered now with shallow snowdrift too hard to meld into ice.

The storm had passed over, and he was still alive. Thankfully, it had been only a modest blizzard, lasting a few hours. He was no more than half a mile from the great portals of VIPR's Nest, the supply doors that had let him escape. Half a mile! It was as far as he had been able to travel in this harsh land, before the elements drove him to cover.

He had dug himself a hole in the lee side of a hard-ice ridge, using flares from VIPR's storehouse to melt the surface. Then, dressed in three layers of woven wool, with goose-down quilted thermal pants, parka, mukluk boots, and mittens over it, he had wrapped himself in blankets, forced the little tent into the hole, and burrowed inside.

By the time he had zipped the nylon flap, he was shivering violently. The air temperature, he guessed, was at most minus thirty-five degrees Fahrenheit, and the howling frontal wind of the storm was gusting to fifty knots.

A mild storm for the Antarctic, he told himself wryly. A stroll through the meadow, compared with the polar cyclones that were common in this latitude. "Think it's cold now?" he muttered, rocking this way and that to loosen the weight of snow pressing the tent down on him. "Why, this is summer weather! Just think what winter is like."

When he could move freely, he opened the flap of the buried tent and crawled out, little avalanches of crystal ice cascading around him. The sky above was as clear now as a dark blue pool, fading to purple in the direction opposite the low-riding sun, so clear and so shallow that he could see stars directly overhead, even in the long daylight.

He had taken bearings earlier, and knew that downhill led away from VIPR. The supply port was somewhere on the white slopes above him. How far was it from here to . . . to anyplace else? He could only guess. The nearest seacoast must be straight ahead—downhill. But it might be two hundred miles, even to the mile-deep ice shelf that covered the water farther than the eye could see.

The silence was broken suddenly by a muted, deep roar, like a drawn-out explosion. Logan recognized the sound. Somewhere beneath the ice, beneath the rising slope of the mountain, a timesled had been launched.

Placing the lofty mountains at his back, facing the downward slopes, he tried to orient himself. The sun was no help here, unless one knew the time of day. In high summer in the antarctic interior, the sun did not rise and fall. It simply moved in a vast arc, just above the horizon, going all the way around each twenty-four hours. But the terrain gave him some clues. He was facing toward the South Atlantic, he surmised. Byrd Station was to his left, beyond reach behind a mountain range. Somewhere behind him, beyond the VIPR's lair, was the South Pole.

Gathering his possessions together, dragging the tent as a sled, he set out northward. Everything he knew about the Antarctic told him that there was nothing ahead to help him—no shelter, no habitation, nothing. Yet, just above him—inside the ice shell of a frozen mountain—VIPR had accumulated the resources to build a seat of empire.

The materials had to come from somewhere, and they had to get here somehow.

Somewhere ahead, he hoped, was the supply route to VIPR's Nest. There had to be an access—a hidden airfield, a tractor base, something. Those thousands of tons of cargo in VIPR's supply depots hadn't walked there unaided.

Far out ahead, miles away, the receding horizon had a vaguely patterned, striated look.

The sun was over his right shoulder, heading for the cover of the mountains behind him, when he stopped to rest. In a little depression he melted snow over a tiny canned-heat flame, and made a meal from a few ounces of dried food. Then he climbed an ice crest and shielded his eyes, looking into the distance. The striations were a little closer now, a widening pattern of quiltwork seams and crisscross jagged lines.

Crevasses, he decided. The snowfield out there, starting a few miles ahead and extending as far as he could see, was a maze of cracks and sheer-ice canyons, increasing in size as they extended northward toward the distant ice-clad sea.

A man could die in a maze like that. But then, a man could die just wondering whether or not to proceed. Gathering up his meager supplies, Jack Logan trudged onward, toward the frozen horizon ahead.

XIII

Boston
September 11, 1939

No fewer than twelve claves of bells were within earshot of Boston Common, and it was a mark of Calvin Graham's enthusiastic pride, as well as of his influence in the city, that all of them sang on the morning of his pronouncement. After nine years of marriage, the Merchant Prince of Back Bay had just learned that his Agatha had conceived a child. In keeping with his philosophy that "every honorable event is a public event and should be held so," Calvin set out to proclaim the news to the world—which, to him, was Boston.

A little embarrassed at the whole thing, Agatha Graham stayed at home while her husband set out to tell everyone about her condition. From the paned drawing room windows of their fashionable Back Bay home, she watched him drive away in his elegant new Lincoln. The big car's passage left little red and gold storms of swirling leaves in its wake.

At ten o'clock the bells began to ring, and Agatha shook her head, resignedly. Calvin never did anything by halves, she told herself. Not only were the Congregational churches for a mile around joining in the enthusiastic chorus, but others, as well. Distinctly, she could hear the soundings of

164

Holy Cross Cathedral and St. Paul's, as well as the chimes of Trinity Church and the Campanile across the Charles.

"Old North only showed lights for Paul Revere," Agatha mused. "For my husband, it rings bells."

Drawn by the sound, she stepped out onto the trellised veranda, listening. A chill wind rustled fall leaves around her, but the sun was high and the day bright. For one full minute the bells pealed, powered by—she estimated—two hundred dollars' worth of pledged donations per second. Then, as one, they rang down and only the whisper of the wind echoed them.

Agatha pictured Calvin standing tall and proud—ridiculous, but proud—on the forum box in the Commons, raising his arms high to still the crowd, then announcing in stentorian baritone that a new Graham would enter the world in the spring. A son, naturally. Agatha doubted whether Calvin would ever consider any alternative.

She stood for a moment, shaking her head slowly as she thought about her husband, then she turned, stepped inside, and gasped.

A man stood there, facing her—a swarthy, hook-nosed man with a rodent's grin. "Mrs. Calvin Graham, yes?" he said, his words thickly accented. Before Agatha could react, he lunged at her, and she saw the vicious-looking knife in his hand.

What happened then was beyond her understanding. The air between them seemed to shimmer, and suddenly a young woman stood there—a very young, auburn-haired woman, hardly more than a girl, wearing some kind of shiny red garment that looked like armor, yet fitted her as snugly as a second skin.

The rodent-faced man's eyes widened and he tried to stop his lunge, but momentum carried him forward, directly into a stiff-armed hand that collided with his chin. The sound of teeth breaking fairly echoed around the room.

"That's enough of that!" the girl snapped. Lithe as a cat, she sidestepped and grabbed his wrist, twisting it downward and back. The knife clattered to the floor. The man hissed in pain, bright droplets spraying from his bleeding lips, and his slim assailant completed her pivot, forcing him to his knees. She looped a shiny strap around his wrist, kicked him forward, facedown, and grabbed the other wrist, completing her tie with a flourish.

"I arrest you under general Timecourt warrant," she said. "If you have anything to say, save it for the judge."

"Mercy," Agatha Graham breathed, both hands at her mouth.

The astounding girl looked up. Despite her athletic figure and her air of authority—like a policeman making an arrest—she was very pretty, and quite young, probably not yet twenty. "I doubt it, ma'am," she drawled. "Timecourt isn't lenient with temporal assassins." She stooped, dragged the whimpering man up to his knees, and said, "Come on, bozo. Retrieval time."

The air shimmered again then, and a heavy-shouldered man in black clothing and black mask appeared, holding something that might have been a gun except that there never had been such a gun. Without comment he pointed it at the girl. Where it aimed, a tiny beam of bright red light shone from it, aligning itself as a red dot on her chest, just below her shoulder.

The shot did not sound like a gunshot at all. It was more the sound of bacon frying in a skillet. Agatha stifled a scream . . . then noticed that it wasn't the young woman who fell. It was the masked man. Just beyond him, in the parlor doorway, another woman lowered a gun and said, "Knew it was a trap. 'E'd 'ave winged you, Julie. Then VIPR would 'ave 'ad some questions for you, I expect."

Feeling dazed and unsteady, Agatha stared at the strangers, one by one. The new arrival was small, blond, with wide-set blue eyes as angelic as a child's. She wore a close-fitting armor uniform like the younger one's, except that it was dark gray.

"Who—who are you people?" Agatha managed.

"Sorry about th' mess, mum," the blonde said, and shrugged. "Couldn't be 'elped. That's Julie. She came to save you from what's-'is-name there, an' I came along as backup. I'm 'Arriet. We're cops . . . that is, police officers . . . after a fashion. W'at you do about all this is up to you, but my advice would be to forget it, if you can. Folks'll just think you've gone balmy, otherwise."

The two policewomen dragged the groaning, whining man with the bloody face a few feet and dropped him unceremoniously atop the inert black-suited one. Julie sat on them while Harriet picked up the fallen gun and knife, and removed little black boxes with tiny, sparkling lights on their surfaces from both men. "It's your collar," she told the younger girl. "You take the dead one in. I'll bring Bozo 'ere and be right behind you."

Julie stood, rolled the whimpering, jibbering assassin off the black-suited body, and flipped a loop around the masked man's limp wrist. Holding the strap firmly, she smiled at Agatha. "Nice to meet you, Mrs. Graham," she said. She touched a bracelet on her wrist. The air shimmered again and she was gone, along with the body of the black-garbed killer. Harriet scanned the parlor with practiced eyes, borrowed a tea towel to wipe up some bloodstains, and straightened a rug. "Take good care of young Charlie," she said, indicating Agatha's abdomen. " 'E'll be an important man one day."

With a wink, she took the assassin's come-along, touched her own bracelet, and they both disappeared. It was as though no one had ever been there.

Agatha Graham turned, slowly, full around, with eyes

as big as walnuts. What had that been all about? Had it actually happened at all? Had she dreamed it? Who knew what illusions a belated pregnancy might conjure in the mind of a thirty-eight-year-old woman? Calvin, damn you anyway, why aren't you here?

Maybe a cup of hot tea would help her to sort things out.

TEC Headquarters
2007

"The dead man's name was Ille Galeska," Eugene Matuzek said. "A renegade Serb, under death sentence in four countries. He disappeared six years ago from a prison in Brussels. Obviously recruited by VIPR as an *enmascarado*." He cocked a judicious brow at Harriet. "It was a good shoot, if that matters to you."

"Not in the slightest." She grinned. "I play by Aussie rules. Any shoot you can walk away from's a fair dinkum shoot, Down Under."

"Which brings us to your prisoner." Matuzek's quizzical look became a frown. "Jamail, you called him?"

"Righto. Jamail Akhbar Hussein. Had quite a famous old man, y'know. 'E was a client of VIPR, tradin' favors for a crack at Middle East 'istory. Viper 'imself sent 'im to kill Charles Graham's mother before Graham was born. 'Ow would that 'ave set with TEC, right?"

"God help us all," Bob O'Donnelly muttered, immersed in his keyboards and monitors.

Matuzek ignored the interruption. "But what happened to him, Harriet? I understood that Julie broke a few of his teeth and maybe dislocated his shoulder, but my God! The man's a wreck! It's a wonder he's still alive!"

"Blighter 'ad a 'ard time on the trip in." Harriet shrugged. "Poor soul, some folks just don't travel well. We did 'ave a nice chat, though." Her smile was angelic. "Th' bloke told me just all sorts of things I was interested in knowing about."

"But he was a prisoner in custody! You can't just—oh, I know. Aussie rules. Right?" He turned away, shaking his head. "Full debriefing in ten minutes, Agent Blevins. I want to know everything you learned from that—that unfortunate traveler . . . no matter how you got it!"

"Righto, Cap'n."

At the door to his office, Matuzek turned. "Amy, I want a line out."

Amy Fuller, correlating overlays at a chart screen, stopped and stared at him. "Line out? But we're sealed, Captain. Total shield."

"Then break it!" he snapped. "I want a hard line, now. To Charles Graham, person-to-person only, and scramble."

"Yes, sir!" Amy turned to the comm banks, opened a single channel, and coded in the access for Charles Graham, head of NSSA's black-ops division.

"Gee." Julie Price paused as the code went through. "Charles Graham? *The* Charles Graham? I just met his mother."

A few feet away, a slim, blond woman with two S and R techs tagging behind her paused and turned. "Memo for S and R," she said. "Would time-circuit communications be immune to ripple effect? Check out possibility of routing calls uptime for storage and retransmittal."

As the three moved on, Julie asked, "Who was that?"

"That's Claire Hemmings," Amy told her. "Scientist from S and R, assigned as an observer."

"She looks just a little bit like Harriet," Julie noted. "Don't you think so?"

Captain Eugene Matuzek went in person to escort Charles Graham through the screen of TEC's total-seal security.

He met the NSSA chief in a dingy corridor at the back of a CPA office complex, which was part of TEC's facade to the outside world.

"You understand the situation, sir?" Matuzek pressed. "This is a total-shield seal. Once in, you're here for the duration, with no outside contact except the president himself on a secured line."

"I understand," Graham assured him. "Now let's bring me up-to-date, shall we?"

At a touch of Matuzek's palm against a nine-by-six-inch scanner panel that seemed only to be three of the ordinary bricks in an ordinary fire wall, a hidden door swung open and the two men passed through into the working heart of the Time Enforcement Commission. Graham paused, looking around. He had seen TEC headquarters before, but never under siege. "It's quiet," he observed.

"Yes, sir, it seems that way at first," Matuzek said. "We're on skeleton staff—security-sealed to all but essential TEC personnel."

Graham glanced at him. "You also have a transfer, I believe. An AusTEC agent?"

"Yes, sir. Harriet Blevins. I've accepted her as a TEC assignee, pending further notice."

"Well, you have that notice now," Graham said. "Agent Blevins is sanctioned, by both AusTEC and EuroTEC, under 'host nations' treaty provisions. I was advised personally, by Wilkins."

"Does that mean she doesn't answer to TEC?"

"She's still TEC, Eugene. What it does mean is that she's also a foreign precinct agent, with discretion, and we cooperate with her in that capacity. In essence, it gives her the power to play by Australian rules."

In the briefing room, the captain made introductions, then got down to business. One by one, the historians and techs briefed Graham on the situation with VIPR—what they had encountered, what they had learned, and what was happening now.

Through it all, Graham sat quietly and listened, only now and then interjecting a question as he digested the details.

When the overview was completed, he looked up at the Dome of History. "So with those . . . those blips on the E-warp stream," he said, "you can't be sure from moment to moment what subtle changes may already have occurred, historically."

"That's the reason for total seal-down," Dale Easter agreed. "TEC can't operate consistently from a shifting landscape. With the security seal, we're relatively secure here, at least from minor alterations."

"Hard to hit a moving target if your gun melts every time you aim," Bob O'Donnelly elaborated.

"Yes." Graham pursed his lips thoughtfully. "Quite graphic." He gazed upward again, at the blips. "Also hard to know just who to trust, isn't it?"

"Everybody is suspect," Matuzek said grimly. "From the president right on down. Nobody is really immune to history. I decided to call on you, sir, only after we learned firsthand that VIPR had tried to eliminate you."

"Understandable," Graham said, smiling slightly. "Paranoia isn't paranoia if everybody really is out to get you. And you have an agent unaccounted for?"

"Yes, sir. Jack Logan. He managed to penetrate VIPR, up to a point, because they thought he was dead. But now, obviously, they know otherwise. We have reason to think they have him—if they haven't already killed him—at VIPR's headquarters, somewhere in West Antarctica."

"And you want to get him out."

"Damn right we do!" Harriet Blevins snapped. "Bloody Yank owes me somethin'!"

Matuzek glared at her, then turned to the chief of black

ops. "Pardon the outburst, sir. We're all a little tight-wound right now. We need Logan. He's TEC's number one cop. The best we've got. Also, we need whatever evidence he's gathered. We're 80 percent sure where VIPR's Nest is, and about 50 percent sure what their capabilities are. I know Logan, sir. By now—if he's still alive—he has the rest of what we need to know to go in and put them out of business."

"And if he's dead?"

"Time travel, sir. If he's dead, maybe we can go back and get him before he died. But that gets very chancy."

"Chancy, nothing," Dale Easter interrupted. "The prime rule of time travel is: Don't make tracks. If they've killed him, then the circumstances of his death are part of the fabric of history. And not knowing the circumstances, we can't even predict what all we'd upset by changing them."

Amy Fuller indicated the dome above them. "On that point," she said, "I have to agree with Dr. Easter. Every blip up there is an unknown factor right now. Maybe they're just anomalies . . . some of them. And maybe some of them are customers of VIPR, running around in the past doing their own little felonies, and no high-level ripples have developed yet. But at least one of them is another time bomb aimed squarely at TEC—at everything that stands between us and temporal chaos. And the bomb goes off within the next three years. There's too much uncertainty there for a headlong frontal attack. We'd be charging in blindfolded."

"Then let's draw the buggers out." Harriet's blue eyes were as cold as antarctic ice. "We could buy some time, at least."

Matuzek, bowed over his transcriber-playback, looked up at the Australian. "And how would we do that?"

"Good, old-fashioned police 'arassment," the woman

sometimes called Angel purred, fingering the butt of her laser-sight pistol. "Same as if you've got a drug lord on your streets and you know 'is operation inside out but you can't bust 'im for lack of good evidence. You 'aul in 'is dealers every time they spit on the walk, plaster 'is cars with parking violations, scare off 'is customers, issue fire marshal inspection warrants on 'is bloody 'ouse, flash badges at 'is business associates, arrest 'im every twelve hours or so on every misdemeanor charge you can dredge up, 'ell, you might even get 'is dog impounded for out-of-date tags.

"You make life miserable for th' bugger, try to push 'im off balance so 'e'll make a mistake. And pretty soon, when 'e does, you nail 'im."

"You're speaking metaphorically, of course," Charles Graham mused. "This VIPR is no squalid, urban criminal enterprise. How on earth can you harass something you can't even find?"

Matuzek studied the Australian agent, thoughtfully. In some ways, she reminded him of Jack Logan—unpredictable and determined. And she was sanctioned. "You have an idea about that, Agent Blevins?"

"Bet yer tucker I do," she said.

Graham looked from one to another of them, sizing them up. Historians, technicians, theorists, and policemen. Still, they were the best of the best, each of them, and in this situation they were the ones in the driver's seat. "What do you want from me?" he asked.

"Your presence," Matuzek said. "And your line to the president. VIPR may be a criminal organization in the classic sense, but in terms of capability for destruction it is a world power. We're police, sir, not military. We'll do what we can, but when the target and its circumstances are known, it will be up to you to call in our backup."

82°6′ S, 72°3′ W
2007

Logan had no way to measure how far he had traveled. Miles, certainly. A lot of miles. He knew he had been lucky. The sky had remained clear, allowing him at least a trace of solar warmth in this frozen land. The path he had chosen lay across fairly even terrain, with no great cliffs to scale, no major chasms to cross, and only modest, descending hills to climb. And the wind—the constant, killing wind that blew always across the drifts and dunes of endless snowfields—had been relatively light since that first storm.

Five times now the sun had circled the horizon, and he had pushed his endurance to its limits, putting the miles behind him, using constant, distant landmarks as his compass. A hundred miles? Maybe a hundred and fifty? He had no clear idea, except that he was traveling as fast as humanly possible, and had descended to an elevation where the act of breathing was no longer a constant battle.

His eyes burned constantly now—from the bitter cold, the dryness of the atmosphere, and the unceasing glare of a white landscape that extended to the horizons in all directions. Even through the dark goggles that were part of the insulated face flap in his parka hood, the glare was barely tolerable at times. Unshielded human eyes would have been burned blind in the first few hours of such exposure.

As to temperature, comfort was out of the question. The task here was to retain enough body heat to keep moving, despite the overpowering urge sometimes to just lie down and rest on the nice, white snow. To do that, Logan knew, would be to die. Once at rest, in this kind of cold, a person would never move again.

To keep a sense of time, he had chosen those times when the sun was directly behind him—beyond the high mountains of the Horlick range—to get a few hours' sleep. Each sleep was a problem in itself—finding a suitable drift or ridge to provide a slope away from the wind, then digging in, using the little thermal tent as a cocoon. It was the nearest he came to physical comfort, those sleeps, and he steeled himself each time to limit them to his own somnal minimum of four hours, then dig out, pack up, and move on.

His meager provisions were running low, his strength was more and more based on adrenaline boost, and the constant, colorless white landscape was beginning to play tricks with his mind, but still he kept going.

The sun was in its sixth circuit, riding down toward the now-distant peaks behind him, when he saw the smoking crevasse. Less than a mile ahead, a long, jagged crack in the ice—one of many deep, narrow chasms in the icescape now—widened into a vast, bottomless canyon. It seemed to split the world into two halves, with nothing between them except distance, immense depth, and an odd, abrupt puff of cloud—or smoke—that drifted from below and hung for a moment in view before disappearing in the crosswind.

He stopped, closed his eyes tightly, and shook his head. Then he looked again. The crevasse was still there, too clear and detailed to be a mirage or illusion. And as he watched, another tendril of gray smoke rose lazily from somewhere below, found the wind, and was swept away.

Logan stared at the apparition, disbelieving, then started toward it. When once again he saw a trace of smoke, he increased his pace. He tried to run on protesting legs, and found himself sprawled facedown in the sand-hard powder of a low drift.

For a moment he lay there, understanding why the simple act of lying down was deadly in these conditions. His exhausted muscles, his reflexes, his nerves, his very fibers reacted instantly to the prone position, and he found himself suddenly feeling very contented—very comfortable just to be where he was and let the winds cover him over with their sweeping, drifting loose snow.

He felt the pleasant, insidious sensations of the ice death, and raged at himself to resist them. He moved one arm, then the other, sweeping them up and down, gouging arcs in the loose snow around him. Then he forced his legs to move, increasing the circulation of his bloodstream. Finally, agonizingly, he managed to lift himself, then to stand. Grabbing the towline on his pack desperately, he moved on. Only when he had gone nearly fifty yards did he feel his common sense returning to him, and he stopped for a moment to look back.

There where he had fallen, where his arms and legs had swept the snow, was a perfect pattern—a snow angel just the way he had made them as a child.

"Angel," he whispered. "Angel."

He turned northward again and walked, as though nothing in this world could ever stop him from walking. "Code name Angel," he muttered to himself. "Harriet, you little nuisance, if I ever see a warm bed again, I won't complain about you being in it."

XIV

"You should have a partner for this." Amy Fuller worried as Harriet Blevins, scrubbed and refreshed, clipped on a side arm and a slim backpack. "You know they'll have to react. You won't have any backup, most of the way."

"I'll 'ave all the partner I need," Harriet said. "If your technicians know w'at they're doin', I'll 'ave the best partner a cop could 'ave. Myself."

"And that's another problem," Eugene Matuzek said. "There's just you. We have a procedure rule in TEC about repeat launches. One in twelve. Only one launch in twelve hours. Acceleration to Q-velocity is serious stress. Even with tachyon thrust, that's a punch of eight gravities. The human body needs time to recuperate."

"You bloody Yanks are so conservative," Harriet scoffed. "One in twelve, huh? Well, it's only a rule. Rules can be broken. If I get a nosebleed or two, so be it. I've 'ad 'em before."

Amy Fuller frowned, moving around to help the Australian with her packstraps. "We're already breaking every rule in the probabilities manual," she warned. "There's no way this won't make some tracks in time. And then there's

177

spatial redundancy. That's tricky business, Harriet. You know the limitations?"

"Sure." Harriet grinned. "Don't be two places at once if I can 'elp it, and never be in the same place, at the same time, twice. Same matter, same space . . . stay away from myself at all costs, right?"

"Right. I'd feel better if somebody else could take a share of these launches. Maybe Julie could—"

"Wouldn't work, luv," Harriet said, and shrugged. "You know that as well as I do. The kid's got blips to see about. An' even if you 'ad a spare cop, I'm the only one available as knows the lay of the land. Besides—" She turned, fixing Matuzek with level, no-nonsense blue eyes. "—you're all Yanks. Americans, fair reekin' with the American Way. Tell the truth, Captain. Would you send a Yank cop to do w'at I'm doin', if you 'ad one?"

Matuzek hesitated, then shook his head, slowly.

"Thought not." Harriet smiled coldly. "You've got three centuries of 'never shoot first,' and 'never endanger by-standers' be'ind you. John Wayne an' Roy Rogers an' th' Marquis of Queensberry. Good Yank cops don't open fire in a crowd, do they, ducks?"

Matuzek sighed. "I'm letting you go," he said. "Your sanctions require that. Don't ask me to personally approve, though, because I can't."

"O' course not." Harriet's smile softened. "You're a Yank. Well, I took an oath of office, too, y'know. The TEC part's the same as yours, even if the nationality clause isn't. Besides, you know that w'atever I do back then, VIPR's goin' to undo it. They bloody well 'ave to."

With a quick glance around her, Harriet headed for the launch bay. "Make sure the techs double-check their vec-tors," she said. "And keep the 'ardware coming. I'll be right back."

Matuzek looked after her, frowning. Police harassment, he thought bleakly. Harassment with C4 and detonating timers. He didn't know how Charles Graham had managed to get a stockpile of saboteurs' ordnance into a security-sealed building, but it was here. And a little blond angel with the soul of a seasoned terrorist was on her way now to make some things go bang.

Charles Graham also watched Harriet heading for the sled. The shrewd, gray eyes that some reporter had once called "uncannily canny" held a genuine hint of respect. "That's a formidable young woman," he commented. "I'm glad she's on our side."

Matuzek nodded. "Harriet lost her whole family a few years ago . . . wiped out in a Melbourne shoot-out that wouldn't have happened but for some lunatic playing around with Pastime's experimental timefield. TEC recruited her direct out of academy at Adelaide, when AusTEC was formed. She really hates time travel. Probably why she's so good at it. Wilkins says she's the best timecop AusTEC has, and her record's equal to anyone in any branch of TEC . . . even Logan, probably, give her another year or two."

"She's obsessed, then." Graham pursed his lips. "Sometimes obsession is the key to greatness."

"I think there's more going on with Harriet than just a hatred of time-hopping scum," Amy Fuller allowed. "This is personal with her. She's trying to find Jack Logan, the best way she knows how."

"Time bombs," Bob O'Donnelly mused. "She got the idea from VIPR's own blips, didn't she? Might work, too. They'll launch back to stop the detonations, but they won't find her. The setting of a bomb won't start a ripple, any more than intent would. The history ripple comes with detonation. She'll have gone, before they get there."

Camino del Río, the Outskirts of Buenos Aires
1920

The big, yellow car with its escort of armed gauchos ran alongside the La Plata–Buenos Aires train for half a mile, then pulled away when the city came into view ahead. Don Fernando Vargas glanced aside at his wife and daughter, straightened his bolo tie, and leaned forward to instruct the chauffeur. *"Avenida Camisa, Manuel,"* he said. *"El Quartel, por favor."*

The driver glanced at his windscreen mirror. *"Sí, patrón,"* he said. Ahead the road widened, and the gauchos on their racing horses eased to both sides as the Deusenberg's horns sounded. Manuel eased the throttle a turn and the big engine purred like a kitten as the Deusenberg's wheels left the gravel road behind and rolled along a wide, brick-paved avenue. In the distance a clock tower said three-eighteen.

Manuel cocked his head slightly, listening. There was still that barely perceptible sound beneath the hood, that he had noticed all the way up from La Plata. It had been drowned for a time by the roar of the gravel road, but it was still there—as though the car's fan blades were touching something, barely ticking against a surface as they spun past.

It was nothing, he decided. When he had the opportunity, he would raise the vented bonnets and look inside, but right now the sound—whatever it was—seemed not to alter the big machine's performance.

He leaned back, both hands on the wide steering wheel. Ahead was a small, stone-abutment viaduct and beyond it a residential section where low houses flanked the streets.

Abruptly, the world exploded around him. The big car bucked, reared like a wild thing, and was engulfed in brilliant, blinding fire. It was over so quickly that he never heard the sound of the explosion, never felt the car roll and tumble, never heard the screams of the Vargas family as they were crushed between buckling steel and the unyielding stone of a low viaduct . . .

. . . In the distance a clock tower said three-seventeen. There was still that barely perceptible sound beneath the hood—as though the car's fan blades were ticking against something as they spun. Whatever it was, though, it did not alter the big machine's performance.

Manuel leaned back, both hands on the steering wheel, then gasped and hit the brakes. Just ahead, three black-masked men with strange-looking guns stood in the road, demanding that he stop.

There was no choice. Skidding the car half-around, Manuel brought it to a halt, then raised his arms as one of the masked men thrust a gun muzzle into the car. "Just sit still," the man said in accented Spanish. "Please do not move."

The other two men were at the hood of the Deusenberg. One of them raised the right bonnet, reached inside, and killed the engine. Then he pulled something loose and held it up—something like a squashed gray brick, with black tape dangling from it and a little black box attached. He handed it to the third masked man, who ran across the road, swung his arm, and heaved the thing as far as he could. It disappeared over the bank of a ditch. A second passed, then another, and there was a roar as muddy water geysered up from the ditch, showering everything for fifty yards around.

The three masked men stepped off the road then, and joined hands. In an instant they were gone, as though they had never been there.

Manuel scrambled out of the Deusenberg and looked in

at his passengers, still untangling themselves on the limousine's wide, carpeted floor. They appeared to be unharmed—shaken by the sudden stop, but not injured. Manuel realized abruptly that they probably had seen nothing of what happened. Hoofbeats echoed on the road, as green-banded gauchos raced in from behind, their guns in their hands.

Many times that day, the stunned Manuel would be questioned about the incident. All he would say was, "There were men with a bomb. I had to stop to avoid it. It blew up in the creek. The men went away."

How could a simple chauffeur explain what Manuel thought he had seen—masked men, a gray lump that exploded like jelled nitroglycerin . . . it was better not to try. Still, Manuel would have nightmares for a long time to come, about what would have happened if that thing had exploded under the hood of the patron's automobile.

Drake Passage, Southeast of Cape Horn
1994

The rebuilt old steamer, *Krofft*, rolled on rough seas as Captain Voigt stared into the muzzle of an efficient-looking riot gun and ordered his helmsman to come astarboard to course 177.

The ship had been seized ten minutes before, by masked, dark-clad men who seemed to come from nowhere. Voigt didn't even know how many of them there were. They swarmed over the ship, carrying ready guns, and simply and efficiently took control. None of them even spoke until their leader—a dark-browed, middle-aged man with a mane of gray-streaked dark hair and a foppish little spade beard—stepped onto the con deck and into the wheelhouse.

"I am Emilio Vargas von Steuben," the man said. "I am

the owner of your ship, *Capitán* Voigt, and I am taking charge. We will set a new course. Come to one hundred seventy-seven degrees."

Voigt had balked. "I am the captain of this vessel, and I have my sailing orders," he snapped. "Owner or no owner—" He had subsided quickly when one of the masked men flanking Emilio thrust a riot gun under his nose.

Now Voigt stood bleakly next to his nervous helmsman, watching the hard waves march against *Krofft*'s starboard bow and listening to the whine of the icy wind, which was a perpetual nemesis to ships in this troubled sea south of the roving ring of riptides known as the Antarctic Convergence. "There's nothing ahead of us on this course but pack ice," he said, not looking around at the spade-bearded man behind him. "This heading will take us between the South Shetlands and the South Orkneys, into the Weddell Sea east of the peninsula. There is nothing beyond, except the ice."

"I know where we are going, Captain," Emilio told him. "We will maintain heading one hundred seventy-seven for approximately six days. Then we will correct to one hundred eighty-two and navigate by sight."

Despite himself, Voigt went pale. Ignoring the guns around him, he turned to the chart tables and pulled out a seaman's chart, unrolling it on the surface. He studied it for a moment, then turned to Emilio. "You'll take us right into the Filchner Ice Shelf! That's madness. Not even ice-breakers go there, man! Have you any idea what—"

"I told you—" Emilio's dark eyes seemed to burn through him like cold fire. "—I know where we are going. You are expendable, Captain—"

The ship rocked violently as an earsplitting roar echoed through her superstructure. Forward of the con deck, panels buckled, twisting upward, and blinding fire mushroomed from below. The force of the blast sent men tumbling, and a whirling davit, torn loose from its stanchions, flew upward to crash through the glass of the control cabin, smashing everything and everyone in its path . . .

. . . "I know where we are going, Captain," Emilio told the stunned, angry old seaman as the refitted fifty-year-old steamship *Krofft* wallowed through the marching waves of the Antarctic Convergence. "We will maintain heading one hundred seventy-seven for approximately six days, then—"

The air in the chilly command booth seemed to shimmer, and suddenly there were two more people there—a hulking, grinning giant and . . . Emilio's eyes widened . . . and himself! Another himself, a few years older, grayer at the temples, and with streaks of snowy white in his beard, but unquestionably himself, from somewhere in the future.

"There is an explosive device aboard this ship," the older Emilio told the younger one. "Time police—from my time—they are trying to destroy us." Without waiting for a response, he turned and gestured. "Kurt, go and get the bomb."

The giant hurried out of the cabin, jostling people aside right and left. Moving with a quick agility that belied his size, he swung down the topside ladder to the operations deck and from there to the foredeck, sprinted to the forward hold hatch, sprung it open as deftly as a normal man might open the lid of a shoe box, and disappeared down the gaping hole. Seconds passed, then he reappeared, carrying a football-sized wad of gray putty with a little electronic timer attached to it.

Emilio—the 1994 Emilio—gaped at the device through the pilothouse glass. "What is that?" he demanded. "Is that plastique?"

"C4 explosive," the older Emilio muttered. "With a thousand-hour timer. It is set for now."

On the foredeck, the giant Kurt ran to the port rail and heaved the bomb outward, to arc above the rolling waves for nearly a hundred yards before it disappeared into the whitecapped, cobalt-gray water. Two minutes passed, then three. Kurt was at the top of the starboard operations ladder when a huge gout of water erupted from the sea astern, rising up and up, higher than the cargo mast tops of *Krofft*. A rumbling, sullen thump echoed through the old ship's hull, and shock waves crashed against her iron stern.

"Divergence corrected," the future Emilio snapped, fury lashing from his dark eyes. "The sheer arrogance! And this isn't the first attempt." He turned toward his younger self, keeping a cautious distance between them. "Continue your voyage," he said. "The timefield sensors you are carrying belowdecks—that I carried here when I was you— just saved our life. Again." He turned to the giant, who had just entered from starboard. "Retrieve, Kurt," he snapped. "We must find out who is doing this."

TEC Headquarters
2007

Harriet Blevins closed the launch bay doors behind her, and leaned back against them, closing her eyes. "Whoo!" she said. "I'm beginnin' to 'urt in places I didn't even know I 'ad." With a grimace, she opened her eyes, straightened, and headed for the squad room. "Slight change of plans, lads," she told the vector team techs as she passed the open field controls booth. "Next launch as planned, then set up another one right after that, same spatial coordinates but a bit later in time. ThinkTank will give you the figures."

In the squad room, Harriet slouched in a chair while Amy Fuller checked her over for acceleration traumas.

Above them, the E-warp screen displayed its normal patterns except for the scattering of unidentified blips that still remained there.

"Was 'at last one a pretty sight?" Harriet asked, gazing upward.

"Marvelous." Amy frowned. "Hold still while I take your blood pressure. Any special pains this time?"

"They're all special," Harriet sighed. "Lor' but I'm sore! Damn the perps anyway, I ought to be raisin' a batch of kids, not blowin' up cars an' ships. But then, I reckon somebody's got to do it."

"I'm on record," Julie Price called from a nearby desk. "I'll help, if you want me."

"Sorry, luv." Harriet grinned. "You're not checked out on high explosives. Better stick to the blips."

"She's brought in two of the blippers so far," Amy said. "That girl's racking up almost as much launch time as you are. I think Bob O'Donnelly would have kittens if the captain let her go out again right away. Your eyes are a little bloodshot, Harriet. Are you bleeding anywhere that you're not supposed to?"

"Not a drop. Maybe I should try 'arder."

Captain Matuzek appeared from the briefing room and squatted beside Harriet's chair. "What's this about a change of plans?" he demanded. "You want two more launches?"

"Little idea I 'ad," the Angel of AusTEC said, straightening up in the chair. "We don't know 'oo's jumping back to undo w'at I'm doin', but my 'unch is it was Emilio 'imself this last time. After all, 'e was aboard the *Krofft*, an' I don't reckon 'e'd trust anybody else to save 'is own skin. So I'm thinkin', let's 'it 'em with a redundancy now an' see 'ow they 'andle it."

"Redundancy? You mean two strikes, same time and place? Two bombs?"

"One bomb. I'll use w'at's 'andy on the second one.

Maybe I'll get a target of opportunity, if I'm there when they mop up."

"I want to see a probability chart on this," Matuzek said, frowning. "Your chances of getting out the second time—"

"It's a 'unch, Captain," she said.

"I don't believe in hunches, Agent Blevins!"

"The 'ell you don't." She shrugged. "You're a cop. You play 'unches every day."

Nearby, Charles Graham had been sitting quietly, just listening. Now he said, "She's right, Eugene. That's probably why some people make fine policemen, while the rest of us couldn't do it if we tried."

"If your internal organs make it through two more launches without serious trauma," Amy Fuller said, "it'll be a miracle."

Harriet got to her feet, wincing. "I'll need at least three pounds this time," she said. "Twelve-hour timer with remote pickup, an' a bye-bye button. And while I'm out, 'ow 'bout diggin' up some instructions on 'ow to drive a steam locomotive."

XV

Estancia Vargas
The Argentine Pampas
1945

On the rolling pampas west of Buenos Aires, where widely scattered villages dotted a landscape dominated by fields of waving wheat and the broad grasslands that were the domain of fine cattle and gaucho horsemen, Estancia Vargas stood as a monument to four generations of cunning, ruthless, and ambitious men—the *patrónes* of *familia* Vargas.

Within Estancia Vargas, which spread across vast miles above the Salados, the estate was a fortress. High, whitewashed walls encircled two hundred acres of sandy highland, protecting a settlement that was in fact a self-contained little town of cottages, barns, barracks, shops, and all the structures of a large, working ranch. The rails approaching from the northeast ran right through the main portal, where huge iron-bound doors swung aside to admit rail or road traffic, and into the central compound. Beyond the end of the rail stood the *casa grande*, the main house, a rambling, palatial structure with two guest wings and a formal courtyard.

Guest accommodations were prepared on this evening for a dozen distinguished exiles from Nazi Germany, and their retinues. The entire east wing blazed with lights, as did the central house where Don Fernando Vargas and his family resided. Six Rolls-Royce limousines were on hand to carry the guests the last hundred yards from the rail platforms in the main yard, up to the grand house.

The guest list read like a partial roster of Adolf Hitler's National Socialist elite—military, industrial, and financial leaders now fled from the *Vaterland* in exile, and possessing the means to pay handsomely for their comforts.

For these, it was the end of various long, harrowing journeys—first to Lisbon, each in secrecy, then across the Atlantic and across the Equator aboard a sturdy but hardly luxurious steamship, the SS *Krofft*, and finally by rail from Buenos Aires to Estancia Vargas, where each of them, in coming weeks, would arrange and pay for the means to disappear into the mainstream of Argentine life.

Evening had settled on the pampas when telephone calls—first from Pergamino and then from the little village of Cresta—alerted the *estancia* that the guest train from Buenos Aires was approaching. It was fully dark when the big gates were opened and the train crept into the compound to come to a steaming, hissing halt at the platforms. The gates were closed behind it, and the limousines rolled down the gravel drive to meet their passengers.

The confusion and commotion in the courtyard began when the passengers transferred to their limousines for the ride up to the house. One of the limousines veered crazily, bounded across a rose garden, and roared away toward the barns and outbuildings beyond the estate's tended lawns.

What occurred there, few of the rest saw, though there were running men—gauchos and some of Don Fernando's trusted black-clad *enmascarados*—and the swerving and skidding of a big automobile in chase. Some among the guests thought they had glimpsed a panzer in the distance, beyond the main barn, but then they were hurried on to the house, ushered inside, and told nothing.

It was nearly a half hour later when Helmut von Steuben appeared at the house, angry and silent, cradling an injured right hand. The young woman he had brought all the way from La Plata—a spy who had boarded the *Krofft* as a rescuee and then been identified as an enemy—had escaped somehow. Also missing now were Herr von Steuben's sinister associate, a man called only Emilio, and the giant who had seemed to be his bodyguard.

But none of this was the concern of the guests of Estancia Vargas, and they were told nothing about it. They were greeted cordially by Don Fernando and his pretty, dark-eyed daughter—who, it seemed, was betrothed to Herr von Steuben—then shown to their accommodations. Everywhere were the scents of fresh paint and polish. The casa had been two days, servants admitted, in preparation for their visit. A hundred people had been here at one time or another, just making ready for honored guests.

For a time, the great house hummed with activity. Then, just as it was settling down for the night, it exploded. With a blast that could be heard miles away, the entire south wall of the great house disappeared in flying rubble, and a fireball as blinding as noonday sun erupted from the aperture to climb into the sky.

Sean McGinty was just returning home to Cresta, his old taxi weaving from ditch to ditch in time with his enthusiastic rendition of "Mother Macree." He had spent the evening at Monty's, thoroughly sampling the Irish whiskey there as the *Norteamericano* gent had instructed him to do. Sean might still have been at Monty's, perfecting his singing voice, except that Monty had finally thrown him out for waking the neighbors down the road.

The more Irish whiskey Sean consumed, the better his fine tenor became, and he was just hitting the high notes in the old ballad when a fireball grew in the southern sky. The taxi swerved into the ditch. McGinty sat for a moment, stunned, then dragged himself out from behind the wheel and stood, unsteadily, staring at the fireball across the pampas.

"Holy Mother," he breathed. "It's Armageddon!"

Harriet Blevins stepped out of the shimmer of a time warp and climbed into the shadowy cab of the train's idling locomotive, just in time to see the Rolls-Royce skid to a stop several hundred yards away, near the main barn. It was too far to see distinctly, but she knew the scene from memory. Tiny figures darted here and there in the uncertain light of Rolls-Royce headlights diffused by dust, and in her mind she saw again the lithe, angry figure of Jack Logan being held by masked men in the headlights' beam. She saw Helmut von Steuben raving and cursing, Emilio strutting arrogantly, taunting the TEC agent, and she heard Logan playing out his wild, impossible bluff.

She felt again the thump of the Wehrmacht Luger as her earlier self killed the knife-wielding *enmascarado*, and saw again the retrieval bracelet—Logan's own bracelet—as he tossed it toward her just as the giant hit him.

And she saw Logan with Emilio clinging to his back, disappearing into time the instant before her earlier self activated the retrieve and reverse-launched, back to TEC.

Now, in the shadows of the locomotive's cab, she glanced at her watch, and settled down to wait.

She didn't have long to wait. The arrival of VIPR's countermeasure personnel was a shimmer directly under the lights of Casa Vargas's wide veranda. She wasn't surprised to see who had come. It was Emilio himself, with his lumbering giant tagging behind him. The giant's knuckles thundered against the polished wood of the main entrance, and when the door was opened they both pushed through.

They knew, of course, what they were looking for and where to find it. It would be only a matter of minutes before Kurt, or maybe both of them, reappeared, carrying her C4 package, to dispose of it over a wall or down a well. But Harriet didn't wait for them. The clock ticking down, the C4 in the house only minutes from detonation, Harriet fed coal to the engine's boilers, closed the fire door, and set the valves for full steam. As the boilers began to rumble she swung down behind the engine, slipped the tender coupling, and climbed to the cab again. Seconds passed, as the pressure gauges climbed. When she could wait no longer she released the brake, pushed the throttle home, and felt the big drive wheels spinning on steel rails as the train jolted forward, massive and unstoppable.

She dived from the cab, rolled into the shadows of a loading platform, and watched.

The locomotive hit the timer guards at the end of the track the way a fist might hit a sparrow's nest. Ties screamed, bolts snapped, and splinters flew as the engine threw the barricade aside and jolted off the rails onto the sandy slope beyond, heading for the great house. A hundred yards closed to fifty, then to twenty, and everywhere there were people, running and screaming.

The locomotive didn't climb the veranda. It simply smashed it and carried its tangled debris as a shield when it punched through the front wall and into the house, still gaining speed. Segments of roof collapsed behind the behemoth, and just beyond, within the house, she saw the great silhouette of Kurt, dodging aside, trying to get to the open front wall. In the glare and smoke a girder slammed down from above, directly onto him, and he disappeared in a pile of rubble as the locomotive destroyed the columns of the house's central rise.

In growing pandemonium, people clambered here and there in the wreckage . . . and then a glare and a thunder erupted within. The C4's detonation sent debris tumbling in all directions, and a fireball as blinding as the noonday sun rose through the destroyed central roof and climbed into the sky.

Several miles to the north, Sean McGinty crawled from his taxi, removed his hat, and made the sign of the cross.

As the pressure gauges climbed, Harriet released the locomotive's brake and pushed the throttle home. She felt big wheels spinning on steel rails, and the engine lurched forward toward its barricade.

Harriet dived from the cab, rolled into the shadows beneath a platform, and looked out just in time to see the shimmer of time-transfer at the very gate of the engine. Three men appeared there, mere silhouettes in the darkness. As the first one swung aboard the moving locomotive, Harriet took careful aim and shot him. The other two paused, surprised, but only for an instant. Then one of them crouched and returned her fire, his laser beam dancing beneath the platform. A shot singed her arm, causing her to miss once, but she fired again and the man fell.

Even as he hit the ground, she heard the locomotive's brakes lock and the shrill hiss of steam being vented. The third man had made it into the cab. Scrambling from beneath the platform, Harriet ran to the engine, swung to its oilers' rail, and fired again. The masked man at the reversed throttle never knew what hit him. As he toppled, she caught him, rolled him over in the gateway, and removed a small, plastic object from his belt.

VIPR's retrieval devices were not exactly like those used by TEC and the other legitimate timefield operators, but the differences were mostly cosmetic. A retrieve is a retrieve.

With a touch of a tab, Harriet Blevins was gone—back to the year 2007, but not back to TEC. It was a strange timesled that materialized around her in reverse-launch—a long, lightly built, boatlike device that despite its future-time technology still reminded her vaguely of the Heindl prototype she and Logan had seen and used at Krakenfjord.

" 'Come into my parlor,' said the spider to the fly," she murmured to herself as the punishing pressures of deceleration pummeled her. Her glimpse of VIPR's timebase was momentary, but it was enough for the impression of a long, blurred tunnel where everything was ice-white and ice-cold.

In the village of Cresta, Sean McGinty slewed his taxi around in the sandy yard of his little house, clambered out unsteadily, and sighed. He had enjoyed the fine singing at Monty's, but now it was time to sleep.

"A humdrum life for an Irishman," he muttered. "Nothin' ever happens around here."

82°1′ S, 71°0′ W
2007

Here the surface was a patchwork quilt of crevasses, extending into the distance like a vast chessboard viewed by an ant. Logan had been among the chasms for an hour or more—a few miles, at least—before his slowing mind began to recognize that there were chasms beyond chasms, with a distinct pattern to them.

The ones that more or less paralleled his direction of travel—jagged, zigzagging cracks in the ice that seemed to go on forever—were wider and, it seemed, deeper than the cross-path cracks that he veered this way and that to approach at their narrowest points.

Polar stress, something told him, dimly. Rotational pull against unanchored ice could cause a texture like that. And if so, then he had crossed from the mainland to the ice shelf, where beneath these thousands of feet of ancient ice lay liquid water.

It almost made him want to laugh, the sheer cussedness of a continent where the only difference between land and sea is in how its cover cracks. Yet, somehow, it was significant that—at least technically—he was now walking across a frozen sea. Somehow it tied in to the progressing width of the long crevasse he was following, and to the ghostly traces of smoke he had seen rising from those depths.

He hadn't seen the smoke again, but the crevasse at his right had widened now to a vertiginous, blue-white canyon a hundred yards or more across. And more and more, he had the impression that there was something down in that crack that he should know about.

Once he had crawled toward the edge of it, wanting to look over the side. But as he neared it, his weight caused little spiderwebs to form in the ice, accompanied by a crackling sound. He had withdrawn barely in time. The entire field where he had been had shifted slowly, seeming to break up into little blocks, then had simply disappeared. He had waited for several seconds before the sound of ice crashing below came to him.

Still, that had been a long way back. He must be lower now, the bottom nearer. His strength was nearly gone, and the sun had gone behind the distant mountains to the south, casting everything in blue shade. He would try one more time, then rest.

On hands and knees, he approached the crevasse. The nylon tent he had been dragging he now pushed ahead, because it had frozen stiff. Along the way it had come unfolded, collecting snow in its outer texture. The snow had softened slightly in the sun's reflected heat, but now that the sun was gone the tent was a wide, flat thing, frozen as stiff as a board.

As he neared the edge of the crack, the ice sloped downward slightly and he could see the far side. It was a wall of ice, dropping almost straight down from the rim to tumbles of broken ice below, a hundred feet or so down. Below the rim of ice debris was another drop-off, but he couldn't see the bottom of that incline.

He inched forward, straining to see farther down, and suddenly the ice beneath him collapsed, a shelf sliding downward into the unknown. Logan felt himself falling, and grabbed the only thing that came to hand—the edge of his frozen tent. He rolled, sprawled atop the plummeting nylon, and spiraled downward, smothered in a battering, shattering cloud of broken ice and crystal shards.

The tent-sled hit a bump that almost knocked the wind out of him, but he clung frantically and an instant later the wild plunge slowed, slowed again, and stopped with a thump.

Logan dug his way upward, out of a mound of fallen ice, and crawled out of the hole he had left. He was at the bottom of a high gorge, just below a massive wall of sheer ice. Drifted snow, collecting under the lee cliff of the ice chasm, had broken his fall.

He felt bruised, battered, and stunned, but could find nothing broken. Cautiously, he set his feet, skidded down a ten-foot slope and onto a nearly level floor of ice. In the distance, northward, the canyon widened more and more, and out near the end of visible range it became a broken, textured mass of ice plates and tumbled shards.

It looked like nothing more than the skim of an icebreaker, like the drifts of skim the tugs on the Potomac left in winter . . . except that no Potomac tugboat had ever pushed aside slabs that big.

A modern, deep-sea icebreaker might do it, though, he told himself. A glimmer of hope grew in him as he realized what he was seeing, off there in the distance where the chasm cliffs bent away to cut back into other chasms. If an icebreaker had been at work here, that meant there was a channel. And where there was a channel, there might be ships. That hint of smoke—that could have been the plume from diesel engines, passing out of sight below the jutting edge of high pack ice.

He started walking in that direction, then stopped. Almost beside him, the ice cliff bulged outward and when he looked into its clear, dark surface he saw a faint outline—precise, tapering shapes and dark lines that formed a pattern, like the bowsprit and stays of an old sailing ship.

He moved along the bulge, peering into it, exploring its surface with numb hands. The pattern within the ice changed with each step, becoming larger, sweeping out toward the sheared surface of the cliff until, just at the first outward curve, the thing in the ice was almost exposed. Only an inch or so of ice crusted it here, and he could see exactly what it was. It was a ship—a very old, square-rigged sailing vessel—sealed up in an icy tomb.

A galleon, he thought. An honest-to-God, full-grown galleon, of a style that had disappeared with the discovery of staysails and spreader rigging. Columbus had used ships like this on his later voyages to the New World. Through the sixteenth century, the galleon had been the finest design of ship afloat. These things had ruled the seas in the 1500s.

Using one of his precious flares, Logan melted away the ice from a looming bow higher than his head, and stepped back to read the escutcheon fastened there. SANTA YSABELA, it proclaimed.

A Spaniard! A Spanish galleon, frozen for centuries in the pack ice of the antarctic shelf! Dimly Logan recalled a tale of ancient ships caught adrift in the west Sargasso, preserved by seaweed as they drifted southward on the trade currents. A few of them, supposedly, had been found by future generations of sailors.

On impulse, Logan got out another flare, his climber's pick, and a tin of jelled alcohol. It took an hour or more, but he managed to tunnel into the ice above the old ship's bow rail, and reach the little hatch of its forward companionway. Praying, he broke the hatch loose and looked inside. The hull was open belowdecks. Above the bilges, no ice had gotten in!

He let himself down into the dark space and collapsed there for a time, out of the constant wind. When he could move again, he found his pocket lamp and looked around. Everywhere was frozen antiquity, and among the bales and bundles and clumps were dead men—withered, freeze-dried corpses still clad in the clothing they had worn when they died. But these were no antique Spaniards. These men wore uniforms—or at least bits and pieces of uniforms—and the attire was that of World War II German soldiers. Here and there he could see the insignia of the SS and Wehrmacht.

From the forward lockers to the little galley and the hammock bins, he explored as much of the ship as he could reach. Here and there, German soldiers lay in perpetual rest, and the placement and condition of the corpses said they had died of hunger, or maybe of thirst. How had men of the middle twentieth century come to die on a ship of the middle sixteenth century? And how long had *Santa Ysabela* drifted, without sail or steerage, before she found her way to this frozen grave?

The galley stores and larders were stripped bare, emptied of every drop of drinking water, every crumb of food. But the Germans apparently didn't know about galleons. Beneath the larders were the rat bins, hidey-holes of extra storage covered over by the lap boards of the working galley, and here Logan found food. It was four-hundred-year-old food, and it had been practically inedible even when it was new. But the ice had sustained it—frozen salt pork, frozen hardtack, frozen blood sausage, and even a supply of frozen Madeira wine.

And the ship and everything in it was made of wood. Logan got a campfire going on the frozen copper plate of the galley floor, with his crawlway and a cannon run-out as ventilation ports, and settled in for a little R and R.

XVI

Jerusalem: The Old City
1924

Julie Price was having the time of her life. With the enthusiastic support of Bob O'Donnelly, the young courier-become-agent had tackled the problem of the blips, and had made three launches in as many days.

She had delivered two prisoners to Timecourt—a retired U.S. Special Forces colonel from 2009 whose attempt to escalate the Vietnamese conflict in 1974 had almost resulted in the massacre of a marine platoon, and a renegade IRS auditor who had infiltrated 1779 Philadelphia to assassinate Benjamin Franklin. That one had remained a small blip because Dr. Franklin was in Paris at the time.

This one, though, had just become a write-off. Under a bright, full moon Julie sagged against the pillars of the Saq Menyada and put her gun away. Only seconds before, she had been in full pursuit of a man in long robes, sandals, and a fez, down the shadowy ways of the ancient Holy City. Now she shook her head sadly, panting to catch her breath. The perp, a privately funded zealot from 2008, had tried to bomb a mosque. Now his remains smoldered on the paving stones, as the echoes of his device died away in the distance.

Sheer panic, she told herself. The man who had tried to change history had become clumsy at the sight of a timecop. The historic alteration—which had grown suddenly from an E-warp blip on the Dome of History to a level-one ripple—would be gone now. His mission had accomplished nothing more than another little splash of blood on the Wailing Wall.

She didn't hear the man behind her until he spoke, and when she whirled around, it was to face a uniform not much different from her own blast suit, except for the insignia.

"So much for that," he said, looking past her at the smoking lump that had been a time saboteur. "I'm George Spiros," he said, shrugging. "EuroTEC field ops. And you?" He stepped closer, squinting at her in the night shadows, then straightened as Julie stepped into full moonlight. He seemed to tower over her, looking incredulous. "A girl!" he mused, as though to himself. "No more than a child. And from TEC? I thought you people were out of business."

"Since when?" Julie demanded.

"Since about two years ago . . . my time. Didn't Ameri-TEC shut down in 2010? After the antitime riots?"

"I trained in 2010," Julie corrected him. "We were under tight security seal. Had been for several months. But we didn't shut down." She cocked her head, suspiciously. "What antitime riots?"

It was Spiros's turn to look incredulous. "You're from 2010 and don't know about the riots? They started right after the Hankins Committee released the TEC story to the American public . . . with some editorial comment. That was a nasty business. Came near to ruining all of us." He paused, thoughtfully. "You really don't know? Then was all that an alteration?"

"I think we'd better talk," Julie decided.

TEC Headquarters
2007

"So you think that one's the time bomb?" Eugene Matuzek demanded, glancing up at the Dome of History. "Have you tracked it?"

"Yes, sir." Bob O'Donnelly nodded. "The most significant corollary we can find is Victor Hankins's election as the representative from Illinois's ninety-seventh district. The blip's first vectors on the dome equate to when he was sworn into office. It looks like someone from the future—his future—may have tampered with the campaign."

"That's probably why it has remained only a blip," Charles Graham suggested. "I've met Congressman Hankins. He came to my office, a year ago, trying to get my endorsement for some kind of research grant having to do with feed grains. He hasn't accomplished anything notable in his first term in office, but he was reelected in his district. Sometimes I wonder if voters send people to Washington just to get them out of their hair at home."

O'Donnelly glanced at a pad of notes. "Julie's informant says it was Hankins himself who leaked—or, rather, will leak—the timefield data to the tabloids and networks," he said. "He was reprimanded and kicked out of office, but he got rich in the process. Our guess is that he was—I mean, is—another VIPR mole. The material he put out—that he will put out in two years—includes names, dates, and places. He even had mission records and technical data on the timefield apparatus. In other words, he went public with incontrovertible proof that time travel exists, and that the government funds it. The spin he'll put on it makes TEC look like a social control mechanism. It's no wonder people rebelled. I'd rebel, too."

Dale Easter had moved to a ChronComp monitor. His fingers danced on the keyboard. "Mr. Graham, I don't find anything here about a feed grain research project. What was it called?"

"Nothing." Graham spread his hands. "We didn't include it in NSSA's program. It wasn't true research, just a gambit to create an import opportunity for foreign grain dealers . . ." He paused, rubbed his chin thoughtfully, and added, "Argentine grains, to be specific."

Eugene Matuzek paced the length of the room, and back. "Mission records? Timefield technical data?" he growled. "Where would Hankins get information like that? TEC is the best-kept secret in this country. Isn't it? Those records never leave this office, except—"

"Except under strict security, eyes-only to the president, through me." Charles Graham took a deep breath and stood. "Captain Matuzek, would you do me the honor of swearing me in as a special agent or deputy or something? Just pro tem? No pun intended." His grin was only momentary, and didn't hide the hard anger behind it.

Matuzek gawked at the aging chief of the National Science Security Agency's black-ops section. "Agent or deputy of what?"

"Of the Time Enforcement Commission, of course. With investigative and warrant authority, please. Could you do that?"

"Sir? You—you want to serve as a TEC agent?"

"No time jumps, of course," Graham said, nodding. "I'm far too old for that kind of punishment. The time we're in right now will do, for what I have in mind. Just swear me in. And if I may, I'd like the assistance of Agent Price."

"Yes, sir!"

Julie leaned close to Amy Fuller. "Does that mean we're partners?" she whispered. "Me and—and Mr. Graham?"

"Looks like it." Amy shrugged. "Technically, you'll be the senior partner, but I suggest you don't push it."

Aside, Bob O'Donnelly's grin spread so wide it threatened his ears. "I'd like to see this," he murmured to Julie. "You and Charles Graham taking on a sleazy congressman. Like sending in a tiger cub and an elephant to step on an ant. I'll bet you a dinner at Luigi's that blip disappears within twenty-four hours."

"I don't gamble," Julie whispered. "But I'd love to have dinner with you . . . Bob. If I ever get out of whatever this is I'm getting into."

VIPR's Nest
2007

There was no one at the sled ramps, no one in the launching bay—no one visible anywhere when Harriet Blevins stepped out of the VIPR timesled into a huge cavern of ice—the steel-hard ice of eons, frozen and compacted by tens of thousands of years of unrelenting cold. Yet the walls glistened and dripped, and there were runoff trenches here and there.

Harriet looked around, pausing to wipe away the trickle of blood on her lip. This last deceleration, in a strange vehicle not fitted to her blast suit, had done what all those back-to-back jumps had not done. She had a nosebleed.

The cavern was awesome. Just this one tunnel—the timefield launch facility—was at least half a mile long and several hundred yards across. An ice cave, deep within the perpetual overburden of a polar landscape, it was like being inside a hollow glacier. And yet, the ambient air was not too uncomfortable.

Carefully, she inspected the settings of the vector controls in the launch bay, and knew where she was. Eighty-three degrees, four minutes south, one hundred eight degrees, two minutes west. The Horlick Mountains in the interior of Antarctica, midway between Byrd Station and the Amundsen-Scott Station at the South Pole.

She got out her reports pen and wrote on the palm of her left hand: 83-4-S, 108-2-W. Those numbers were all they would need—Wilkins or Captain Matuzek or any of them— to bring the wrath of nations down upon this place.

The metal surfaces of the vector controls were cool to the touch, but not cold, and again she noticed that the air temperature was comfortable. A thermostat on the bay wall was set at sixty degrees Fahrenheit. A livable place, in a region where the average air temperature even in the warmest season was subzero!

The cavern had forced-air heating, she realized. Convection heating, with exhaust ventilation. Somewhere there were furnaces, and heat ducts and a fuel source. Banks of fluorescent lights marched away down the tunnel, and in the distance she could see the timefield armatures—great, standing rigs with massive clusters of electrodes along their inner rims. In design, they resembled the primitive armatures of that grandfather field in Krakenfjord's Lundsgrofenwerk, though vastly more complex—just as the long, slender sled resting now at its bays resembled that first timesled, which looked like a cross between a canoe and an arrow.

The entire time-launch complex seemed deserted, sealed behind steel doors. But the blast screens were still warm from recent use, and Harriet reasoned that since someone had been at the timefield's vector controls to send the sled out—only moments ago in real time—someone would be expecting the sled's return with its three masked passengers.

She tried the doors. They were locked. But the locks were intended to keep people out of the launch area, not to keep them in. On the sled side, the bolts could be rolled back with a simple hand crank.

She was just reaching for the mechanism when the locks

turned and one of the doors swung open. She dived behind a control console and peered out. Two dark-clad men carrying modern automatic weapons and wearing the woolen face covers of *enmascarados* stepped into the launch chamber and looked around. "Petrov!" one of them called. "Mikhail? Joder?"

When there was no response, they stepped out onto the sled platform. One of them glanced at the launch recorder. "They have returned," he said in clear Russian. "But where are they? Petrov?"

The other knelt by the timesled and touched a finger to its surface, then stood. "Maybe they went to medical," he growled. "It looks as though Petrov has a nosebleed again."

The two did a peremptory inspection of the launch area, but found no one. There was no one to find. Harriet Blevins had ducked through the open portal behind them, and out into the immense subglacial catacombs of VIPR's Nest.

Never in her wildest dreams had Harriet imagined a place like this—an ice cavern, or series of caverns, resting on the slopes and shelves of a bare, stone mountainside with a solid ice roof maybe a mile thick. There were whole farms in this cavern, where stooped, dark-haired people clothed in ragged fabrics and filthy old blankets toiled under the watchful eyes of armed mercenaries clad in black uniforms and black stocking-masks. Beyond them the dark-white walls soared upward, curving overhead to become great, carved arches above catwalks and bridges traversing the spans. Though the entire cavern was at least a mile beneath the surface ice of Antarctica, overhead lights and flood lamps illuminated everything to daylight brightness.

Over each field, crop shelf, and hydroponic bank hung lamps that Harriet suspected were in the ultraviolet range, bathing the greenery below with canned sunlight.

How had VIPR done all this? Even assuming forty or

fifty years of excavation, with unlimited slave labor, the place was enormous! Looking closer at the ice pillars and the immense, soaring perimeter walls, though, she noticed that only portions of the surface showed the marks of excavation. Most of the ceiling and large portions of the walls were glass-slick, as though formed by melting and refreezing.

Volcanic origin, she surmised. There is volcanic activity in central Antarctica, and in some of the buried mountains. This must at one time have been a great volcanic vent, hollowed out by subterranean steam issuing from seams somewhere in the stone strata. The actual volcano might be hundreds of miles away, but superheated gases could have erupted in this range and hollowed vent routes through the ice.

She wished Papa Hank could see this. The old Australian National Exploration Society geologist—whose passion in life had been his three expeditions to Mawson Station— would have loved it.

Clouds of vapor hung and condensed around the perimeters of the cavern, where ranked furnaces produced the heat and the power to run the installation. At a shielded juncture where narrow-gauge tracks curved around a massive pillar of ice, she stooped to pick up a pebble, her eyes narrowing. It was black and shiny, with little striations along its broken edges. She tasted it. "Coal," she muttered. "Hard coal. Pure anthracite."

Tracking back, a shadow among shadows, she found the source of the coal—a full-scale mining operation in caverns of its own, with mills, float tanks, dumps, and ranks of hoppers standing above a wide basin of open water where barges and seagoing tugs moved. And all of this under a vast, tunnelized roof of pure, solid ice!

Here the masked men were everywhere, dozens of them

alert and watchful as smudged, bowed Indians in rags trundled hand-cut fragments of coal from underlying shelves in the surrounding stone.

Along a remote wall, within view of them all, hung the bodies of sixteen workers—pegged to the black stone as though crucified, and left there on display.

Slaves, Harriet realized. Slaves who misbehaved and were punished as examples.

Picking her way carefully, staying out of sight, Harriet had gone nearly a half mile, working upward along the subglacial slopes, when the upslope extent of the cave came into view above a quarried shelf of reddish stone. A solid wall of shiny black had been carved into a series of steeply rising steps there, and set back from sturdy railings were living quarters—apartments delved from the living heart of a huge vein of exposed coal.

"Lord luv us all," Harriet told herself. "It's a bloody city-state in a 'ole."

She wanted a closer look at those places in the wall. Reason told her she had enough, that it was time to find a way out of here and back to TEC. The launch controls and vector setting on the VIPR sled were simple enough, and she knew she could activate a time-lapse launch. From inspection of the equipment, she knew, too, that the timefield was interlinked. It would—at least, it should—trigger itself by the sled's controls. It was time to leave. Still, plain curiosity goaded her onward—the intense curiosity of a tracker hot on a scent, of a policeman following a hot lead.

And there was another matter, too. The Yank. Emilio Vargas von Steuben had drawn Jack Logan into his retrieve mode, so this was where Logan had been brought.

"Bloody Yank," she whispered angrily, hiding under a conduit bridge as masked guards tramped overhead, "you're goin' to get me killed yet!"

82°1′ S, 71°0′ W
2007

A fissure tunnel! Logan jerked awake, shivering and miserable but refreshed. Dreams scattered around him like puffs of vapor breath freezing into little snowstorms that clung to the half-inch stubble on his cheeks and chin. He clung to sleep, dreaming of acceleration, of the thundering ride down a railed tunnel toward a blank wall that careened headlong toward him. In his tumbling dream the rippling, swirling timefield within its armature was a too-fragile thing that faded as he approached it, retreating beyond the wall. His silent dream voice screamed, again and again, 2,994! 2,994! Two thousand nine hundred ninety-four feet per second! Q-velocity! But there was no one to hear the voice that was no voice, and there was only the wall—a wall of steel, of solid stone, a wall of ice that became intense, hot steam, gushing toward him with molten lava and raw magma lighting it from behind.

Two thousand nine hundred ninety-four! The voice—his silent, seeking voice—screamed it and was drowned out by the sounds of distant gunfire. Giants roared across a savage land and deep down, somewhere, there was the roll of thunder.

Abruptly he was awake. Dream fragments faded, and there should have been only silence and the tiny crackle of his fire. But the sounds continued, distantly—a hard, erratic crackle like machine guns and fragmentation bombs, punctuated by the call of a strident horn.

Quickly he refastened his antarctic gear and crawled out of the darkness of the old ship, into the clear, slanting glare of polar sunlight. Now the sounds came clearly, echoing up the canyon of ice. He let himself down to the solid, frozen surface and hurried sunward—northward. Three hundred yards, and the mouth of the crevasse lay ahead, with vistas of pack ice beyond it. Tiny dots flocking out there on the far ice were a colony of curious penguins, their white bellies brilliant as they shuffled and gawked, looking inland.

Five hundred yards more and he was at the mouth of the crevasse—and like the penguins, he turned and gawked at what lay to his left. Huge, tumbled mounds of broken pack ice lay there like a wall, coming straight in from the north. And beyond the wall an intricate shape moved landward— the superstructure of a cargo ship!

Logan watched it until it was past, then he ran. When he reached the wall of broken ice he climbed it. Open water lay beyond—a wide ditch between ice jetties. The dark water still swirled lazily in the wake of the ship that had passed, but already it was becoming slushy, beginning to crust over with skim ice between the swells.

Logan looked to his left, where the ship lumbered on its way, and knew what sounds he had heard. Ships' horns, calling to each other between the cargo vessel and the smaller, knife-hulled icebreaker working out ahead of it. Just beyond the icebreaker, clouds of steam billowed outward from the ice ledge ahead—thick, white vapor seeming to fill the wide crevasse in the ice, rising above its rim to disperse on the wind, freezing as it spread.

Logan had slept, and dreamed, and in waking he found the answer to a question his exhausted mind had not even asked before he slept: how can there be an open channel in waters that are perpetually frozen?

Vulcanism, of course! Western Antarctica was not solid land. Melt away the ice and it would be an archipelago, a group of closely gathered islands surrounded and separated by water. And the tops of those islands were peaks of volcanic rock—the deposits of eons of volcanic activity deep within the earth below. Ice over magma . . . water and lava . . . steam!

How long had the polar continent—one of the highest landmasses on earth in terms of average elevation—been mixing and venting steam? Maybe a million years, maybe more. And where did the steam go? It went where it could, escaping through rock fissures in the underlying strata of the rising mountain-islands, directly into and beneath the ice that covered them!

Two centuries of whalers, explorers, adventurers, and scientists had barely touched the surface of the ice continent's mysteries. Oh, the ship channel through the pack ice, the ship tunnel leading into the heart of a huge, unpopulated land, had been discovered, all right. But those who discovered it hadn't told anybody.

This, then, was how contraband minerals were carried away from VIPR's Nest, and how supplies, materials, and equipment were carried in—through a water passage, deep below the surface, hidden by the pack and then by the continent itself.

His breath flowing back around his shielded face, Logan went to catch the ship to VIPR's Nest.

XVII

The Office of Charles Graham
McNair Federal Office Building
Washington, D.C.
November 18, 2006

Charles Graham returned to his office looking puzzled. He strode through the reception area, past the glass panel and Rachel's domain, to his private door. He opened it and glanced in. The man he had left there was still there, sitting in one of the visitors' chairs.

"Sorry about the interruption," Graham said. "Be with you in just a moment now." He stepped out again, closed the door behind him, and leaned his hands on Rachel's desk. "Didn't you tell me, just five minutes ago, that Senators Carson and Brown were waiting to see me downstairs?"

"Yes, sir," the secretary said. "Senator Carson's aide phoned up, said the senators needed a moment of your time, privately and urgently. He asked if you could come to the building security office. That's the message I gave you, sir."

"Well, they weren't there. And the security officer on duty says no one has called from there. Are you sure it was Senator Carson's aide?"

"I haven't met the senator's aide, sir." Rachel frowned.

"But I did check the register, and the name he gave was correct."

"A prank, then?" Graham muttered. "Rachel, I want a routine security check on this building, and a phone log for the past hour. Get right on it, please."

"Yes, sir."

"Oh, and, Rachel, that congressman in my office—the one with the soybeans or whatever—what's his name, again?"

"Hankins, sir. Representative Victor Hankins, ninety-seventh district, Illinois. He's bucking for a research grant for Hull Enterprises. Your, ah, crank call or whatever did give me a chance to check that out. Hull Enterprises has a milling plant in the congressman's district, but that's about all. Hull's parent company, though, is on the State Department's flag list. It's a front for an Argentinian entity, SteuVar Limited. I thought you might want to know."

"Interesting," Graham said, and nodded. "Thank you, Rachel. I think you can send in my next appointment very shortly." He glanced around as someone entered the reception area beyond the glass partition. Not the usual politician or lobbyist this time, but a young woman in a green smock, her arms full of large books. A few thick strands of auburn hair fell from the stained painter's cap on her head to frame a pixielike face hiding behind large-rimmed glasses. She glanced this way and that, nodded to the business-suited men already waiting there, and took a chair.

"Who's that?" Graham asked.

"One of the building maintenance people." Rachel shrugged. "You're scheduled for a new carpet. She was here earlier to measure. Guess she's waiting to test some samples now."

Returning to his office, Graham favored his visitor with a wry grin. "Very sorry, Congressman," he apologized. "Gets hectic, sometimes." He crossed to his Byzantine desk, sat, and picked up the sheaf of papers lying there. "I'd like to take this under advisement, for the moment. Of course, we'll review the proposal carefully. The gist as I understand it is a test-marketing of certain domestic and imported grains, to provide the basis for a study of disease resistance in fed livestock. Have you anything to add?"

"My constituents are interested in improved profit margins for beef cattle feedlots," Victor Hankins recited, sounding both authoritative and thoroughly coached—characteristics that Graham had found to be fairly universal among junior congressmen. "Naturally, they have a degree of vested interest, being in the milling business . . ."

"Naturally."

". . . but I sincerely believe them to be individuals of the highest integrity, genuinely interested in the public good. I hope we can count on the NSSA for your support."

Quite a speech, Graham thought. Wonder who writes his crib notes for him. Aloud he said, "I have no question of your sincerity, Congressman, though I wonder how you came to bring this matter to my particular division of NSSA."

Hankins smiled—a smooth, political smile. "I'm kind of a rookie where agencies are concerned," he confessed. "I really don't know one division from another, but this is a scientific matter—a proposal for scientific study. And I was advised that you, ah, swing a good bit of weight in high places, so I came to you."

"I'm flattered," Graham said. "May I ask who advised you, Congressman?"

"The Hull people, of course." Hankins shrugged. "It's their project. They are, by the way, substantial contributors to our party—mine and the president's."

"I see." Graham stood, came around the desk, and extended his hand. "It's a pleasure to meet you, Congressman. I can assure you, since you have placed this matter in my hands, that I will give it the attention it truly warrants."

When Hankins was gone and the door closed, Graham sighed. There is simply no end of them, he thought. He returned to his desk, tossed the Hankins proposal into the disposal bin, and thumbed his intercom. "Rachel, I'll see the next one now. And let me have those security reports as soon as you can, please."

Now, almost a year later, Charles Graham once again sat behind his Byzantine desk, watching Victor Hankins, but the circumstances were very different now. Hankins wasn't here. What Graham and Julie Price were watching was a video recording of the interior of this office, dated November 18, 2006. The scene had the telltale fishbowl look of a wide-angle surveillance lens, but there was no distortion in the image it displayed.

Alone in the office, Congressman Victor Hankins knelt beside an open file folder in front of an open safe, turning pages and taking pictures with a camera no bigger than a pocketwatch.

"That's how he did it, then," Graham growled. "I was out of my office for nearly ten minutes. I remember having to leave the son of a bitch there alone, and now I know why. That urgent conference call was a ruse, to get me out while he opened my safe."

"Are those time-travel files he's copying?" Julie asked. "TEC files?"

"What else? That low wall safe is a dedicated depository. Nothing goes in there but TEC reports and documents. That's where he got all that information that he'll release to the media two years from now. He got it from me!"

"So what do we do? Call the FBI or Secret Service or somebody?"

"And have everything he has become public record

through the courts?" Graham snapped. "Absolutely not. This has to go to Timecourt."

"But he hasn't committed any temporal crime! Espionage, of course, breaking and entering, tampering with federal property, maybe even treason, but those are all standard, nontemporal crimes."

"Intent to commit a temporal crime, evidenced by preparatory action, is a temporal felony," Graham said. "All that's required is proof that, in the absence of explicit deterrence, the crime would have been committed. This video and your testimony will put this clown out of circulation for a long time."

"Yes, sir. Should I go find him and arrest him, then?"

Graham looked at his clock. It was nearly midnight. "We'll both go," he decided. "You can make the arrest, I'll get us back into TEC, and Captain Matuzek can order an emergency session of Timecourt, on my warrant. I don't want Hankins talking to anyone outside TEC and Timecourt facilities, from now on."

TEC Headquarters
2007

The blip was gone. With Victor Hankins's summary sentencing by Timecourt, it had disappeared from the E-warp dome.

Eugene Matuzek himself congratulated Julie on the arrest of Hankins, then he sat her down and explained some of the harsh realities of temporal adjustment. When she left his office she had agent's patches in her hand and tears in her eyes. "I can't go back," she told Bob O'Donnelly. "I'd meet myself there if I did."

"Yeah." He took her hand, sympathetically. "I know.

Three years from now Julie Price is a recruit just finishing her training with TEC and being assigned as a courier."

"Three years from last month." She nodded, gazing at the new patches in her hand. They were the circular shoulder emblems of a full-fledged timefield agent. She glanced toward the launch bay where her old, red, courier's suit hung in the prep wing. "Just about now, then, I'm logging in for my first launch. To now."

"Yeah." O'Donnelly put an arm around her shoulders. "I guess you'll be listed as lost, when you don't come back."

"They'll have to," Julie said. "Because I'll still be there, but from three years before. I'd meet myself when I came upstairs. But I don't see how I can be Julie Price then, because that's who I am now. I mean, if I'm working in this squad room and just down there there's another Julie Price . . . who's also me, going through training . . ."

Somehow they had gravitated to the empty interrogation room, and they sat there, very close. "It's just a name," O'Donnelly suggested. "People change their names."

"But I'll still know! I mean, the me upstairs will know about the me downstairs . . ."

Bob O'Donnelly sighed. "My grandmother wouldn't have a problem with this," he said. "She wades through paradoxes all the time. They don't even faze her."

"They don't?" She looked up at him. "How does she cope with them?"

"No problem." O'Donnelly shrugged. "Grandma just figures life is full of things that can't be understood, so she doesn't dwell on them. I guess she has plenty to talk about without getting into esoterics."

Julie gazed at him, and moisture pooled in her eyes. "I accept how it is," she said. "It's just sort of a kick in the head, realizing that I can't ever go back to 2010."

"Oh, but you can!" O'Donnelly assured her. "You'll just

have to reach the future the same way everybody else does.
One day at a time."

79°9' S, 70°0' W
2007

The big, seagoing tug eased its string of empty barges to
the left as its helmsman glassed the object on the tumbled
ice ahead. He wondered why *Extempor* hadn't investigated
whatever that was over there, or at least signaled about the
sighting. The fact remained, though, that the icebreaker
was past that floe now, and probably not looking back. He
decided to check it out himself. Without altering the tug's
plodding speed, he watched as his two crewmen put the
dinghy over and sped out ahead, along the port flank of the
barges, for a better look. The ice made it hard to see just
what was there. Something red, mostly obscured.

By the time the tug approached the anomaly, the crewmen were climbing out of the dinghy fifty yards away,
lashing it to a spar of broken ice. They waved at him,
turned, and began clambering over the wall of tumbled ice
left behind by *Extempor*.

The helmsman squinted through his goggles and altered
his port screw to correct the string's course, keeping it in
midchannel. For several minutes he was thoroughly occupied with navigation. When the string was clear and true
again, he raised his binoculars and looked back. The two
crewmen were a little astern now, just reappearing atop
the ice heap, one of them carrying something red. The man
held it high. It looked like a nylon pup tent, ice-coated and
frozen into a flat, misshapen mass.

The second crewman waved his arms wildly, and the
helmsman turned farther, looking back over the tug's short
stern.

The dinghy was no longer tied to the ice back there. It floated adrift in the slushy channel, bobbing on the tug's wake. With a curse, the helmsman reduced power to his screws, feeling the pull of inertia and the barges' momentum pulling at their moorings, reluctant to stop. Those idiots! the helmsman cursed to himself, raising a delay pennant for the icebreaker now three hundred yards ahead.

To bring the barge string to a halt, reverse the tow, pick up the dinghy, and rescue his frantic crewmen would take at least half an hour.

They would hear about this. He would hear about it, and the reaction would not be pleasant. For a long moment, the helmsman considered just leaving those two idiots behind, out there on the unsheltered ice. It would serve them right. But that would be a more serious mistake than the loss of a little time to bring them back.

When the dinghy was secured, he climbed down and dropped into it, shouting angry oaths at a large leopard seal that poked its whiskered snout out of the freezing water a yard from the little boat's wales. Then, leaving his tug and tows in midchannel, he cranked up the dinghy's engine and went to get his crew.

He was on the ice, roaring curses at them, when a familiar sound brought him around. Nearly a quarter mile away, his tug and its barges were under way, heading inland into the great maw of the ice shelf where *Extempor* had now disappeared from sight. It was as though the icebreaker had sailed into a solid wall of freeze, and now the tug aimed its barges at that same recessed wall and chugged toward it. The tug's delay pennant had been lowered, its skim foils spread, and as its baffled crew watched helplessly from the ice pack, it revved its big engines, kicked up a bow wake, and headed for the wide, dark cavern. The string of barges arrowed ahead of it on bow wakes of their own.

VIPR's Nest
2007

Where catwalks and tram ramps merged, four stories up on the anthracite wall, a neat cubicle forty feet wide, twenty high, and fifty deep had been excavated and fitted out as a luxurious apartment, adjacent to a complex of monitors, computer banks, communications controls, and surveillance screens. This was the control center for VIPR's Nest. Glass partitions displayed slate-tiled floors, fixtures of gleaming metal and polished ebony, furnished in lavish taste with cedars, leathers, richly hued rugs and tapestries. And above it all, nearly filling the high ceiling, spread the bright swirling patterns of a timestream display—an E-warp.

Emilio Vargas von Steuben didn't notice it at first, when the little counterswirl that was his Hankins blip winked out. He was relaxing at that moment, sprawled in the misting warmth of a hot bath while several pubescent *Indio* girls attended him. But the machines noticed, and triggered an alarm tone that brought the heir of *Verteidigung Innung Provozieren Rache* half out of his ornate tub.

He looked up at the timestream display and his dark eyes narrowed in rage. *"Schweinehundten!"* he muttered. *"Perros! Basta!"* Scattering startled nymphs around him, he clambered from the tub and flung a wrap over his shoulders, just as a group of *enmascarados* appeared beyond the glass, with Kurt lumbering after them. Emilio's shout had brought them from their stations at the catwalks, and Kurt from the littered hole that was his preferred quarters.

The glass door was bolted, and for a moment it appeared the guards would break out the glass to come in. But Emilio waved them away. *"No entren!"* he shouted. *"Está nada! A sus estaciones!"*

They hesitated, then backed away, looking sheepish even behind their woolen masks. One by one they turned away.

Emilio glared at the cluster of dark-haired girls. "Get out!" he waved at them. *"Váyanse!"* As one, they scampered around a partition of Oriental silk and disappeared through a side entrance. Stairs from there, spiraling down through a shaft, led to the household servants' quarters below.

Snarling, Emilio strode from the bath chamber through his wide central living area and into the control center beyond. He heard the hiss of another door, and knew that his father also had heard the alarm.

At the age of eighty-nine, Helmut von Steuben still was a striking man. A clipped mane of snowy hair haloed his seamed face and highlighted the pale blue of his eyes, and his stance was still that of a Prussian officer—straight, rigid, and unforgiving.

They met in the control room and Emilio tapped orders into a keypad. Around him, several monitors sprang to life, scrolling and weaving their various patterns as they drew from the main banks, from the archive analyzers, and from E-warp itself. While Helmut looked over his shoulder, Emilio read the screens, and hot anger grew within him. There was no hint of the Hankins eventuality. Victor Hankins, just completing his first two-year term as a United States congressman, had simply dropped out of sight. He had liquidated his holdings in the Chicago area, and gone away. Vague surmises of a sudden illness were suggested, but there really was no serious inquiry. Emilio knew there never would be.

"They found him," he muttered.

"And his TEC data?" Helmut demanded, squinting at the electronic images. "Where is the intelligence he gathered, about the other timefields? The location of this TEC?"

"The data is gone," Emilio said. "They have eliminated all traces of themselves."

"Then we must get it back," Helmut decreed. "And this time we play no little games." With a snort of disgust the old man turned and stepped away, looking upward at the E-warp display. "You are too much Spanish, I think, Emilio. Always you must be the slithering snake, hiding and darting away, waiting too long to strike. Deceit and subtlety! The German way is better. We choose our enemies. We seek them out. When we find them, we obliterate them without warning."

" 'At's a bloody interesting comparison of cultural proclivities," a feminine voice said, behind them. They spun around and stared into the business end of a laser-fitted machine pistol with the face of an angry angel behind it. "Now 'ere's some Australian philosophy, mates," Harriet Blevins purred. "When we're on walkabout we take th' target of opportunity." The bantering tone disappeared as she stepped into the open, facing them. "Helmut von Steuben and Emilio Vargas von Steuben, by my authority as an officer of AusTEC an' on be'alf of TEC and Euro-TEC, I arrest you both for capitemporal crimes. You are 'ereby tried and adjudged guilty of—"

"Now, Kurt!" Emilio snapped. Before Harriet could react, a huge hand lashed out from behind to send the blond timecop tumbling. She slammed against the front of a computer cabinet and lay stunned for an instant, then tried to level her gun and found that she could not lift her arm. She could barely move it. She tried to roll and her legs failed her. Nothing below her shoulders seemed to work as it should.

Emilio stood over her, his beard twitching, his eyes ablaze. "You!" he hissed. "You know where TEC's launcher is hidden . . . and the others. You will tell me now."

In a voice barely above a whisper, Harriet said, "You go to 'ell, Junior."

Helmut von Steuben shook his head. "It is no use," he said. "She will tell us nothing."

"Kill the bitch, Kurt," Emilio said.

With a leering grin, Kurt strode across to a heavy file cabinet, stooped, and lifted it, then hoisted it over his head. Carrying the two-hundred-pound cabinet high, like a huge child with a new toy, he stood over Harriet for a moment, then brought the cabinet smashing down on her. It almost covered her small form. Harriet's right leg from the thigh down, her right arm with the small hand still holding the gun, and a welling seep of blood were all that could be seen beneath the metal frame of the object.

In the moment of silence then, distantly and muffled, a sound grew—a deep, broken, shuddering sound like a wail of grief . . . or like a scream of rage.

XVIII

A few hundred yards into the overhung cavern of the seaway, permanent fog shrouded the channel—a heavy, blind fog that smelled vaguely of sulfur and was impossible to see through. "It's no wonder nobody has spotted this place," Jack Logan told himself, switching on the tug's sophisticated hull sonars. "It can't be seen from the air, and from offshore it just looks like another ice cave. The mist hides it."

As the string of barges crept on, holding to a steady seven knots and guided now by head foils linked to the sonar signals, Jack noticed that the mushy, crackling sound had gone from the tug's thrusting wales. He peered over the rail, barely able to see the water below in the thick mist, then lowered a bucket and brought it up. The water was warm! Somewhere beneath the channel, polar vulcanism was still brewing steam and venting it into this subterranean cleft. In a stretch where the mist was almost too thick to breathe, he tested again. Bubbles rose around the tug's hull, and the water was as warm as a bath.

An hour passed, and then another, and Jack let the sonars guide the barges while he adjusted speed by the occasional, distant wails of the icebreaker's horns somewhere ahead. He didn't want to get too close. Diffuse lighting haloed the fog now, and high above he caught glimpses of arc lights.

He tried to reckon the distance traveled, but gave up. The great cavern seemed to go on forever, and when he tried to locate himself in his mind he brought up images of the rising surface above, the massive landscape of Antarctica—ice cap maybe several miles deep, with stony crags rising through it, an inverted mountainscape where the snow line began at the bottom and faded out in the too-thin air of sky-reaching peaks.

He had no idea how far he had come, except that it was a long way. Then, finally, he noticed that the mist was thinning. He could see the barges ahead of him now, and after a while he could see again the walls of the huge tunnel. It was as wide as a great river at flood crest, maybe a mile or so across.

When next he heard *Extempor*'s pipes, he could dimly see the ship ahead, and beyond it a wide turning basin lined with barges, tugs, and various other vessels. Cutting the sonars, he eased the barge string to starboard. Here engines thrummed, and rank upon rank of barges lay side by side below a busy shipyard where great hoppers poured black coal into waiting vessels. Carefully he eased alongside the outermost barges, almost touching them, and cut the tug's engines.

By the time the string of barges had slowed to a halt, Jack Logan was long gone from the coal docks and making his way up into the ice-roofed mountain heart of the *Verteidigung Innung Provozieren Rache*—the lair of the viper.

He followed the cart rails for a mile, through chill tunnels and murky sumps—always angling upward. Once again he wore the dark clothing and black woolen mask of an *enmascarado*, and carried a long-clip AR-15-20. The mercenary whose insignia emblazoned the shoulders of the sweater—a VIPR recruit from some Turkish prison—wouldn't need clothing or guns anymore.

Logan made no attempt to hide himself now, and those he passed along the way stepped aside or scattered ahead of a *capitán jefe de enmascarados* who was obviously in no mood to be crossed.

Only once did he hesitate. In a brightly lit cavern above the hydroponic banks, a trio of laughing, taunting masked bullies was tormenting several ragged Indians, shouting insults at them, forcing them one after another to strip naked and crawl across a steam vent—a scorching, painful bed of hot gravel. It was a little too much for Logan. Stepping up to the armed mercenaries, he coldcocked the first one with his rifle butt and flattened the second with a kick to the groin and a gunstock to the jaw, both in the instant that it took them to react.

The third man apparently had trained in Oriental martial arts. Realizing the threat, he attacked. Whirling like a dervish, he feinted once and spun. His extended boot narrowly missed Logan on the first twirl, then swept around again to connect solidly . . . with the unforgiving steel of a braced AR-15-20. The leg snapped, the man howled and toppled across the gravel vent, and Logan crushed his larynx with a chop of his gunstock.

Pulling off his own mask momentarily, Logan stripped the bullies of their weapons and handed them over to their victims. "To work is a proud thing," he told the gawking Indians in clear Spanish, "but there is no pride in brutality, and even less in tolerating it."

He didn't look back. Maybe what he had started there would spread. The glint in some of those dark eyes said it might. If it did, so much the better.

Above the subterranean grainfields, Logan followed the catwalks upward, toward the rising cliff of anthracite—the black castle of VIPR. Where tramways crossed he helped himself to a second weapon—a modern, laser-sight handgun—and left two guards sprawled over the underrails.

He was striding along a suspended catwalk when he spotted the glass-fronted abode of the masters of this place. Drawing nearer, in the shadows of the looming cliff, he saw Emilio leave his bath and hurry into the adjoining command center. Through the open panes of glass he saw Helmut von Steuben join his son there, and saw Harriet Blevins appear from between data bins to confront them.

And he saw Kurt enter through a sliding portal in the back wall.

Logan was still sixty yards from the pristine glass of the lair when Kurt struck—near enough to see it all but too far away to do anything about it.

As the heavy cabinet smashed down on the sprawled form of the little, blond angel from Australia, all the anger and pain of untold past days blended with even older pains— the pains of lost partners—and welled up in Jack Logan's throat. His scream was a negation, and a battle cry.

Startled *enmascarados* whirled toward him as he charged down the ramp, but they were too late to stop him. The AR-15-20 drummed like sharp thunder, and there was no one there to slow the raging man whose calling cards shattered the glass panes ahead of him as he came.

In a heartbeat, Logan was in the control center with VIPR's leaders. He erupted through showering glass fragments as instruments and displays shattered and sparked all around them. With a glance at the fallen file cabinet and the still, bleeding form beneath it, he spun, leveling his rifle. "Agent Blevins read you your rights," he growled. "Now you're mine."

His eyes bulging with shock and anger, Emilio Vargas von Steuben snapped, "Kurt! Kill him!"

The giant moved with surprising speed, launching his huge bulk at the TEC agent, knocking the rifle aside as he closed with him. Only by an instant did Logan escape being crushed by those huge arms. He ducked, falling to one knee, and Kurt went over him, toppling a standing bank of electronic gear. He turned, charging again. Logan side-stepped, slammed the giant across the belly with the rifle, and lost the rifle to a big hand that wrenched it from his grasp and tossed it aside.

Kurt doubled back, swatted Logan to the floor, and stood tall, raising his arms high as though for applause.

A wrestler! Logan realized. The huge man was more than just a circus freak. He had been a professional wrestler! His instincts were those of the gaming arena.

Rolling to the side, Logan scurried through the shattered glass-frame to the high, railed veranda and pulled himself upright, clinging unsteadily to the railing. He let his legs wobble just a bit, then braced himself as though pushing off from the railing to strike.

Kurt came at him like a juggernaut, intent on "pinning him to the ropes," and Logan let him come. At the last instant, just as those big arms closed, the TEC agent dropped to a low crouch, grabbed both of the giant's legs, and heaved upright. Kurt hung suspended above the railing for a second, then flew outward, twisting as he fell. Four stories below, he crashed down headfirst onto a trundling coal cart.

Logan turned, took a few deep breaths, and sprang back into the control center.

Emilio was just picking up the fallen AR-15-20 when Logan swatted him aside and retrieved it from him. He turned the rifle, leveled it, and aimed it at Emilio.

Emilio raised his hands. "All right!" he snapped. "Arrest me, then!"

"You've already been arrested," Jack Logan growled. "We're going by Aussie rules now." Without remorse or hesitation, he shot the chief of VIPR through the head.

The sound that followed the gunshot was a high-pitched, warbling cry like nothing human—a harsh, despairing howl that grew and grew, a wail like erupting grief tinged with rage and madness. Logan spun around, and old Helmut von Steuben stood there, wild-eyed, holding a Wehrmacht Luger.

The Luger bucked, its report as loud as lightning, and Logan felt a sting at one shoulder. He braced himself for the next bullet. But it was von Steuben who staggered as the next shot rang out—a step forward, then another, then the old man toppled, face forward. The little hole between his shoulder blades seemed ridiculously small, but it was enough. Viper had joined the Viper's spawn. Helmut von Steuben was dead.

Logan heaved the heavy file case away. He didn't bother looking at the damage it had done, only at the blue eyes that gazed up at him from the bloody floor. Her laser pistol dropped from her hand, still hot from its final shot, and there was nothing left but the broken body, the pooling blood, and the dimming blue eyes. Crouched over Harriet, Logan felt the tears welling up in his eyes. "We got them . . . partner," he said. "We got them both."

Her lips moved weakly and he lowered his head to hear.

"Left 'and, Yank," she breathed. "Co . . . coordinates." She paused for a breath that was almost no breath, then murmured, "Think I'll go walkabout now, Yank. See ya."

And with that, Harriet Blevins was gone.

Logan closed her eyes with gentle fingers, and covered her with one of Emilio's fine tapestries. Among the still-functioning electronics he found a powerful shortwave radio and set a message into its repeater. It was a code, known to TEC, EuroTEC, and AusTEC officials. Dudley Wilkins would be the first to receive the signal, in Australia. But it would go to all three agencies, and they would take it from there.

The key sequence in the message, repeating endlessly

on the transmitter's beam, were the numbers written on the palm of Harriet's left hand: 83-4-S, 108-2-W.

The location of VIPR's Nest.

He wrapped her in a tapestry and carried her away—out along the catwalks, down a tramway and a ramp, and out across the subglacial landscape where gunshots rang out here and there in the distance as thousands of rampaging slave Indians picked up more and more weapons to use on fewer and fewer *enmascarados*.

At the vaulted portal to the time tunnel, armed men had fortified themselves, but even before Logan approached with his burden they were overrun. Indians with new weapons stood aside and lowered their heads as the tall man strode past, carrying his tapestry bundle, looking straight ahead. When he had passed through the portal and closed it behind him, the Indians went looking for more *enmascarados* to kill.

At the launch bay, Logan placed Harriet's body in the forward cockpit of the long, boatlike timesled. He set the vector controls, set them with the precision of long deliberation: TEC central, the squad room right where two wide corridors crossed in front of the Dome of History—the triad coordinates that were the prime reference for all of TEC's vector equations—in the immediate past. One hour ago. The timesled was not a transporter, but it did transfer spatially to any point in the historic past. An hour ago was history.

With his settings locked, he time-set the field controls as he and Harriet had figured out. Then he relinquished to manual and climbed in behind her still, frail body, holding her in his arms as he strapped down.

He was just reaching for the trigger when a huge form thundered across the launch ramp toward him. Kurt roared like a bull, his impact shaking the sled as he missed his hold, skidded across the top shield, and sprawled on the far side. But it was only for an instant. Gibbering inanities, the giant picked himself up, sprang again, and Logan touched the ignition trigger. The sled careened away, down the track, and in a quick glance around, Logan saw Kurt standing like a raging statue, his legs spread, feet straddling the sled-trough, his fists high and threatening.

"Hold that pose," Logan muttered as the gravities thrust him back against the sled's restraints. "I'll tend to you in a minute." Riding its tachyon thrusters, the sled plummeted down the groove, toward the huge armatures where the time-field would spring to life at a precise, split-second point in time—spring to life and capture that instant for the duration of its charge.

The sled raced toward it, gaining momentum as its velocity doubled and redoubled—passing Q-velocity as the air shimmered between the armatures.

Even outside the launch tunnel, in those vast caverns where ex-slaves with machine guns hunted down their tormentors, the sound of the VIPR timesled when the wormhole of collapsed dimensions closed around it was like distant, rolling thunder, echoing through the expanses of what Harriet Blevins had called "a city-state in a 'ole."

TEC Headquarters
2007

Abrupt silence fell on the TEC squad room when the air shimmered and a wild, dark-clad figure appeared there, holding a wrapped corpse in gentle arms.

Logan swept off the top of a desk, and laid the tapestry bundle on it. For a moment, the others in the place simply gaped at the apparition among them, then Amy Fuller saw past the shaggy beard, wild hair, and gaunt, haunted features. "Jack!" she whispered. "You made it!"

Logan whirled to Dr. Dale Easter. "Can you lock coordinates on an open wormhole?" He scrawled numbers on the day-sheet pad. "These coordinates?"

Easter gaped at him. "Well, it's never been done before . . . synchronizing two timefields. But theoretically, maybe we could—"

"Then do it!" Jack snapped. "Now."

He whirled away, sprinted to the evidence lockers, and dug out a long, heavy object wrapped in plastic sheeting.

"Go ahead," Eugene Matuzek told Easter. "You heard him. Do it."

Carrying his bundle, Logan ran to the launch area and out into the sled bay. As he unwrapped hardware, Easter's voice came over the intercom. "We've got it, Logan! We're actually vectored in on a four-dimensional anomaly. Our timefield is interfaced with another timefield!"

"Hold the fix!" Logan shouted.

The thing he pulled out of the plastic wrapping was a gun—a big, ugly gun fitted with bipod mounts and a huge awkward-looking diode sight. It was one of fewer than fifty of its breed—a Baldwin Custom sniper rifle, the rifle recovered from B. J. Simms's attempt to assassinate Haile Selassie in Ethiopia.

Logan snapped open the bipod, checked the big rifle's .50-caliber loads, and lay prone on the launch track in front of the TEC sled. He aimed the rifle straight downtrack, squarely at the center of the shimmering timefield between the armatures half a mile away. He squeezed the set-trigger, checked his aim, and muttered, "Hold the pose, Kurt. Harriet Blevins sends you her regards."

The fourth factor in temporal transit was always the projectile hurled into the field, Harriet had told him. The projectile—the timesled itself—became the catalyst for the formation of the wormhole it entered. But it wasn't the timesled itself that caused that. The timesled was just a piece of hardware. The converting catalyst was the velocity of the projectile . . . any projectile. The catalyst was Q-velocity.

The big gun bucked like a mule as Logan fired it, its bullet racing down-track, into one time interface and out another. Even with deceleration at the far end of its trajectory, it was still moving at more than 2,994 feet per second—well over Q-velocity—when it ripped through the chest of the giant standing astraddle the launch trough in VIPR's Nest.

XIX

TEC Headquarters
December 31, 2007

Jack Logan dumped a pile of reports on Eugene Matuzek's desk and glanced at the E-warp dome overhead. For
once, it was serene. There were no ripples, no rifts, not
even a blip to mar the tranquillity of a graceful, flowing
pattern that represented the unaltered course of history.

"Happy New Year, Gene," Logan said. "See you next
year."

Matuzek glanced up. "Where do you think you're going?" he asked crossly. "You're on duty, remember?"

"Special duty, for purpose of these reports." Logan
shrugged. "The reports are completed. Have a nice New
Year's." He turned away. "I have a new apartment, and
there's a new bed in it, and miles to go before I sleep. See
you."

"Hold on, Logan!" Matuzek snapped. "Get back here!
You're logged in until eight A.M., and I've got work for you."

"Give it to somebody else." Logan gestured toward the
squad room beyond. Even though it was New Year's Eve,
the place bustled with people—field agents coming and
going, two teams at work in ThinkTank, techs hurrying
here and there.

"I've already given it to you," Matuzek growled. "Here

I'm trying to wrap up a year's reports, and Oversight sends in a systems analyst to recalibrate all of our controls and inspect all our equipment. God almighty, do they think we've got nothing but time on our hands?"

"Okay," Logan sighed. "What do you need me to do? Day sheets? A reality check for the historians? What?"

A nasty grin spread across the captain's face. "Just baby-sit, Logan. I'm turning the systems analyst over to you."

"Oh, come on, Gene . . ."

Matuzek's gaze shifted, looking past him. "Here she is now," he said. "Agent Logan, I'd like you to meet Claire Hemmings. She'll be with us for a while, and I want you to give her every assistance."

Jack turned, lowered his gaze a bit, and looked into big, blue eyes. He felt his breath go ragged for an instant, as a resemblance hit him. The blond hair, the blue eyes, the determined, stubborn little chin . . . "Hello," he said.

"Agent Logan . . ." She glanced at a sheaf of notes in her hand, then looked up at him. "Jack Logan, is that right?"

"Right." He studied her features, candidly. This wasn't the face of an angel. More the face of an impatient pixie. "Ah, I was just breaking for dinner," he said. "My car's in the back lot, and I was thinking of Luigi's. Have you eaten?"

As the two of them left Matuzek's office, Logan shot the captain a glance, over his shoulder. "Miles to go, Gene," he said. "See you."

Miles to go, the words seemed to say, before I sleep.

Please turn the page
for an excerpt
from another exciting time-travel adventure

The Whispers

Book One of The Gates of Time

by Dan Parkinson

The Anomaly Man

Lucas Hawthorn came awake abruptly, with an eerie feeling that something profound had changed. He had dreamed of hearing voices, but the words ringing in his head didn't mean anything and didn't seem to have come through his ears. Still, he was sure someone had spoken to him. "What?" he slurred. "Didn' hear you, hon."

There was no response, and Lucas opened his eyes. Thin morning light outlined the little slats in the window's shutters. It was early—too early to be awake. Yet he was, and something wasn't right. "What did you say?" he prompted, more awake now. There was an odd feeling about the room, as if there were a lot of people around him. But he didn't see anyone.

Behind him, Maude snored softly. Lucas yawned, stretched, and looked around. Then he sat up. Something was definitely strange here. He glanced around the dawn-lit room. Nothing seemed out of place. It was their bedroom, just as it was every morning. But something seemed odd. And a lingering odor made his nose twitch—a new, live scent as if someone who didn't live here had just passed by.

Like an echo, clear and close but not quite real sound, the odd voice came again. "Funny doog," it said.

"What?" Turning this way and that, Lucas peered about the room, then nudged Maude with ungentle fingers. "Did you say that?"

"Mmfff . . . ," she muttered, pulling the covers higher around her head.

"Maude! Wake up!"

She stirred beside him and opened her eyes. "Wha'?"

"What did you just say?"

"I didn' say anything." She covered her head again, then gasped and peered out from under the blanket. "Who's here?" she muttered. "Somebody's here, Lucas." She sat up, clutching the covers around her, and they both peered around at the empty room.

Except for the fact that he couldn't exactly see anybody, Lucas would have sworn that their bedroom was full of busy people. He squinted, his eyes flicking here and there. All around was the *sense* of presences, but he couldn't quite see them. Each hint of shadow was gone before his eyes could find it. But still they were here. With a growl he clenched big fists, edging toward the bedside table. "What is this?" he muttered. They seemed to be all around—a dozen or more figures, moving here and there, looking closely at walls and ceiling, measuring the window frames, making notes on little pads. Lucas had the feeling he had awakened into a dream—a nightmare.

Beside him, Maude whispered, "What are they doing? Remodeling?"

With a grunt, Lucas pivoted to the bedside table and pulled the drawer open. The S&W wasn't there. "What the hell is going on?" he muttered. After pushing the covers back, he swung his legs over the side of the bed, then jerked them back as someone not quite visible raised an imperious hand.

"Tnemom asudge," a soundless voice ordered. Then: "Ayko."

"Lucas? . . ." Maude's voice was a frightened whimper. Lucas bounded out of bed and turned full around, a defender in rumpled pajamas. He felt—sensed somehow—that people he couldn't quite see were scampering aside, out of his way.

Abruptly the bedroom door opened and a man stepped in. This was no specter but a sturdy, middle-aged man wearing odd-looking old coveralls and a St. Louis Cardinals baseball cap. "You're awake," the man said, without formality. "Sorry to bother you. These delegates needed to verify dimensions."

"Leave my dimensions alone!" Maude shrilled. Lucas swung around, barely glimpsing a furtive shadow that scampered back as Maude swung a businesslike fist at it. The shadow had a measuring tape.

"Sorry," the man in the doorway said. "That's just Peedy. His specialty is mammalian evolution."

Lucas and Maude gawked at the man, who had started past Lucas, toward the east window. The man paused, then touched a finger to his baseball cap in casual salute. There seemed to be a gap between his hand and his wrist, as if he were wearing an invisible watch. "Guess you're a little confused," he said. "Didn't introduce myself. Name's Limmer. Edwin Limmer. You won't remember, Lucas, but I met you a long time ago."

"Limmer?" Lucas blinked at him, sleepy-eyed. "I know that name, all right, but you're not him. You can't be. He's dead."

"Not so you'd notice." The man smiled. "It's a common misconception. I used to be a lot older. But I'm the same Ed Limmer. Look in your old trust portfolio. Does three hundred dollars' worth of soybean futures ring any bells?"

"That's ridiculous! Get out of my house!"

"Can't," the man said. "I came with this group to inspect the place. Have you forgotten the reciprocal service clause?"

"How do you know about that? Nobody knows about that."

"Well, I do. It says that in return for your beneficiary status, I claim access to and limited use of your domicile at an unspecified future time. Well, the time is now and I'm specifying it."

"That's a sealed document! It's in my safe! It's . . . it was written more than forty years ago."

"I know. By A.J. Thornton, attorney-at-law. I dictated it. Now, about your house here. What's the total square footage?"

"Uh . . . about eighteen hundred," Lucas said. Then he bristled. "What are you doing in our bedroom?"

"Measuring," Limmer said. "We'll just be a moment. Where do you keep your coffee?"

"In the kitchen." Maude pointed. "Left cabinet over the counter. Lucas, don't just stand there! Call the police!"

"I'll call the police," Lucas said. "Get the hell out of our bedroom!"

"Okay." Limmer nodded. "I think we're through here. That wall will have to be reinforced, naturally. We'll be doing structural modification on the other side of it. Studs on sixteen-inch centers, I suppose?"

"Of course they are. The building code requires . . . what do you mean, *we*?"

"Us." Limmer gestured vaguely. "You and me and them. Oh, that's right, you can't see them too well. There's a knack to it. They're Whispers. They're just passing through." He glanced past Lucas. Something less than shadow was hovering by the bed where Maude sat. "Peedy, behave yourself! Remember you're a professional!" The hint of shadow flitted away and Limmer spread his hands apologetically. "Too much time on his hands," he explained.

"Whispers get like that. You folks get dressed and I'll go put some coffee on, then we can talk. George is in the kitchen, seeing what he can find to eat. He's pretty well starved, after four days up on that hill."

Lucas blinked, trying to think of something to say.

"Call the police, Lucas!" Maude wailed.

"Call them yourself." Lucas growled. "I'm going to . . . where the hell *is* that thing?" He looked into the table drawer again, then stooped to peer under the bed.

"Your gun?" Limmer asked. "It's over there on the dresser. Do you want it?"

"Hell, yes, I want it! You . . . people are in my house!"

Limmer shrugged, retrieved the revolver, and handed it to Lucas. It was still loaded. Rims of shells glinted at the rear of the cylinder. Lucas checked it, nodded, and pointed it at Limmer. "Get out of my house!" he ordered.

"Let's have coffee first," Limmer suggested. He looked around approvingly. "This place'll do just fine, with some modifications. Do either of you have any experience with electronics? Or maybe crowd control? That might be helpful."

"What the bald-headed hell is going on here?" Lucas demanded. "I'll shoot . . ."

Somewhere beyond the open bedroom door, cooking utensils cascaded to the floor with a resounding crash. Limmer stepped to the door and looked beyond, down the hall. "I'd better go see about George," he said. "I'll be in the kitchen. We'll talk there." With a reassuring smile he touched his baseball cap again, in salute, then disappeared down the hall.

Maude had the bedside phone and was tapping busily at buttons. "Want something done, do it yourself," she muttered. Then: "Lucas, the line's dead. I can't call out."

"Ertal we ees," a voice that was no voice seemed to say,

then the room hollowed out, as rooms do when crowds leave.

Lucas closed the door firmly. "Let's get dressed," he suggested. "Then maybe we'll get to the bottom of this."

"You're really him, then? I mean, *that* Ed Limmer?"

"The very same." Limmer shrugged. "Don't worry. You'll get used to it. Technology is always perplexing to those who haven't lived when it was developed. I was born in the future, and I've been in the past. Now I'm on my way back."

"And a . . . a way station?" Lucas squinted over his coffee. The more Edwin Limmer explained—if that was what he was doing—the more confused the Hawthorns became. "You want to use our house for a depot?"

"Not exactly." Edwin Limmer shrugged. "More like a booster station on a pipeline. We could be looking at quite a bit of traffic before long. Handy, the business you're in. The Whispers had a part in that, I guess. You can handle everything as general contractor."

"We only have one extra bathroom," Maude said. "I suppose we could put up two or three people for a day or so with the kids away, but . . ."

"I'm talking about hundreds of people." Limmer shook his head. "But once we're set up they'll be no trouble. They'll just be passing through. You won't even notice them, except for the relegation pips. And that brings me to my point. We're counting on you folks to tend the generator and keep the conduits open."

"Where are they going then, those people?" Maude asked.

"Back in time," Limmer said, as if explaining a trip around the block. "They're time travelers."

"Sure they are," Maude muttered. Cautiously she edged away, to where the kitchen telephone hung over the bar. Her eyes flicked back and forth between the kitchen table, where her husband and the crazy man sat sipping hot coffee, and the pantry shelf, where a gaunt, tattered young man with scratches and smudges all over him was wolfing down a pint of cottage cheese. He had already eaten two apples and all the leftover pizza. Cautiously Maude reached for the phone.

"That one won't work either," Limmer told her. "But don't worry. It's only temporary. Toojay had to rewire the circuit to move the box away from the dining room wall. What do you think? Could you folks handle things here for a while?"

"Handle things?"

"Tend the generator. Keep the conduit open. Operate the station."

"What's in it for us?" Lucas frowned.

"What do you want? Money? You'll be paid, of course. I'll cover all expenses, plus a nice retainer and fee for the use of your property. That and found."

"What's found?"

"Well, you'll have more or less free use of the . . . ah . . . apparatus, when the Whispers aren't using it. There really isn't that much damage that you can do."

"You said tend the generator and keep the whatever open. What do we do, oil and clean, or something?"

"Nothing so primitive." Limmer smiled. "I'll teach you what to do. I'll need to stay on for a while anyway, to get you started."

"No way," Maude snapped.

"What about him?" Lucas indicated the hungry young man, who had now polished off the cottage cheese and was rummaging through the refrigerator. That one hadn't said a word, but when he glanced at them his eyes were distant and haunted.

"George is the technician," Limmer explained. "The Whispers picked him up forty-four years from now. Under rather trying circumstances, I might add. But he'll be all right. He'll install the mechanisms. We'll clear everything out of that dining room there. It's about the right size. That will be the booster stage."

Maude took a deep breath, stepped to the back porch door, and glanced around at her husband. "I'm going to the Johnsons', Lucas," she said. "I'll call the police from there." She turned the knob on the door, then paused, puzzled. "This is locked. So's the other one. How did you people get in here?"

"We came in while the wall was open." Limmer shrugged. "Those stacks of sheet metal wouldn't go through the door."

"What sheet metal? What wall?"

"Oh, you don't know about that, of course. It didn't happen until this afternoon. You can't even order the metal before nine. That's when the supply shops open. By the way, you'll need some welding gear, too, and protective clothing for the four of us. It gets hot in here when the focalizer is first tuned. But don't worry. Booster fields don't burn."

Maude stared at him, the way a box-trained cat might stare at the dunes of the Sahara. It was just too much to contemplate.

"Now hang on," Lucas growled, struggling to get the drift of it. "Just supposing you did jump back in time, through a hole in the wall that we open because you say to. Then if you aren't here to tell us what to do, there won't be a hole for you to have come through in the first place . . . before you told us. And if there isn't going to be a hole in the wall—because you aren't here now telling us there will be, so there isn't any way for you to get here later so you can . . . so you can be here earlier to make later happen . . . I mean, before it does . . . if it doesn't . . ." He trailed off into muttering confusion.

Edwin Limmer nodded his approval. "You're getting

the hang of it," he said. "Anachronisms are always a problem. But in this case it doesn't matter. The wall will be open when we arrive, but we're already here so we won't really need it to get here. You see? That's called an empty loop—an anachronism that allows something to happen but no longer matters before it happens because it is already going to happen. Some of them, when the Whispers are from, think that's how the universe began. They call it an accomplished improbability. It cancels itself out."

"Oh," Lucas said.

"I'll go get the police myself," Maude decided.

"Hold it, hon." Lucas raised a hand. "The man mentioned money. I guess we ought to hear him out."

"Oh, that," Limmer said. "Yes, we'll pay you money. As much as you want. It's only money. But I think you'll want something a little more tangible than that for your services. The currency collapse is only a few years away. After that Federal Reserve scrip isn't worth shit. Of course, it already isn't, but when the IRS stops accepting it, nobody will pretend anymore. That's what starts the paper revolts. Inflation, multiple taxation, all the usual government lunacy, then they'll change the design plates and that's what sets it off. I favor commodity futures myself, but you might want to look at venture enterprise."

"Like what?" Lucas glared at him.

"Well, water pumps and hang gliders have a bright future. Also road and bridge consortiums and some real estate. That's tricky, though. Claims and titles get pretty uncertain when court systems collapse. How about travel? That's a good industry. There's always somebody wanting to be somewhere else. Just don't honor credit or cash. Keep it on a barter basis. Tradable goods only. That's pretty depression-proof."

"My aunt Irene and her husband had a travel agency," Maude said scornfully. "They went bust."

"They didn't have a temporal field to play with." Limmer smiled. "Anywhen has a lot more appeal than anywhere."

"We can't run a business here," Lucas argued. "This whole district is zoned residential-only."

"Then don't put up a sign." Limmer shrugged. "Keep it discreet. Letters of recommendation only. Just think! Package tours to the Cenozoic. Organized dinosaur-watching! Or how about reserved seats to watch Rome burn?"

Over by the refrigerator, George Wilson was peeling an orange. "Be careful," he said quietly. "You're talking major anachronisms here, if you plan to let tourists loose in the past."

"There'll have to be some defined limits," Limmer agreed. "But I think the idea would sell. Just a select group at first. Show them what can be done. Then let them talk it over and think about it. People will always travel if you give them time."

"Leo Whitehead's always talking about how nice Colorado used to be," Lucas said thoughtfully.

"The Brents would love to see Custer's last stand," Maude offered, taken by it all. "They fight all the time about who won."

"Like a look at last year's county ballots myself," Lucas added. "If that water authority vote wasn't rigged, there's no fenceposts in Kansas."

"Then it's settled." Limmer beamed. "George can get to work on the conversion chamber. And we need to order some materials."

"Who pays for it?" Lucas demanded.

"You do." Limmer gestured. "I told you, it's only money. We'll use the Limmer Trust reserve. Good as gold. Built on commodity futures in the past. In the meantime, for petty cash, that bag in the hall is full of U.S. federal currency. Help yourself."

"What is it? Counterfeit?" Lucas glared at him threateningly.

"Absolutely not! Why counterfeit money when there's so much of it just lying around in warehouses and shipping depots?"

"There is?"

"Sure. Always been that way. Back when I was old it was bootleggers and gunrunners. Nowadays it's dope dealers and headbrokers. And there are always lawyers and politicians with cash to stash. You don't think they use banks, do you?"

Across the kitchen, George Wilson frowned, opened a stained vinyl pouch at his waist, and drew out a shining object the size of a milk carton. It was cone-shaped and glinted with a deep luster like melded metals in glass. "There are so many of these now, coming upstream," he said, sadly. "When Magda left Long Mesa, there were only three." He set the thing on the kitchen table. "Arthur had one, and we had the others at Long Mesa. Magda took one with her. I never knew what happened to the third one."

"Magda?" Maude groped, searching for some clue as to what he was talking about.

"His wife," Limmer said quietly.

Wilson turned toward the hall. "I'd like to rest a bit before I go to work," he said. "I feel like I've been through a war."

"You have," Limmer said.

"What war?" Maude stared at the smoke-darkened, sweat-stained man who had just decimated her refrigerator's contents. "Guest bedroom is second on the left. What war? Where? Or . . . I mean, when?"

Wilson nodded tiredly and trudged away, looking for a bed.

"Arthur's Cimarron Siege," Limmer said. "George was with the Revivalists. And he's worried about his wife. She was there, too. That's a little over forty years from now. I'll be involved in that one, too, I guess."

"You were?" Lucas managed.

"Will. It hasn't happened yet, but I'll be there. Or so they tell me. I was only ten years old the first time I made that trip, and I was just in passage. You can't see much from retrosync, especially that close to a major anachronism."

George Wilson reappeared at the hall entrance. "Okay if I use the shower?"

Maude barely heard him. She was staring at Limmer. "So you've actually *been* to the future?"

"That's what I said." Limmer shrugged. "I was born there, but I never saw much of it. I passed through, but I haven't actually been where I seem to be going. I'm not a Whisper, you know. I'm sort of a stowaway. I've been out of time most of my life. Now I'm going back."

"To the future?"

"Back to the future, just like the movies." Limmer grimaced. "My future's the same as yours, except that I was born there. Everybody's headed for the future, except the Whispers. They've already been there. It's where they started. They just picked me up along the way."

"You mean you're an anach—ana—a whatzit yourself?" Lucas gaped at Limmer.

"Anachronism," Limmer said slowly. "No, not exactly. But my base mode is retrosync, so I guess that makes me an anomaly. Step right up, folks." He sneered. "See the world's only living stopwatch. Spent ninety years going the wrong direction and now working his way back to where he started." He sighed, shaking his head. "It's all King Arthur's fault. I'll get that son of a bitch—beg pardon, ma'am—if it takes the rest of my life, which is exactly what it will do."

"It ... you will?" Maude felt dazed, trying to make sense out of so many things that didn't.

Limmer's ironic smile disappeared and his eyes narrowed. "Damn right I will," he swore. "I know I will, because I already did, even though I haven't done it yet. I was—will be—the paradox in Arthur's Anachronism. And it's all because of him. That bastard! May he bounce forever within the stroke of twelve! I only wish I could be there to see it."

Lucas and Maude shook their heads convulsively, as if besieged by gnats. As one, they turned toward the other stranger. The quiet, somber man in the tattered, smoke-darkened clothing still stood in the hall entry. Though no longer ravenous, he looked exhausted, bleak, and somehow tragic.

"Don't ask me to explain it," George Wilson said, dismissing their stares. His tired, disinterested eyes lingered on Limmer, then shifted to the shining focalizer on the table. "I invented the damn thing, but I'm not proud of it. And I've never understood this juggling of redundancies. That gets into probability equations. It's all aftermath to me. I'm just a technician."

✎ FREE DRINKS ✎

Take the Del Rey® survey and get a free newsletter! Answer the questions below and we will send you complimentary copies of the DRINK (Del Rey® Ink) newsletter free for one year. Here's where you will find out all about upcoming books, read articles by top authors, artists, and editors, and get the inside scoop on your favorite books.

Age _____ Sex ❑ M ❑ F

Highest education level: ❑ high school ❑ college ❑ graduate degree

Annual income: ❑ $0-30,000 ❑ $30,001-60,000 ❑ over $60,000

Number of books you read per month: ❑ 0-2 ❑ 3-5 ❑ 6 or more

Preference: ❑ fantasy ❑ science fiction ❑ horror ❑ other fiction ❑ nonfiction

I buy books in hardcover: ❑ frequently ❑ sometimes ❑ rarely

I buy books at: ❑ superstores ❑ mall bookstores ❑ independent bookstores
❑ mail order

I read books by new authors: ❑ frequently ❑ sometimes ❑ rarely

I read comic books: ❑ frequently ❑ sometimes ❑ rarely

I watch the Sci-Fi cable TV channel: ❑ frequently ❑ sometimes ❑ rarely

I am interested in collector editions (signed by the author or illustrated):
❑ yes ❑ no ❑ maybe

I read Star Wars novels: ❑ frequently ❑ sometimes ❑ rarely

I read Star Trek novels: ❑ frequently ❑ sometimes ❑ rarely

I read the following newspapers and magazines:

❑ Analog	❑ Locus	❑ Popular Science
❑ Asimov	❑ Wired	❑ USA Today
❑ SF Universe	❑ Realms of Fantasy	❑ The New York Times

Check the box if you do not want your name and address shared with qualified vendors ❑

Name _____
Address _____
City/State/Zip _____
E-mail _____
timecop

PLEASE SEND TO: DEL REY®/The DRINK
201 EAST 50TH STREET, NEW YORK, NY 10022 OR FAX TO
THE ATTENTION OF DEL REY PUBLICITY 212/572-2676

DEL REY® ONLINE!

The Del Rey Internet Newsletter...

A monthly electronic publication e-mailed to subscribers and posted on the rec.arts.sf.written Usenet newsgroup and on our Del Rey Books Web site (www.randomhouse.com/delrey). It features hype-free descriptions of books that are new in the stores, a list of our upcoming books, special promotional programs and offers, announcements and news, a signing/reading/convention-attendance calendar for Del Rey authors and editors, "In Depth" essays in which professionals in the field (authors, artists, cover designers, salespeople, etc.) talk about their jobs in science fiction, a question-and-answer section, and more!

Subscribe to the DRIN: send a message reading "subscribe" in the subject or body to drin-dist@cruises.randomhouse.com

The Del Rey Books Web Site!

We make a lot of information available on our Web site at
www.randomhouse.com/delrey
- all back issues and the current issue of the Del Rey Internet Newsletter
- sample chapters of almost every new book
- detailed interactive features of some of our books
- special features on various authors and SF/F worlds
- ordering information (and online ordering)
- reader reviews of upcoming books
- news and announcements
- our Works in Progress report, detailing the doings of our most popular authors
- bargain offers in our Del Rey Online Store
- manuscript transmission requirements
- and more!

If You're Not on the Web...

You can subscribe to the DRIN via e-mail (send a message reading "subscribe" in the subject or body to drin-dist@cruises.randomhouse.com), read it on the rec.arts.sf.written Usenet newsgroup the first few days of every month, or visit our gopher site (gopher.panix.com) for back issues of the DRIN and about a hundred sample chapters. We also have editors and other representatives who participate in America Online and CompuServe SF/F forums and rec.arts.sf.written, making contact and sharing information with SF/F readers.

Questions? E-mail us...

at delrey@randomhouse.com (though it sometimes takes us a little while to answer).